"THE WORLD'S GOING TO END, OR THE VIOLENCE WILL STOP.

"No matter which one of those scenarios happens, all of us at Stony Man are going to be out of a job. If that's the case, what better finale than for us to go out snuffing a monster who decided to loose a plague on the world so he could set himself up as a tin god?"

"That's part of the problem the President's facing, Barb. There's no way he can get any kind of political backing for targeting a religious leader."

"Religion isn't a hot topic for debate around this place. All I care about is that people who do abhorrent things should pay for them. To put it in religious terms, he excommunicated himself from the human race the day he decided to commit a crime against humanity. So I guess the only question left is, are you with us or not?"

DON PENDLETON'S
MACK BOLAN.

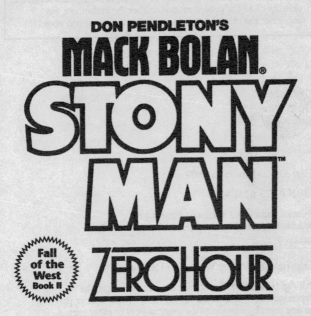

STONY MAN™

Fall of the West Book II

ZEROHOUR

A GOLD EAGLE BOOK FROM
WORLDWIDE.

TORONTO • NEW YORK • LONDON
AMSTERDAM • PARIS • SYDNEY • HAMBURG
STOCKHOLM • ATHENS • TOKYO • MILAN
MADRID • WARSAW • BUDAPEST • AUCKLAND

First edition November 1999

ISBN 0-373-61927-8

Special thanks and acknowledgment to
Michael Kasner for his contribution to this work.

ZERO HOUR

CHAPTER ONE

Beirut, Lebanon

Mack Bolan and Yakov Katzenelenbogen walked side by side down the palm-lined esplanade along the beach of Beirut's Corniche district. Once this had been the most fashionable part of a glittering city that had rivaled any as the premier fun-in-the-sun spot for Europe's jet set. The glittering all-night casinos and clubs, beaches crowded with sleek bikini-clad beauties, expensive boutiques and exclusive restaurants had been legendary.

Then in 1975, the good life of Beirut came to an abrupt end. The next fifteen years were hell as the various religious sects in the city battled for dominance. If that wasn't enough, the Israelis had sided with the Christians and the Druze while the Syrians and Jordanians had backed the Muslims and the PLO. It had been unremittingly brutal as only a factions war could be, and the United States had foolishly allowed itself to be drawn into the bloody conflict.

The Americans had gone to Lebanon as "peacekeepers,'' but one of the greatest truisms of all time was that it took both sides to make a peace. With neither major faction willing to make the first move, America soon became the third combatant force. A suicide car bomb delivered to the American Embassy and another to the Marine barracks caused great loss of life and even greater loss of face when the U.S. was forced to pull out to keep from taking more casualties.

The frenzied killing came to an end only when Syria occupied Lebanon and imposed a cease-fire by force of arms. Like all enforced settlements, though, it was an uneasy peace and no one could predict how long it would last.

It had been some time since either of the two warriors had been in the embattled city, and they had decided to take the walk to get a feel for the local situation before they went to work. They were surprised to see how quickly the city was being rebuilt. That wasn't to say that all traces of the civil war had been erased. It would take decades before that happened. Nonetheless, even with bombed-out buildings still the norm, the people seemed to have shaken off the psychic trauma of suffering eighty-five thousand deaths in the fighting.

Nowadays, the people weren't reflexively ducking at loud noises. Sleek young women again sunbathed on the beach, very much aware of the admiring glances of the young men. Brightly colored umbrellas shaded well-dressed patrons of sidewalk cafés as they sipped their coffee and tea and talked of plans for their reborn city. Normal life had returned, but one thing Bolan and Katz noticed was that there were almost no Westerners in the crowds. And that was why they were there.

It wasn't sight-seeing that had brought Katzenelenbogen and Bolan back to Beirut, but grim business. As the millennium approached, the Middle East hadn't escaped becoming wrapped up in the apocalyptic frenzy that was affecting the Christian world. In fact, the year 2000 anno Domini shouldn't have had any meaning at all to Islam. But for some reason, the Millennium Madness, as the media was calling it, had hit the Muslim world full force.

The first sign had been when a reputedly ancient Islamic manuscript had turned up filled with prophecies of the end of the Christian world in the year 2000 A.D. Then a mysterious plague swept through Western embassies and corporate headquarters in the Middle East. Hundreds of Westerners died, even more were incurably ill and expected to die, but no Muslim had succumbed to the disease.

The millennium plague, however, wasn't a disease that had been sent by a vengeful God to strike down the unbelievers as so many imams preached from their mosques. In fact, there was nothing divine about it. It was simply a laboratory-mutated form of an age-old scourge, anthrax. Normal anthrax was a bacterial disease of domesticated animals and, while it could pass to humans, normally it could be cured quickly. This version, however, had been engineered to withstand every antibiotic known to man. Virus genes had been spliced into the anthrax bacteria DNA, rendering it immune to the arsenal of modern medicine.

Beirut wasn't known as a center of bioengineering, but the man who was believed to be responsible for this horror had been spotted in Beirut a few days earlier. He was a Bosnian Muslim doctor who had worked at the Sarajevo medical university before becoming a wanted war criminal for his activities during the Bosnian war. He had been spotted by a Croatian nurse working for the French, who, after reporting him to the UN, had been assassinated in her clinic.

It was Yakov Katzenelenbogen's contacts that had sent him to join Phoenix Force in the once-divided city. The one-armed Israeli was a legend among the Christian as well as Israeli interests in the region. The complexities of Beirut required someone who knew his way around the town.

Bolan was a legend in the Middle East as well, but not as the Executioner. In Arabic, he was known as al-Askari, the Soldier. He was not, though, as "real" a figure as was Katz. People who really should have known better often regarded him as pure mythology. Part of that was because when al-Askari operated in the Middle East, he left few live enemies behind and the dead could hardly tell of what they had seen.

BOLAN AND KATZ BOTH carried identification that let them into the UN compound without question. Once inside the main building, the duty officer directed them to see a René Clostermann. The UN man introduced himself and asked how he could be of assistance. When Katz asked of Wendelmann, he seemed to pause for a moment before answering.

"Georg Wendelmann, yes," Clostermann said. "I'm sorry to have to tell you gentlemen that Mr. Wendelmann was killed a few days ago."

"What happened?" Katz asked.

"He was gunned down in the street. A most unfortunate incident."

"Did any witnesses happen to say that he was killed by men who came in a dark Mercedes and who were wearing ski masks?" Bolan asked.

"Yes." Clostermann seemed surprised. "How did you know?"

Katz's face was grim. "They also killed the woman who visited Wendelmann here. She was a Croatian nurse with the French medical team."

"I'm afraid that I don't know anything about the details of his death." Clostermann seemed disturbed. "You will have to talk to the city authorities for that. Now—" he made a show of glancing at his watch "—if you will excuse me, gentlemen, I have to get back to my duties."

As soon as the two men left his office, René Clostermann picked up his phone and dialed a number. When his call was picked up on the other end, he identified himself, ordered a sandwich to go and said that he would be right down to pick it up. Telling his secretary that he was going out for a moment, he walked out of the UN compound to the café around the corner.

Taking a seat in the rear of the café, Clostermann didn't have to wait very long before his contact arrived. He didn't know the man's name, only that he paid very well for information about certain subjects of interest. One of those topics was anyone who showed interest in the late Georg Wendelmann.

After telling the man what his two visitors had talked to him about, an envelope was passed under the table. Clostermann slipped it into the side pocket of his suit coat and got up to leave. Like Wendelmann, he, too, always had more expenses than he had income, particularly in a city like Beirut. In fact, with the money in his pocket, he would visit one of his major expenses that night and share most of it with her.

As he walked out of the café, his contact was speaking into a cellular phone.

KATZ AND BOLAN WERE continuing their recon on foot when a dark blue Mercedes four-door locked its brakes and skidded to a halt blocking the road in front of them. The two men didn't need to be told what was going to happen next and dived for cover.

The four gunmen who emerged from the Mercedes were wearing the uniform of sectarian violence in the city, dark clothing with ski masks, and carrying folding-stock AK-47s. No ID tags were needed to know who they were and what they had in mind.

Bolan's Beretta 93-R appeared in his hand like magic and spit a series of 3-round bursts of 9 mm hollowpoint slugs. The first burst took out the lead gunman before he could get his AK off his shoulder. The second burst drilled into the thug bringing his AK to bear on Katz.

By that time, Katz had his mini-Uzi out from under his jacket and, firing one-handed, swept the last two gunners with a sustained burst. Only one of them had managed to get off a short burst, and it hadn't connected.

Seeing his comrades on the ground, the Mercedes driver cranked the wheel around and trod on the gas. Engine roaring and tires squealing, the powerful sedan fishtailed as the driver fought to control it.

Bolan stepped out into the street, took a two-handed stance and sent a single shot through the rear window of the accelerating car. The driver's head snapped back reflexively when the slug mushroomed inside his skull. The Mercedes rammed a concrete power pole at the end of the block and came to an abrupt halt.

"Welcome to Beirut," Katz said, as he slipped a fresh magazine into the butt of his minisubgun.

"I think we hit a nerve," Bolan commented, "and I think we need to have another talk with Clostermann."

"Exactly my thought as well."

"But we need to get out of here first." Bolan looked down the street. "Talking to the authorities at this point in time will be counterproductive."

Katz looked around to get his bearings. "Follow me."

IN HIS FORTRESS inside a mountain in northern Syria, the man known as the Old Man of the Mountain had taken the news of the previous week's successful raid against Pakistan's nuclear arsenal calmly. He had long ago learned how to banish anger from his life. It was a gift God had given him so he could better implement the plan to bring all of the world under the rule of Islam. A man whose mind was clouded with anger was in no state to listen to God's word.

God spoke softly, and a man needed to have a clear mind to hear him. The Old Man had the clarity of mind to hear God and the strength of will to carry out His purpose. God was telling him to speed the spread of Islam over all the earth and to do that, the Old Man had to go to war against the Western infidels.

The Old Man of the Mountain hadn't always been known by his title. He had been born with a real name, Malik al-Ismaili. In English it meant high chief of the Ismaili. It, too, was a title, but more important it meant that he was the inheritor of a lineage that went back all the way to Hasan ibn-Sabbah, the founder of the Brotherhood of Assassins.

Much of the mysticism of the Nizari sect of the Assassins' founder had dissipated over the centuries. The Old Man was a true Ismaili, but he didn't despise the technology of the West, not when he could turn it to his own use. The Assassins of old had used carrier pigeons to pass information from the far reaches of the Muslim world to their master's hideaway. Al-Ismaili's men did it via the Internet.

So far, Western technology had been critical to winning his battles, and the first stage of his plan had worked well. A refugee Bosnian medical researcher working for him had developed a mutated strain of anthrax, and it had been used to good effect. The Western embassies and companies doing business in the Middle East had been hard hit, and those who hadn't been infected had fled.

The second part of his plan was to have seen a nuclear war break out between India and Pakistan, but it had been foiled. An unknown group of commandos had struck at both Gandara and Palimiro, the two Pakistani nuclear bases. Both their ballistic missiles and the delivery systems for their aircraft bombs had been destroyed. That the foiling strike had been aimed against Pakistan, a Muslim nation, instead of India's nuclear arsenal told al-Ismaili that the Western powers had once again acted to thwart the march of Islam.

That war would have done two things for the plan: it would have created tens of thousands of new holy martyrs for Islam and it would have let the nuclear genie out of the bottle. But there was more than one tool that could bring the Islamic masses together for this undertaking and even a more powerful tool than nuclear weapons.

Al-Ismaili was an expert on the yearnings of his people. He knew better, though, than to hope and pray for something that could be accomplished only by direct action. In contests between prayer and action, action won out every time. He truly believed that God was great. But he knew that God worked his miracles through the hands of men. Islam would triumph, but not because of anything God did himself. The prophet had personally spread the word of God and the Old Man of the Mountain could do no less.

Almost every people on earth had a legend of a savior figure who would return at a time of great need to save "his" people or to create a paradise for them on earth. The English had their King Arthur, the French had Roland, the Jews had their Messiah, the Christians had Jesus and the Muslims had Muhammad. That none of these heroes had ever returned made no difference, people always yearned for a Golden Age that was just around the corner.

Muslims the world over knew of the Twelfth Imam, their Mahdi, and they knew that when he returned, he would bring a new order with him. He would transform the Muslim world into a Golden Age more wonderful than anything that had ever been and everyone wanted that.

CHAPTER TWO

Beirut, Lebanon

Naji Nahas swore under his breath as he surveyed the bullet-ridden Mercedes sedan and the bodies of his men sprawled in the street. He hadn't believed it when the police lieutenant on his payroll had called to tell him about the shootout, but now he did. He had sent five men to do a simple job like those they had done dozens of times before, and now they were all dead. And from the lack of any bloody trails leading away, their killers apparently hadn't even been touched.

Like Nahas, the dead men in the ski masks had all been followers of the Old Man of the Mountain, Assassins. That they had struck openly in daylight was actually a device to disguise who they really were. The dark Mercedes and ski masks marked them as run-of-the-mill Beirut gunmen working for one of the sectarian factions that had torn apart the city.

Even though peace had come to Lebanon, that didn't mean that the fighting was over. The sectarian fighters were still jockeying for position as they waited for the Syrians to get tired of occupying the country and pull out. As in Bosnia, the hatreds in Lebanon had histories longer than the modern nation and wouldn't be easily put aside. More blood would be let as soon as the Syrian troops turned their backs on Beirut.

With hard-eyed Syrian troops enforcing the peace, though, the factions had reduced their warfare to the occasional ambush or assassination. Had this hit been successful, it would have been reported as just another faction affair. Now it looked like a disaster, and he would have to explain his failure to the Old Man. But before he did that, he needed to try to find out what had gone wrong.

Walking over to the sidewalk, Nahas looked around for expended ammunition cases and saw dozens of 9 mm empties on the pavement. Picking one up, he turned it over to look at the headstamp on the base. Where there should have been a manufacturer's identification or a coded lot-number stamp, there was nothing. The case head was blank. Picking up two more cases, he saw that they were blank as well.

Blank headstamp ammunition always meant a clandestine operation. Both the CIA and the Mossad, and even the British MI-6, were known to use blank headstamps so the ammunition couldn't be traced. More and more, though, intelligence agencies were using ammunition from other nations so as not to announce themselves and to throw investigators off the track. For a professional hit like this, he would have expected to see Bulgarian or Czech ammo, or even Spanish.

The use of untraceable ammunition indicated that something was going on in Beirut he needed to know about immediately. One other group that he knew used blank headstamps was the mysterious American commando organization that went by half a dozen different names. It had been a long time since Nahas had heard more than a rumor about this group. Every year, though, someone blamed a disaster on them, crying wolf. Even if these men were avenging angels, they couldn't possibly have done everything that had been credited to them.

Most of the time, Nahas didn't believe that this group even existed. The Yankees were far too inept to get away with anything that subtle. He knew better than to disregard America's ability to use brute force when it wanted. Those who made that mistake suffered. Saddam Hussein had learned that. But when their war machines were taken away from them, the Yankees weren't great warriors. They were a soft, overfed, decadent people who couldn't spend a day without their big cars, their rock and roll music, their television and their Coca-Cola soda. The only warriors in America had been the native Indians, and the Christians had eliminated most of them.

Nonetheless, he would talk to the UN man who had sent his people to their deaths. If Clostermann had set them up, he would pay the price. The Old Man of the Mountain would demand it.

WHEN BOLAN AND Katzenelenbogen returned to their rented villa in Christian East Beirut, they found that the men of Phoenix Force were already restless. They had been in the city a full day now and, after getting their weapons and equipment squared away, they were ready to go into action.

"What did you come up with?" David McCarter wasted no time getting down to business.

"Not much for a place like Beirut." Katz shrugged as he slipped his mini-Uzi from under his jacket to lay it on a table. "We talked to a UN official who told us that the man the nurse talked to also died in an apparent assassination. He was so sorry, but he couldn't help us. Then, as we were continuing our recon, we were attacked by a dark Mercedes full of gunmen."

He grinned boyishly. "Other than that, we just took in the sights."

Seeing how much his old team leader was enjoying himself being back in the field, McCarter repressed a smile. The Israeli war horse had always liked to be in the thick of things.

"Do you have any idea who the gunmen were?" a burley blond man with a slight Texas accent asked.

J. R. Rust had been the CIA field agent at Oman who had first brought the millennium plague to light. When the consulate staff succumbed to the mysterious disease after a diplomatic party, he had been the sole survivor. It had only been his taste for the local cuisine that had kept him from been stricken along with the rest. Upon being evacuated from Oman, he had returned to D.C. for debriefing and had come to the attention of Hal Brognola.

After putting Stony Man on the track of the millennium plague, Rust had been invited to link up with Bolan and Phoenix Force because of his extensive knowledge of the Middle East and his ability with the languages of the region. He proved himself under fire in Pakistan and had volunteered to continue with them in Beirut.

"Not really, J.R.," Katz replied. "But I'm certain that we'll be hearing more from whoever they were."

"Speaking of that," Bolan said, turning to McCarter, "who's on security?"

In typical Mediterranean style, the villa they had rented through one of Katz's contacts was walled. And since it was in Beirut, the top of the wall was further protected with rolls of razor wire, as well as broken glass embedded in the concrete. That wasn't to say that the wall couldn't be breached, just that it would take an attacker a little longer to get over it. For real security, men had to stand watch over the villa. Fortunately, the villa itself had a tower that made a good observation post.

"I've got Gary and T.J. out there now."

The team's best sniper and an ex-Ranger ought to be able to keep things well covered during the day. Once dark fell, though, they would all get into their nightsuits.

"Since someone's on to us," Katz said, "at least on to Striker and me, we need to make sure that this place is well covered in case we were followed. And remember, this is the home of the car bomb.''

"The villa came with a supply of fifty-five-gallon drums filled with concrete,'' McCarter reported. ''And I had the lads roll them out to cover the gate. It's an RPG attack I'm more worried about. Our neighbors are a little too close to us for my taste.''

"Hopefully, we won't be here long enough to attract that much attention,'' Bolan replied.

"Where are we going?'' Rafael Encizo asked.

"First,'' Bolan said, ''I'm going to have a talk with the UN man we spoke to earlier and see if he knows why someone tried to kill us. Apparently, anytime someone asks the UN about Dr. Vedik, they get set up for a hit.''

"Who do you want to take with you?'' McCarter asked.

"I was thinking of having Jack drive so Katz and I can concentrate on the target. I also want him to get acquainted with the terrain around here.''

"How about my tagging along too, Striker?'' Rust interjected. ''I speak good Syrian Arabic.''

Katz spoke Arabic, but in a place like Beirut, it might not hurt to have two linguists. Plus, in Palimiro, Pakistan, the CIA man had proved to be a good man to have around when the situation went bad. His solo rescue of McCarter from the Pakistani Air Police lockup had been a thoroughly professional piece of work.

"Sure.''

LATER THAT AFTERNOON, Bolan and Katzenelenbogen were sitting in a rented Alfa Romeo sedan across the street from the UN building. Jack Grimaldi was glad to be behind the wheel and out of the villa compound. Sitting in a static position always bored him. He didn't mind being the pointman, but he liked to do it behind the controls of an aircraft or a fast car.

After calling and learning that the UN offices closed at six, they took up position a half-hour early in case their man was in a hurry to call it a day.

"Here he comes." Katz lowered his binoculars after making the ID.

"I've got him." Grimaldi reached for the ignition switch and keyed the powerful DOHC Alfa engine to life.

René Clostermann paid no heed to his surroundings as he drove out of the UN compound. The payoff he had received earlier that day was burning a hole in his pocket, and it had been almost three weeks since he had been able to afford the services of Jerzil, she of the golden eyes and skin. Had he not been saddled with a wife who was the daughter of a high-ranking UN official, Clostermann would have dumped her and become an expatriate in Beirut. But that would cost him his job and, as he had found out, Jerzil was allergic to impoverished men.

It was no challenge at all for Grimaldi to follow the UN man's Fiat through the streets. Even though the city was making a strong comeback, vehicular traffic was still sparse by Western standards. When Clostermann pulled into the open gate of an elaborate arabesque building, Grimaldi pulled around the corner and parked on the street.

"We got him," Katz said with a grin. "That's one of the city's better whorehouses. It's been in business since the days of the Turks and if he's seeing someone there, he'd better have a major credit card with him."

"That good?" Grimaldi asked.

"That expensive."

"Maybe we should see if we can save him some money then," Rust suggested. "I'm sure he'll want to thank us for it later."

"You watch the door," Katz said, "and Striker and I will invite him to join us."

UNLIKE IN THE STERILE cash-and-carry sex operations of Europe, a high-class whorehouse in Beirut was more like an exclusive Victorian-era gentlemen's club that offered women along with the other refreshments. The interior looked like something out of the turn of the century as well, but with an Oriental flair.

René Clostermann was sitting on a pile of cushions sipping a cup of cardamom-scented coffee. He was fortunate that Jerzil hadn't been spoken for and, while he waited for her to appear, he watched two scantily clad girls writhing to strains of classical Arabic music. Westerners called it belly dancing, but here it was an art form designed as a warm-up for the pleasures to come.

"Come with us and you won't be killed," the

voice said in French as cold steel was pressed behind his ear.

Clostermann almost lost control of his bladder. "Who are—"

"Keep your head to the front and your mouth shut," Katz hissed. "Get up and walk to the door."

Clostermann wasn't a brave man and did as he was told. Outside the establishment, he offered no resistance as he was put into the backseat of a sedan and blindfolded. "Where are you taking me?" he asked.

"One more word," the man speaking French said, "and you will die."

The UN official fell silent and rode in silence except for the heavy hammering of his heart.

"This is far enough," Katz said in English when they reached a bombed-out, deserted area. "Take off his blindfold."

When he saw where he had been taken, the UN man was certain that he was going to be killed. This was one of the major body-dumping sites for the city. "I don't know what you want, but I'll cooperate in any way with you."

"Do you know who we are?"

Clostermann shook his head. "I just know that you were in my office this morning."

"After we left your office," Katz said, "someone tried to kill us and I think that you can tell me why that happened."

The Israeli shrugged and nodded his head toward the nearest burned-out building. "If you can't, though, you get left here with a bullet in your head.''

The UN man feared the Lebanese man he fed his information to, but that threat was far away right now, and this new one couldn't be escaped. Taking a deep breath, Clostermann quickly recounted his arrangement with the Lebanese. He explained the system of calling the café to arrange a meeting or of being called there to be given a new assignment.

''Do you know your contact's name?'' Katz asked.

''He never would tell me his name, but I can tell you what he looks like, and I am willing to look at photos if you have any and try to pick him out.''

''Describe him.''

Clostermann gave a description that would fit three out of four males in Beirut.

''Does he have any distinctive features?'' Katz asked.

''Only a small scar on the right side of his mouth.''

''One more thing,'' Katz said.

''Yes?'' Clostermann's voice was close to breaking with fear. Throughout the interview, the big, dark-haired man hadn't taken his piercing blue eyes off him, and it was like having death look at him. He couldn't meet that gaze without flinching.

''I advise you to leave Lebanon immediately,'' Katz said. ''In fact, I advise you to find another line of work entirely. The UN isn't well served by men like you.''

"I will." Clostermann let out the breath he had been holding. "I promise."

"And I promise that I will hold you to that."

Syria

THE OLD MAN of the Mountain studied the image of Naji Nahas in the screen of his video-equipped computer. Another gift God had given him was the ability to tell when a man was lying to him, and he could tell that the Assassin leader was telling the truth. If the Brotherhood had unknowingly gone up against the elusive commando unit that turned up in many corners of the world, the failed Beirut hit hadn't been Nahas's fault.

Unlike Nahas, though, al-Ismaili fully believed the rumors about the secret commando force that were so common in the Middle East. In fact, he had once barely escaped death when they had attacked a Hezbollah stronghold in the Bekaa Valley. Had he delayed his departure a half an hour, he, too, would have been killed. He alone had escaped while more than a dozen experienced freedom fighters had died.

For that commando team to be in Beirut meant that the Americans were looking for him. Or at least, that they were looking for whoever was responsible for this latest outbreak of Islamic unrest in the region. He doubted seriously that they had a line on him personally. As had been the tradition since the days of the original Brotherhood of Assassins, his security was tighter than tight. Nonetheless, he could take no chances that they might get a lead on him. He had to wait a few more days before he could announce that the Mahdi had come, and he didn't need anything to complicate that.

"Activate all of your cells," he told Nahas, "and find those two men. When you find them, kill them. Spare no effort to insure success this time."

"As you command, Master," Nahas said, grateful that he hadn't been ordered to kill himself for the debacle in the streets of Beirut. Failure wasn't tolerated in the Brotherhood, and he had clearly failed.

"And, Nahas…"

"Yes, Master?"

"Do not fail me again."

Nahas lowered his head in submission.

CHAPTER THREE

Stony Man Farm, Virginia

Hal Brognola looked at the cluttered desk in front of him in dismay. For the duration, or at least he hoped to God that it was just for the duration, he had taken over Barbara Price's small office in the farmhouse. With her in the hospital with the millennium plague and Yakov Katzenelenbogen in Beirut with Bolan and Phoenix Force, the institution was in danger of being taken over by the inmates. Someone had had to step in to keep things on track, and he had been elected.

That was the problem with running the nation's most secretive government organization. There was no one on the outside he could call upon to come in and give him a hand for a few weeks. The Stony Man Farm crew was a tightly closed society, closed to both the public at large as well as most of the government officials on the federal payroll. Brognola himself was the sole point of contact with the outside world, and he reported only to the President. As the mission controller, Barbara Price was his second in command, and Katz was in the number three slot as the tactical adviser. But with both of them indisposed, he was the man both in Washington and at the Farm.

Price's little cubicle was a far cry from Brognola's spacious Washington, D.C., office on the executive floor of the Justice Department building. For one, it was like trying to work in a shoe box. He didn't have a clue how Barbara was able to get anything done in such cramped quarters.

Even though Brognola was personally focused on the chance to resolve the millennium plague situation, the President was zeroed in on the new threat Carl Lyons and his Able Team had brought back from their last mission in California. So, while most of the Stony Man crew was supporting Phoenix Force's Beirut operation, Brognola was being drawn deeper and deeper into the latest disaster in the making.

While Able Team had been on a weapons-smuggling mission in San Diego, Rosario Blancanales had infiltrated a cult organization that was arming for Armageddon in a big way. The cult leader, however, had been smart enough to plant a female spy with Blancanales to make sure that he was what he purported himself to be—a true believer. Over the course of the mission, the woman, Sarah Carter, had been critical in helping Able Team pull off another success. With her help, they tracked down and destroyed stolen military weapons that were being used to arm a surplus Air Force ballistic missile silo that was being turned into a fortress.

In payment for Blancanales having rescued her, Carter disclosed that she had once been the girl-friend of a Florida computer billionaire, Ian "Dingo" Jones, and was hiding from him. Jones was an Australian who had moved his company, Rainbow Cybertech, to the United States to escape the tax structure of his native land. Once in this country, he quickly built a high-tech empire rivaled only by Microsoft and Intel.

Carter, whose real name was Anne Keegan, had stolen a prototype computer chip from her lover before fleeing for her life. When Able Team offered her sanctuary, she paid them by handing over the chip and explaining that it was at the heart of Jones's plan to take over the world's financial markets by causing them to collapse. According to her, the chip was a cybernetic hunter-killer missile designed to wipe out banking and financial networks the world over.

Aaron Kurtzman had tested the chip and reported that it was everything that she had said it was. Jones had designed a computer virus capable of evading all of the known virus screens and filters in use in the world. It could attach itself to almost any input and hide completely undetected. The activation signal could be as simple as a modem call. If it was intended, as Carter claimed, to destroy the world's financial networks, it could do it in a microsecond.

Kurtzman's team was working on a virus filter to counter the killer program, but he had admitted that it wasn't easy finding a way to block it. It would be best for everyone if it was just never activated.

Needless to say, as the world's leading financial power, the United States would be devastated by such an attack. The President's advisers were in a blind panic at the possible consequences, and the Man had tasked Stony Man with tracking down the threat and eliminating it. With Phoenix in the field and most of the cyber backup crew tied up trying to crack the millennium plague, Able Team was being sent to Florida to try to learn exactly what Ian "Dingo" Jones was up to.

DR. WILLIAM HENDRICKSON of the Atlanta headquarters of the Centers for Disease Control stood in front of the biomonitors silently recording the gradual deterioration of the woman in the bed. Part of him, the private, humane part, wanted the process to speed up so she wouldn't suffer so much. Another part of him, the research scientist, wanted to keep trying to fight for her life.

Though he had several hundred victims of the millennium plague in his own hospital and the other CDC satellites throughout the nation, this one woman, Barbara Price, was his personal poster girl. The fact that she was highly intelligent as well as stunningly beautiful probably had a great deal to do with his interest. He didn't know it, but Barbara Price had that effect on most men.

Like so many others who had been stricken with this mutated form of anthrax, she had responded well to the initial treatments, but had now gone into a relapse. Unlike most of the others, though, she was still alive. For how much longer, he had no way of predicting. It was times like this that he wished that he had gone into cabinetmaking as he had wanted before he passed the MedCats. At least when a piece of wood cracked it could be replaced, or maybe even glued, and the cabinet made well again.

He was watching the insidious destruction of a beautiful woman, and there was damned little he could do to stop it. Nor was there anything he could do for any of her fellow sufferers, either.

He had been told that the government was trying to track down the designer of this plague in hopes that he had also engineered a cure at the same time. He knew, however, that the chance for that to happen before Ms. Price was dead was slim.

After making his final note, he bent and brushed a strand of the woman's honey blond hair out of her face. "I'm sorry," he said. "I really am."

Stony Man Farm, Virginia

AARON KURTZMAN PUT DOWN the phone and stared blankly at the data slowly scrolling down his monitor. He wasn't a man who gave up easily, but he was close to despair this time. He had just spoken with Dr. Hendrickson of CDC Atlanta and had been given an update on Barbara Price's condition.

Hendrickson had reported that she was very gradually slipping deeper and deeper toward an irreversible state. This process had been noted in other patients who had contracted the mysterious plague, and most of them had died. Price was strong and she was still fighting it. But without new information to work with, Hendrickson wasn't optimistic that the CDC would be able to come up with a way to reverse the process in time to save her life.

It wasn't only that Stony Man Farm just wasn't right without her running the show, Kurtzman had a very personal connection to her. It wasn't a romantic connection, but a professional one. Some of the others might have a different view of what went on at the Farm, but as far as he was concerned, the work they did together made Stony Man what it was. Sure, the action teams did the actual work and Brognola greased the skids to make it easier, but he and Barbara made it all come together.

He considered telling Mack Bolan what he had just learned. Bolan and Price did have a long-standing relationship that went beyond the professional. It wasn't a thing of promises and rings, but that didn't diminish the strength of what they felt for each other. It was merely a realistic reflection of the lives they led. No one expected the Executioner to settle down in the suburbs, wear a suit and drive a Volvo wagon to a nine-to-five job. Equally, Barbara Price wasn't cut out to be a soccer mom who did volunteer work for worthy causes when she wasn't baking cookies.

While he knew that motherhood was a worthy occupation in the greater scheme of things, Barbara Price was more important to the average American family than a hundred minivanloads of soccer moms. All mothers took care of their own children, but Barbara took care of everyone's children by working her ass off to keep the bad guys away from them.

He knew that she could be replaced as the Farm's mission controller. No one was irreplaceable to the operation, except maybe Striker. But without her, something indefinable would be lost. Just like Stonewall Jackson's Brigade wasn't the same after his death, Stony Man would be different without her. This meant that he had to work even harder to help Bolan and Katz find the monster who had cooked up the plague. And the way he saw it, one of the things he could do to help was to keep this information to himself for a while.

The mission in Beirut was in a critical phase right now. Developing information from the single lead they had was going to require Bolan's undivided attention. Kurtzman didn't insult Bolan by thinking that he would not be able to absorb the information about Barbara, put it out of his mind and continue doing what he had to do. But every man, even the Executioner, could take only so much.

He also decided not to mention this to Hal Brognola either. The big Fed also had enough on his plate. Even though the last Phoenix Force mission in Pakistan had defused a potential nuclear war on the Indian subcontinent, they hadn't been able to make even a dent in the craziness that was overwhelming the world. The world was coming to an end, and it looked like Stony Man Farm wasn't immune.

ORDERS WERE ORDERS, but Carl Lyons still wasn't used to having Sarah Carter as an appendage to Able Team. It wasn't that the ex-LAPD cop was phobic about women, far from it. But even though she had been crucial to their being able to shut down a dangerous millennium cult in San Diego, he didn't trust her. His well-honed instincts developed over years of dealing with scumbags, made him leery of her.

Both Brognola and Kurtzman had checked her background and had given her a clean bill. Dancing in topless clubs wasn't a crime, nor was it a sign of criminal pathology. And beyond that, all they had been able to find on her was a couple of traffic tickets. Except for having linked up with Ian "Dingo" Jones, she had lived what passed for a normal life in the American nineties. As far as her association with Jones went, she wasn't the first, nor would she be the last, beautiful young woman who had fallen in love with a wealthy, older man. That story was as old as time.

But Lyons didn't depend on computers and records to form his opinion of anyone, not even a beautiful woman. In fact, with women, he rarely bothered even looking at their rap sheets. As he well knew, they had more ways to hide their past than a spider has legs. His main problem with her was the effect she was having on Rosario Blancanales. He was smitten with the woman.

Lyons didn't have a problem with Blancanales getting laid, not at all. But when his involvement with her threatened to break up the relationship the three of them had developed over years of working together, he had a right to be concerned.

Even with all his misgivings, Lyons still couldn't

come up with a single way that the woman could have been planted on the team. There was simply no way that anyone would have predicted that the Temple of Zion would come to the attention of Able Team or that Sarah Carter would be the person Immanuel Zion would choose to keep an eye on Blancanales.

And he also had to admit that, so far, her behavior had been above reproach. She had freely given them everything she could on Dingo Jones and his plans to use his killer chip to take over the world's financial markets.

At first, he'd been suspicious about what she had claimed to know. But she had explained it by pointing out that Jones took great glee in bragging about his coups. Apparently, it served as foreplay for him and was a part of his daily routine.

Still, he was glad that Brognola hadn't wanted her brought into the Farm compound itself. She and Blancanales were camping out at one of the SOG safehouses in the countryside around the Farm. That way, she could be consulted without revealing any of the Farm's secrets to her.

SARAH CARTER, as she wanted to be called now, was starting to have second thoughts about agreeing to come to Virginia with Arthur Corona—and she knew that wasn't his real name—and his partners. It was much too close to Miami where Dingo Jones ruled his empire. She could almost feel his eyes on her back every time she left the safehouse. As she knew all too well, he could very well have a spy in every small town in the South and pay them out of his petty cash. As she had learned, men as rich as Jones lived by their own set of rules.

She had to admit, though, that she couldn't complain about how she had been treated since she had been with these three men. She was guarded day and night, and Harold Brognola assured her that the warrants for her arrest Dingo had put out had been cancelled. To all intents and purposes, she was once again a free woman. And she had to admit that she was enjoying Corona's company. It had been a long time since she had been treated as anything other than a rich man's sex toy or a slave to a charismatic cult leader.

If they were anywhere else in the country, maybe she could relax. But Virginia was too close to Florida.

"WE'RE GOING to Miami," Carl Lyons announced to Blancanales and Carter when he and Gadgets Schwarz walked into the safehouse. "Hal wants us to start working on this Jones guy as soon as possible. He says that the President's advisers are collectively defecating in their pants at the thought of what that chip could do to the markets."

Carter's face froze at those words. "I can't go to Miami." She turned to Blancanales. "I just can't. You didn't say anything about my having to go back to Florida."

Blancanales looked at Lyons. "Does Hal want her in on this too?"

Lyons nodded. "He thinks that we might be able to smoke him out through her."

"But we already know where he is," Blancanales protested. "It's not like this guy is hiding or anything. He's completely out in the open."

"We know where his corporate headquarters is, granted. It's hard to hide a place like that. But we don't know anything about any other facilities he might have. Aaron and his people are running that for us right now, but they're coming across layers of dummy corporations that are signed off on even his known property. Hal's afraid that he's done a 'Family' thing and hidden everything."

"Speaking of 'Family,'" Schwarz said. "We also might want to talk to the Miami Mob and see what they know about him. They have as much to lose as anyone if the markets go tits up."

He glanced Carter's way and muttered, "Sorry."

She ignored Schwarz's reflexive apology. As a one-time exotic dancer, she had heard that word and many more before Dingo Jones had bought her out of the club where she had been the star performer.

Blancanales turned to her, his concern plain on his face. "What do you say, Sarah? I won't let anything happen to you. You know that we'll be able to protect you."

Finding herself in another trap, Sarah had no real choice but to go along with them. One way or another, her only way out of this depended on these men and the powerful organization they worked for. "All right," she said, sighing.

CHAPTER FOUR

Miami, Florida

Dingo Jones stood in front of the floor-to-ceiling windows of his office and looked out over Miami. His building was at the edge of what the local papers usually called a high crime area. That was PC speak for an urban war zone that was both vibrant and chaotic. It was a place where life-and-death scenarios were casually played out on street corners as if they were children's games.

Most people thought that Jones was crazy to have put his corporate headquarters in a place like Miami. The crime rate in the metropolitan Dade County area was among the highest in the world, not just the U.S. It was a war zone as blacks, Haitians and Cubans fought for the control of the drug trade and anything else in the city that was worth controlling. It was truly a jungle down there, and he loved it.

Unlike most men of great wealth in the United States, Jones didn't try to shield himself from the violence of modern urban society. In fact, he often went into Little Havana or the Haitian barrios alone, but not unarmed. His nickname had come from the wild dogs of his homeland, and it was well deserved. Going up against a couple of street punks in a dark alley was his favorite kind of workout.

He also didn't bewail the assault on civilization that was so much a part of the end days of the second millennium. As far as he was concerned, only the strong survived and the weak were their natural prey. If the American people were too weak to protect what was theirs, they deserved everything they got. The Americans had once been a strong people, but the soft living and even softer thinking of the past thirty or forty years had reduced them to helpless whiners. When he came into his own, he would insure that what was his would be protected. To do anything else would be stupid and, if there was one thing that Dingo Jones wasn't, it was stupid.

"Mr. Jones." The honey smooth voice of his personal secretary intruded into his meditations on the world he was about to own. "Roy and Gunner are here to see you, sir."

"Send the lads in." He turned and sat at his desk to await his two most trusted associates.

He could tell by the expressions on their faces that they weren't bringing him good news. Roy Bogs and Gunner Caldwell were the last two of his old Australian outback pals. The three of them had started as teenagers in a backwater, hole-in-the-road town repairing TVs and renting videotapes to stockmen living at remote cattle stations in the bush. They had also dabbled in the transport of drugs and anything else that would make them a buck before Jones discovered computers.

When he found that he was good at writing programs, Jones went to Sydney, taking Roy and Gunner with him, and they had used their outback methods to set themselves up in business. When Jones saw that he could go no farther in Australia, he moved to the United States, first stopping in California's Silicon Valley. After finding a niche in the cyberbusiness that wasn't being covered by the giants of the industry, he hired bright young computer engineers and designers and made that niche his empire. Now he was one of America's top twenty richest men, and he was poised to become the richest man of all history. The only glitch he saw was the matter of Anne Keegan and the microchip she had stolen.

He didn't really need the computer chip she had taken when she failed to return from a mall crawl. Making specialized computer chips was what had built Rainbow Cybertech to be the power that it was, and he could make millions more like it. The chip itself didn't matter, but he wanted Anne Keegan back because, like the wild dog he had been named after, he didn't let go of anything that was his.

"You haven't found her, have you?"

Gunner Caldwell stepped up to take the heat. Of Jones's two henchmen, he was the stronger and the natural leader. He was smart enough, though, to know when to bend to a stronger will rather than try to go head-to-head. That was what had kept him from falling by the wayside when Jones moved into the big leagues. Roy Bogs was a born follower and a man who could carry out instructions without question. Such men were useful.

"No, we haven't, Dingo," he admitted. "But we're making good progress. We've found a way to check the driver's licence photos of all fifty states, and we're running that now. The problem is that no two of the bloody states are using the same bloody kind of computers, so we have to tailor our program to each system. You can't believe some of the crap that's still in use out there."

"You're assuming that she's still in the States."

"We already ran as good an immigration check as our money could buy and—"

"My money," Jones interjected coldly.

"Christ, Dingo," Caldwell said, "I know it's your money. All I'm trying to tell you, mate, is that we're doing everything we can."

"Keep on doing it, and do more."

WHEN THE TWO MEN left his office, Jones walked across the room and laid his hand on the electronic keypad to the door of his inner operations room. Only two people in the company had access to the area—he and his chief programmer, Cliff Jennings. Anyone else who even tried to get in would end up talking to Gunner and Roy, and it would be the last conversation that person would ever have with anyone.

The lights in the room came on automatically when the door closed behind him. Slipping into the leather swivel chair in front of the battery of oversized monitors, he pulled the remote keyboard into place and started calling up the world's stock market figures. As the numbers flashed by almost too fast for the eye to read, Jones inputted it all into his brain.

Considering that the Southeast Asian and Japanese markets were still trying to find a level between repeated currency panics, the general market wasn't doing too badly. Although he hadn't had a hand in it, rather, not a big one, the Asian currency crisis of late 1997 and early 1998 had set a trend for the regional markets. Even Hong Kong was a mere shadow of what it had been at the Chinese takeover in 1997.

Were he a conventional trader, this regional instability would be troubling. But he wasn't a conventional anything, and he didn't speculate on the stock market. Even the most savvy investors were subject to the whims of fate and things beyond their control. Dingo Jones wasn't a man to subject himself to things he couldn't control. Period.

He played the market, but to him it wasn't play, it was all-out war. And, while he wasn't known for having a delicate ego, he wasn't so foolish as to think that even he would be able to foresee everything that might affect the financial world. Instead of opening himself up to uncertainty, he specialized in one thing—precious metals. And even in that narrow arena, he didn't speculate. Every time he stepped into the ring, he won. And he won because he had set up the match beforehand, every last move.

As a result of this, he controlled more gold and silver than most nations. Only the big three, the U.S., China and Russia, owned more gold than he did. The difference was that he didn't have all of his gold in one place like Fort Knox. In fact, much of it wasn't even out of the ground yet. What he owned was gold stocks, precious metal options and gold mines, and he had purchased them when gold had been at its all-time post-World War II low in the 1980s. So, when Singapore devalued its currency, it only made his gold holdings in its banks worth more because the contracts were written in U.S. dollars and were payable in bullion.

Were he to call in all of his assets at one time, the Asian market would really become unstable, and he didn't want that. At least not yet. Instead, he was siphoning off just enough to keep everything in flux and churning. A few million here, a few there, and he was taking all of it in bullion. This, of course, was making gold prices very unstable, so he was selling a little at the high points and using the money to buy out some of his lower-priced options.

In a lesser man, this would have been called risky tactics if not suicidal. But he was Dingo Jones and he never took risks with money.

When he finished the market report, he clicked over to the unedited network news feeds. Being in the line of work that he was, it was child's play for him to break the encryption the networks tried to put on their raw footage. He had once offered CNN an unbeatable 72-bit scrambler system and was turned down. Ever since then, he had enjoyed breaking into every security system the media giant tried to use.

A quick scan of the latest news showed that there had been no lessening of Millennium Madness around the world. The process was racing to its inevitable conclusion and nothing could stop it now. In less than six months, the world was going to come to an end. At least the world as it had been known before the year 1999.

There would still be nations, cities and people left all over the world, of course. But there would be fewer of them in each of the three categories. In the place of the missing entities would be chaos and bringing order to chaos, was a good way for a man to make his mark. Napoleon had done quite well for himself by going up against an unruly street mob in Paris. He had won a European empire with a few well-placed shots from a couple of cannons, but Jones was going for a much bigger prize.

At exactly the right time, he was prepared to send the world's financial markets back to the Dark Ages. The cyberspace revolution had linked and intertwined the entire global economy as it had never been before. That had sped the pace of business and had made the modern world possible. But, relying on electronics had also made this global entity vulnerable. If someone was to kill the cyberspace network that held it all together, every economy in the world would collapse.

As history had shown again and again, in times of social collapse, the Golden Rule applied. He who has the most gold rules. And in his case, he had the gold, not paper accounts, not electronic files, but the real stuff, so he would rule. It was really as simple as that.

Not only did Jones have gold above ground, many of the world's richest gold mines were under his control. As with many of his holdings, the mines weren't in his name, but were owned by shadow corporations. The mines in Australia were ready to go into operation, but the ones in South Africa would probably have to be worked under armed guard. He didn't see that as a problem, though. The millennium was also going to produce hundreds of freelance armies as lesser national governments went up in flames and their soldiers would need employment.

The genesis of this plan went back almost a decade when he had collided with a couple of tequila bottles one night and his drunken brain had concocted a plan to rule the world. Like folklore has it, there is something mystical about the worms in the bottles. At first, he had tried to put the preposterous idea out of his sober mind. But like a worm, it had burrowed deeper into his thoughts. Then one day he locked himself in his office and spent the next several days taking a cold hard look at the world of the nineties.

With weapons technology what it was, ruling through force was no longer practical. Even owning a nuclear strike force was no guarantee of security. Ruling through wealth, however, was a very effective alternative. Never before in the history of man had there been a time when wealth had counted for so much. To be sure, there had been times when a single man had owned most of the world's convertible wealth—Alexander the Great and Ramses came readily to mind. But unlike in Alexander's time, modern wealth wasn't in gold bullion and it wasn't even in paper anymore.

Today's wealth was counted in electrons stored on magnetic media in a computer somewhere. And as with paper money that went up in smoke, no electrons, no wealth. A man like Jones, who knew how to work electrons like few others did, would be able to make those electrons disappear taking all the world's wealth with them. When the computer records of the world's finances disappeared, so would the wealth.

The property, real and otherwise, would remain to be sure, but the value of stocks, bonds and all other promissory notes would drop to that of toilet paper and not a good grade TP at that. In the chaos, a man with gold in hand would have an edge no one would be able to counter.

DINGO JONES WASN'T the only one who was following the raw footage of the world's activities. As if the Stony Man team didn't already have enough to do, Hal Brognola had tasked the Computer Room staff with keeping track of the growing number of Millennium Madness incidents. The countdown to the year 2000 was ticking, and the pulse of the world was quickening in time to it. The only way the United States could keep on top of the situation was to stay informed. Threats and trends had to be caught as early as possible so the danger they represented wouldn't come as a surprise.

Hunt Wethers, Akira Tokaido and Carmen Delahunt were all logging and running threat analysis on each event as it happened. Most of what they were finding was harmless, at least as far as being a threat to the security of the United States. But it was tagged for trend and filed for later reference.

In Latin America and the United States, sightings of the Virgin Mary and the resulting riots were increasing, as was the loss of life when order was restored. Even in the most Catholic of nations, public order had to be maintained. Crowds simply couldn't be allowed to run rampant and close down major cities.

In the U.S. and Western Europe, cult groups, some religious and some New Age, were a box-office business. Otherwise rational people were flocking to join anyone who stood and claimed to know what the future held in store. In the U.S. though, after the problems in California with the Temple of Zion and other cults arming themselves for Armageddon, these groups were being closely watched by everyone from the ATF to the local sheriff.

The hottest action right now, though, was in the Islamic world. The so-called millennium prophecies were getting more attention than ever. In almost every Muslim nation from Afghanistan to Zanzibar, the prophecies were being played on radio and TV daily and imams read from the apocalyptic texts at every mosque service. Even with these broadcasts, though, it was difficult to know what was going on because of a lack of firm intelligence.

Now that the threat of the millennium plague had forced the evacuation of most of the Western embassies in the Middle East, getting on-the-ground intelligence from the region wasn't easy. Even faced with an unknown plague, though, the British were holding out, as were a few of the Russian trade missions, but they weren't venturing far from their compounds. The other source of information, Western businessmen operating in the area, was also gone, so local Arab TV broadcasts had become the major source of input for Stony Man, and what they were showing wasn't good.

Several major cities were experiencing serious unrest, with Cairo leading in the body count. With its huge population of younger, marginally employed, urban poor it was a natural for millennium-inspired unrest. The imams were promising the armies of poverty that their time in the sun was coming, but many of them weren't willing to wait even a few months for the millennium. They wanted theirs now and they knew where they could find it.

Cairo was a city of great contrasts. Many of its people suffered great poverty, but it was also a center of even greater commerce and wealth. The city's elite were proud of their accomplishments and didn't try to hide their wealth. They lived in stunning mansions, drove the world's most expensive cars and ignored the lives of the "lesser" people. They were now learning that ignoring the poor came with a heavy price tag.

In Cairo, the green flags of jihad had been raised against the rich. It started with a street confrontation between a Mercedes sedan and a donkey cart. When the Mercedes driver assaulted the donkey's owner, a small crowd gathered and the driver was severely beaten. In the souks and bazaars, the story grew with each retelling until it had become a story of armed guards of the rich man opening fire on a peaceful crowd. To add insult to injury, the revised version had the rich man himself killing the poor man's donkey.

A march on the justice minister's building to demand justice for the poor man turned into a blood bath when police really did open fire. That night, invoking Allah's protection, masked men armed with gasoline bombs stormed an exclusive Cairo neighborhood. More people blocked the streets preventing fire trucks from getting near the blaze. By the time the riot police arrived to disperse the crowd, several mansions had gone up in flame.

The next several nights, the poor didn't burn out the rich. Instead they stormed their compounds and looted them. In most instances, they also killed the occupants. By the end of the week, the city was under martial law. But since the army drew its troops from the poorer classes of Egyptian society, they, too, were susceptible to millennium dreams. Each confrontation saw fewer and fewer soldiers using their weapons to defend the rich.

CHAPTER FIVE

Beirut, Lebanon

Even though René Clostermann hadn't been able to put a name to his terrorist contact, Katzenelenbogen now had confirmation that someone was closely protecting Dr. Insmir Vedik. The attempted ambush on him and Bolan was tied in with the death of the nurse and Wendelmann. Someone was trying to make sure that no one learned Vedik was in Beirut. Or if they did find out, that they didn't live long enough to pass on the information. The question of who were the watchers had no ready answer. Not in a place like Beirut.

If Vedik was the man behind the millennium plague as Aaron Kurtzman suspected, and if it was tied in with the so-called millennium prophecies, any of the Islamic nationalist or terrorist organizations could be shielding him. The followers of Hamas, Hezbollah, the Taliban, the old Islamic Brotherhood and the PLO were just the more notable suspects in a city that hosted representatives from almost every Islamic revolutionary group in the

Middle East. When the wannabes and the hangers-on were added, the suspects made up a large percentage of the male population of the city.

Finding which group was behind this wasn't going to be easy, but Katz had been in this situation before and had a few ideas about separating the sheep from the goats.

THE LAST THING any of the Phoenix Force commandos wanted to do was to get involved in an Alamo scenario with them playing the Texans and every out-of-work terrorist in Beirut pretending to be Mexicans. But as Katzenelenbogen pointed out, someone knew they were in town, and they needed to find out who that someone was. Since one of the time-honored ways to trap rats was to put out cheese, they would go along with it this time.

The villa the team had leased had a nice stucco-over-concrete tower on the corner of the main house that gave Gary Manning a good 360-degree view of the compound and the neighborhood. It was a nice sniper's nest, and he was playing the team's designated sniper again. This time, though, he had left both his trusty old Winchester Model 700 and his M-21 at home.

When Katz had arranged for a supplemental hardware shipment, he had ordered a new weapon specifically tailored to urban combat. Springfield Armory's 7.62 mm SAR-8 heavy barrel countersniper rifle had been designed for police SWAT team use. As the name implied, it was intended to take out opposing snipers and, since it took a sniper to kill a sniper, it was perfect for this job.

The weapon's 20-round magazine made rapid-fire sniping situations more manageable. There was nothing worse than being in a good firing position and having to pull off target to work a bolt to reload. Stony Man Farm's armorer, Cowboy Kissinger, had threaded the Springfield's barrel to accept a sound suppressor and mounted a folding bipod. Combined with the new Springfield 2d Generation Government Model 4 ranging scope, he could reach out and touch someone right between the eyes at well over a thousand yards.

He turned when the trapdoor behind him opened and T. J. Hawkins stepped on the roof with a steaming mug in his hand. "I brought you some coffee," he said. "It ought to tide you over till dinner."

"Thanks."

"It's quiet around here," Hawkins commented as his eyes scanned the villas and apartments surrounding their compound. The villa's walls allowed good fields of fire.

"Maybe too quiet," Manning replied.

Part and parcel of being a good sniper was to have a well-tuned sense of what was called situational awareness. In simple terms, it meant keeping track of absolutely everything that was going on around you at all times. In a built-up area, that meant keeping close tabs on the activities of the locals. The vehicle traffic, how fast people were walking, how many windows were shut with the curtains drawn and how many shops had closed signs displayed in the windows could all be indicators of a setup.

Being new to the neighborhood, Manning couldn't tell if what he was seeing today was normal activity for the locals. But he was sensing a definite edginess to their movements. For a people who had been hammered as hard as they had been for so long, though, a lingering sense of wariness might be their norm. It would take another day before he would be fully integrated with the rhythms of the neighborhood.

"You want me to spell you on the gun?" Hawkins asked.

"Give me another hour or so," the Canadian replied. "I'm still fresh. You can take over when I switch to the nightscope."

"Is that going to work around here with all this light?"

"I'm going to try it," Manning said. "But if there's too much ambient light, I'll use the light-intensifying scope."

Night-vision devices had come a long way since the Starlight scopes of Vietnam. With the right hardware, a shooter could see as well at night as he could during the day. The only problem now was interference from artificial light, which could still affect even the best night optics.

"Catch you in an hour," Hawkins said as he headed for the trapdoor.

NAJI NAHAS WATCHED from the third-floor window of an apartment across the street and half a block down from the villa the Yankees had holed up in. From his vantage point he could observe the target without being directly in the line of fire.

God had indeed been merciful letting him locate the killers so quickly. And from the report of the watcher assigned to Clostermann, it was obvious that the UN infidel was working with them. He would pay for his treachery later, as Nahas had to deal with the Americans first. His watchers had spotted another two Yankees, so there were at least four staying in the villa, but he had no fears.

Three Assassin cells, fifteen men, were ready to move in on them as soon as they had the cover of darkness. Five more men were standing by in case they were needed, but Nahas didn't expect to have to send them in. Four or five Americans wouldn't be a problem for that many of the Brotherhood.

THE NIGHT FOUND Bolan and Phoenix Force inside the darkened compound patrolling with their night-vision goggles. Katz was in the villa's makeshift communications room as information central, and Bolan was the mobile reserve. There was no hard evidence that they would be attacked this night, but the swift response after they visited the UN building showed that the opposition was taking them seriously. Not to be prepared would be a serious mistake.

Hawkins was taking his shift on the sniper rifle when he spotted movement on the north wall. "Heads up, guys," he whispered over the com link.

"I've got two intruders coming over the seaward wall and they're armed."

"Roger," Katz sent back. "Let them get inside and then drop them. I don't want their bodies falling into the street."

"Roger."

Through the scope, Hawkins saw the intruders in shades of green. They were dressed from head to toe in dark clothing, including a face scarf and gloves. Their weapons appeared to be silenced Italian Beretta Model 12 subguns.

Once they had dropped inside the wall, Hawkins fixed the trailing terrorist in his sight reticle and squeezed off a single shot. Without waiting to see if he had scored, he switched to take out the lead man. As he brought the scope to bear, he saw that his target had heard the 7.62 mm round impact with his partner and was turning to see what had happened.

Not wanting to lose him, Hawkins took a three-quarters shot, catching him behind the left shoulder. A second insurance shot went into the base of his skull. "Two down," he reported.

"It's a feint!" Encizo called out from the opposite corner of the compound. "I've got a dozen of them coming over the south wall."

"Pull back to the garage," Katz ordered as Bolan grabbed his H & K and headed for the door.

By the time Hawkins moved the rifle to the other side of the tower, all the dark-clad attackers except for the one Encizo had dropped, had disappeared under cover. For the moment, the ball was in the attackers' court.

"Rafe," Bolan sent, "I'm coming up on your right."

"I've got your left," McCarter advised him.

Rust, Manning and Calvin James were spread out a few yards apart in front of the west side of the main house waiting for the terrorists to come to them. In preparation for the evening's activities, they had fitted the sound suppressors to their MP-5 SDs, and their magazines were loaded with subsonic 9 mm ammunition.

"Left front," Manning whispered. "By the pool house."

"Got him," James replied.

When the intruder broke cover, James triggered a short burst of 9 mm lead, stitching him from his belt buckle to his neck. Even on full-auto, the MP-5 barely made an audible pop as the subsonic rounds left the silenced muzzle.

Before the terrorist's body had time to hit the ground, a silent return burst sang past James's head and splattered against the wall behind him. Even though the shot was too late, he ducked in reflex.

Sound, as well as sight, was vital to survival in any firefight, particularly one at night. Without the sounds of gunfire to tell them where the opposition was, the Phoenix Force warriors were at a disadvantage. But their attackers were equally hampered.

When the terrorist fired again, Manning spotted his muzzle-flash and fired a burst at it. Instantly, half a dozen more weapons silently opened up on them and the Stony Man commandos were fighting for their lives.

Bolan, Encizo and McCarter waited in the dark until the terrorists were concentrating on the other half of the team before breaking cover. "Go!" Bolan whispered.

Coming in on the attackers' flank, the commandos silently put four of them down before the other terrorists knew they were being hit. It took a long moment for them to react to taking fire from two sides, and the delay cost them two more of their comrades.

Though they were grouped together in cells, the Assassins had been primarily trained to work alone. Bolan and Phoenix Force, however, worked as a team and the teamwork was paying off as they whipsawed the attackers.

In the tower, Hawkins was using his scoped rifle to spot movement and direct fire. He was looking for a clear target so he could take a shot as well, but having his teammates down there made him cautious. "There's one working his way around the hedge behind the patio."

"I'm on him," Rust sent back.

Spinning to face the threat, the CIA man saw the winking of muzzle-flash. Rolling to the side, he snapped out a return burst and rolled again. When another burst chewed up the ground beside him, Rust had had enough.

Spotting the glow of warm muzzle steel in his night optics, he rose to one knee and let loose a long burst. When the MP-5's bolt locked back on an empty magazine, he dropped and quickly exchanged magazines.

When he looked again, the target was gone.

WITHOUT THE SOUNDS of gunfire, it was hard to tell when the battle ended. After waiting several minutes, the Stony Man team moved out to comb every square foot of the compound to make sure that no one was hiding in the dark.

"I'm clear," James radioed to Katz.

"Nada," Encizo reported.

"I think I've got a WIA," Hawkins reported. "South side of the pool house."

"On the way," McCarter replied.

Hawkins had held back to keep from spooking the terrorist until help arrived to take him captive. The man's bloody right arm hung limply at his side, and he had taken another round in the chest. But, even with blood bubbling from his mouth, his eyes glared defiance. When he saw the Phoenix Force commandos, their weapons ready, his left hand snaked down to his waist and came up with a curved dagger.

"Allah akbar!" he shouted as he raked the knife across his own throat. His feet kicked and his eyes fixed on infinity.

"Shit!" James muttered. It was difficult enough to try to keep someone alive to question in a night fight without their doing things like that.

"You know," Hawkins said at he looked at the inlaid handle of the curved bladed dagger imbedded in the terrorist's throat, "that knife looks like an Assassin's dagger."

"A jambiya," Rust stated, identifying the weapon. "It's more or less the standard knife throughout the Arab world."

"No," Hawkins said. "I mean the signature daggers of the old Brotherhood of Assassins. You know, the guys who were around during the Crusades."

"The Old Man of the Mountain," Rust said, "that and the Tales of Sinbad are the most enduring myths to have come out of this region since Islam took over."

"The Assassins weren't a myth," Hawkins replied quickly. "I know that they took the credit, or were given the blame, for damned near every guy who disappeared in a dark alley or who went face first into a dish of poisoned couscous back then. But they were very real, and they were damned good at what they did."

"Some of your heroes?" James grinned.

"You might say that," Hawkins replied. "They were some of the best clandestine warriors of all-time and make the Japanese ninjas look like amateurs. The combined efforts of every caliph and prince in the region couldn't put them down. It took the Mongol hordes to finally accomplish that."

"So you're saying that this guy was an Assassin?"

"I know they've been dead for centuries," Hawkins said, "but that knife sure as hell looks like the only authentic Assassin dagger known to exist. In fact, it looks like it could be its twin.''

"Where's this dagger?'' Rust asked. "The real one, I mean.''

"As I recall,'' Hawkins replied, "it was last seen in Damascus right after World War II before it disappeared. Like the Spear of Casca Longinius, it seems to keep dropping out of sight.''

"That was the spear used to kill Christ, wasn't it?''

Hawkins grinned sheepishly. "I have this thing about legendary weapons. And that spear was found in Syria as well, in Antioch I think.''

Katzenelenbogen had stood silent throughout this exchange. He was a pragmatic man and he had no use for legends and myths, not even for the ones he had helped create. He worked with cold, hard facts and the knife buried in the terrorist's throat was such a fact. If Hawkins was correct in saying that it was a copy of an ancient Assassin's jambiya, that would also be a fact. It was also a fact that the old Assassins were dead. Everyone who had lived back then was dead, even the Roman who had killed Jesus. But if the dagger was an insignia of the Assassins, it could mean that the deadly Brotherhood had been resurrected. And if that was the case, it would also be a fact.

Katz also knew a lot about the Assassins of old, and he, too, knew that many of the stories were fact. Hawkins was right in saying that they were the greatest clandestine warriors of all time. In fact, for the better part of two centuries, they had played a critical role in the history of the Middle East. In the modern age of nation states, a medieval cult of killers might seem to be out of place, but it wasn't impossible.

"I think we'd better pass this one on to the Farm," he said, "and see what Aaron can come up with on resurrected Assassins."

"Whoever these guys were," James said, pointing to the last of the attackers, "what do we do with them?"

"Take their mug shots in duplicate," Katz said, "and then deliver them to the UN compound. Let those bastards sort them out."

"We have a dozen or so to haul away," James reminded him.

Katz shrugged. "Make two trips."

CHAPTER SIX

Miami, Florida

Sarah Carter didn't particularly enjoy being back in Florida. The soft early-evening breeze caressing her skin didn't feel as good as it had before. After having lived in San Diego, the stately royal palms lining the boulevard looked stunted. God knew that California had its problems and then some, but Miami had a tattered, third-world look that she had completely forgotten. Even the spray-painted gang graffiti on the walls looked second-rate. The colors weren't as bright and the words were misspelled.

Rather than it being a homecoming for her, returning to Miami was like returning to the scene of the crime. Contrary to the popular conception of a woman in trouble, though, she didn't see herself as a victim of any crime. She knew full well that she'd made some stupid choices and had played an active part in creating the circumstances that had sent her fleeing for her life to California.

She'd also made some choices in San Diego that had worked to her advantage for a change. But agreeing to come back to Miami with Arthur, rather, Rosario, as he said to call him, and his two sidekicks might turn out to be the stupidest decision she'd ever made.

This was Dingo Jones's home turf. As she knew only too well, he had an army of informants in the greater metro area. Why he had this private army, she had never found out. As far as she knew, he wasn't involved in any of the traditional southern Florida criminal enterprises. He didn't deal drugs, he didn't smuggle illegal immigrants and he didn't deal arms. Beyond Rainbow Cybertech and humiliating her, his only real interests seemed to have been real estate and making even more money. The only thing she had been able to figure was that having an army of street informants made him feel even more powerful.

Rosario Blancanales glanced at her sitting beside him in the red Caddy convertible he had leased. "Are you okay?" he asked.

She suppressed the urge to jump out of the car and run away screaming.

"I'm fine," she said and breathed deeply. "I just never thought that I'd be riding through this part of town in a pimpmobile again. It's too much like the bad old days." Part of why she felt so good around Rosario was that she could talk about her past and it didn't freak him out.

Blancanales laughed. "We always try to get cars that will fit into the local scenery. Caddys are a dime a dozen around here, and most of them are ragtops.

I'm sorry about the color, but it was all they had left on the lot.''

She felt like the flashy car had a blinking neon sign on it announcing that she was riding in it, but she realized that it was just her imagination working overtime again. "It's okay, Rosario. I'm just a little jumpy, that's all."

"I'll take you back to the motel if you want and I can finish this up with Gadgets."

"No," she stated with a shake of her head. "Let's just keep going and get it over with."

As the first part of the exercise, Blancanales was making a street recon of all the known Rainbow Cybertech sites and taking notes. Having Carter riding with him made them look like they were just two more tourists out for a thrill visiting the wild side of the city. The woman had thought that Blancanales had been out of his mind when he suggested doing that. But now that they were in Little Havana, she saw that they weren't the only two well-dressed people in fancy cars cruising the crowded streets.

She didn't understand why anyone in their right mind who didn't have to be here would want to be. She had also never understood why Dingo had so much of his operation located in the high crime areas of the city. It was true that the land was cheaper, but he had so much money that a couple of million more or less was just pocket change for him. He could have built anywhere he wanted.

The thought crossed her mind that it might have been because of his warped love of danger. He might be getting a thrill out of living so close to people who would kill him for his shoes and not think a thing about it. She knew, though, that anyone to try wouldn't live long enough to regret it. It wouldn't be easy to kill Dingo Jones.

"Do you want to stop for lunch?" Blancanales glanced at the clock on the Caddy's dash.

"Sure," she replied. The only thing she had truly missed about Miami was the food. Southern Californians simply had no idea how to cook fish. They kept trying to make it part of a lifestyle statement instead of something to eat.

"If I remember right," she said, looking around to get her bearings, "there's a good place not too far from here, Papa's. I think you'll like it."

"Which way?"

"Keep going."

BACK AT THE MOTEL Able Team had taken up residence in, Hermann Schwarz was downloading the information Kurtzman's team had gathered about Dingo Jones and his operation. Acting on a hunch, he had also requested a listing of any and all crimes that had been reported in a four-block radius around the Rainbow Cybertech sites. He didn't know what he was looking for there, but it would help pass the time until they came up with something worth working.

While Schwarz sorted through the files, Carl Lyons lay on the bed, staring at the ceiling and waiting for night to fall. This was one operation where he knew that he was going to have to be more than patient. Patience wasn't one of the ex-cop's better virtues. Not for the first time, he wished that Sarah Carter had just kept her mouth shut about that damned computer chip. He'd been sent on wild-goose chases before, but this time he didn't even have a decent goose to chase. All they had was the fact that this Dingo Jones made computer chips and operated out of Miami.

Having Blancanales drive around town in a red Caddy with the woman at his side was a crude way to try to develop a lead, but it was all they had. If Carter's story was legitimate, her ex-lover was an out-of-control maniac about her. And considering that he had posted a million dollar reward for information leading to her capture, apparently he was. The average millionaire usually didn't throw money around like that, not when a few thousand in this town could buy just about all the sex a man could handle.

The hope was that Jones would get word that she was back in town and would make a move on her. The way Stony Man Farm worked, that would be considered de facto evidence of his being a bad guy. Whether it really meant that he was more than a little angry about having lost his bed partner was yet to be determined. Even the fact that Kurtzman had confirmed that the chip would do what Sarah said it would, didn't make Jones a criminal.

They still had to establish intent, and that wasn't going to be easy. Just because a man owned a gun and ammunition didn't make him a murderer.

AS WAS TO BE EXPECTED from the name, Papa's was another Hemingway-theme restaurant. But unlike most of the eateries that traded on the famous name, it looked like a place where the writer would actually have enjoyed eating. It had that raw, working-class edge to it, and there wasn't a single fern in sight. Plus, every table had a heavy glass ashtray parked in the middle. Better yet, lunch was served in a room with a real old-fashioned bar at one end just like Papa would have liked, and the bar had a brass foot rail.

The waiter was in the white shirt with bow tie and black pants that went with the thirties theme, and he didn't have a long memorized list of trendy specials. Everything on the menu looked good, but Blancanales ordered the conch stew listed as the house specialty. He ate out so much that he automatically tried the local fare.

The service was quick, and they were both hungry when the food arrived.

"That was great," he said as he washed down the last of the stew with the last of his draft beer, also an excellent choice.

"I always liked the food here," she said as she looked out over the water. The familiar food and strong beer had relaxed her a little. Maybe this would work out after all.

She reached across the table and took his hand. "Look, I'm sorry if I was a little jumpy this morning. It's been a long time and I was—"

"I know," he said. "Going back can be stressful. But like I said, we'll keep you out of it as much as we can. As soon as we have a better feel for what we're dealing with here, we'll keep you completely away from the operation. In fact, I'm sure Hal won't mind if we send you back to Virginia until it's all over.''

"That might be nice.''

"So,'' he said, waving to the waiter, "let's get back out there and finish this up today.''

She smiled. "Let's do it.''

At the other end of the room, Papa's bartender was doing what bartenders traditionally do when there is nothing else to do—he was polishing the bar's glassware. Despite the fact that modern dishwashers and detergents had made spots on glassware an endangered species, the customers expected to see a bartender polishing glasses, and that was okay with him. The mindless chore allowed him to keep an eye on the crowd without seeming to be doing so.

Bars were places where people did and said things that they would never think of doing or saying anywhere else, and that also suited the bartender very well. He made a good living behind the bar at Papa's. The salary was fair and the tips were great. He made even more money, though, by selling information. Miami was a place that valued information above everything except maybe money. And since making money in Miami often depended on having the right information at the right time, knowledge was power.

The fact that a young blond woman was having lunch with an older Hispanic man was going to be worth a lot of money to him because he knew who she was. There was a million-dollar reward floating around out there for information about her, and he could use a little of that. She was good-looking, there was no doubt about that, but he couldn't see what it was that made her worth that much. Someone thought she was, though and that's all that mattered to him.

As soon as they left, he reached for the phone and dialed a number from a card he had tacked on the wall next to the cash register.

"THE FIRST REPORT," Gunner Caldwell told Dingo Jones, "was of her riding around in Little Havana with a guy in a red Caddy convertible. The informant was sure it was her because he used to go to the club to watch her."

Caldwell knew that he could mention the strip club where Anne Keegan had once been a dancer. Some men might try to hide the fact that their woman had worked in a place like that, but Jones seemed to revel in it.

"You get a plate on the car?" Jones asked.

"I ran it and it's a rental from down by the marina." Caldwell looked at his notebook. "The name on the form is Rosario Perez."

"The second sighting?"

"The bartender at Papa's said that she stopped by for lunch with an older Hispanic guy, and that would go with the name on the rental."

Both men knew that Papa's had been one of Anne's favorite lunch spots and, if she was back in town, she would likely go there.

"I want to know who this guy is and what she's doing with him."

"Well, Dingo," Caldwell said, "I don't know who he is yet, but he looks like a player, that's for sure. And as far as what she's doing with him, I saw her hanging all over the guy like he was her—"

The Australian stopped when he saw the look on his boss's face. As long as he had known Dingo, he couldn't understand why in the hell he couldn't just let the woman go and get about taking care of business, but he just couldn't. He had to admit that Anne was a real looker, but women like her were two for a penny in a place like Miami. Maybe three, if you went looking in places like the one where he had found her. Damned near every strip joint in town had half a dozen Miss Universe types flashing their goodies at the customers.

"I want both of them brought here immediately," Jones ordered.

"Doing it that way is likely to be noticed in the barrio. And I know that you don't like that—"

"I don't care if it causes a bloody war," Jones almost screamed. "Get them and bring them here."

"You got it, mate."

As soon as the two were gone, Jones went to the window and looked out. He had known that she would come back sooner or later. And he wasn't too surprised that she had a man with her. Being alone wasn't something she did well. But now that she was back, she would never be alone again. He would make sure of that.

THE TAKEDOWN in Little Havana went like clock-work. It was late afternoon and Rosario Blancanales was headed back to the motel when a delivery van backed out of an alley in front of him, so he stopped the Caddy to let the truck get past. An instant later, two men came from behind and had guns to Carter's head before he could react.

"Take it easy," he said, making sure to keep his hands in plain sight on the steering wheel.

The shorter of the two gunmen reaimed his pistol to target Blancanales. "Bring your hands up slowly, mate," he snapped.

Blancanales did as he was told and allowed the gunman to slip plastic riot cuffs over his wrists.

Once his hands were bound, the gunman backed off. "Get out of the front seat," he ordered, "and get in the back on your side. You try to run, and I'll shoot your legs out."

Again, Blancanales was careful to follow instructions. With his options exactly zero, he had no choice. As soon as he was reseated, the shorter gunman slipped into the back with him while his partner got into the driver's seat.

"Where are you taking us?" Blancanales ventured to ask.

"Shut your gob or I'll blow it off," the man beside him said.

Blancanales did as he was told. He did notice, however, that after the first shock, Carter hadn't reacted as he had expected anyone would when they were being carjacked. She sat stiffly, staring out the windshield as if in a trance. Remembering how she had come through in San Diego when the three Temple of Zion goons broke in on them that night, he was surprised. He had thought that she was more of a fighter than that.

Carter kept silent while Caldwell drove the Caddy out of the barrio and headed for Jones's headquarters. She had been in a state of shock since she recognized Gunner Caldwell and Roy Bogs behind the pistols aimed at her face. Dingo Jones's two henchmen were the last people she had expected to see. Or at least she hadn't expected to see them so soon. She had tried to warn Rosario and his partners about the dangers of going into Jones's home ground, but they hadn't believed her. Now they would, but it would be too late for both her and Rosario.

There was a small chance that Jones might let her live, but there was no way that her companion would leave the building alive. Once he was in Jones's glass-and-steel fortress he would die.

CHAPTER SEVEN

Miami, Florida

Rosario Blancanales wasn't surprised to see that the carjacker's destination was the headquarters of Dingo Jones's Rainbow Cybertech. He would have been shocked if that hadn't been the case. From the faint Australian accents of the two gunmen, they had to be Dingo Jones's sidekicks. Plus, white guys in their late thirties didn't fit the profile of the average barrio carjackers.

Throughout the long ride, Sarah Carter continued to sit almost motionless. As soon as the Caddy was driven into an underground garage and parked, she stepped out and walked to the elevator. She knew her way into the building from Jones's private parking bay. The two gunmen let her walk alone and concentrated on making sure that Blancanales didn't try anything.

The elevator smoothly whisked them up several floors before opening onto a wide corridor. Again, a zombielike Sarah Carter led the way, turning to the right for a short walk to a pillared entry and a set of mirrored double doors. The electronic lock opened to her touch, and she led the party into a spacious office with floor-to-ceiling windows that looked out over the city's lights.

"Nice view," Blancanales said to break the silence.

"I'd keep my bloody mouth shut if I were you, mate," the shorter thug replied.

Carter shivered when she saw Jones come out of the side door. The suite behind the door was his bedroom away from home and was the site of many of the humiliations she had experienced at his hands.

"Anne." The Australian smiled not unlike a crocodile from the outback he had been raised in. "I'm so glad that you decided to come back."

"I'm called Sarah now," she said, trying to keep her voice even. "Anne died when I left here."

"I'll call you anything I want, bitch." His voice whiplashed her. "And you won't die until I tell you to."

She closed her eyes and ducked her head as if expecting to be hit, but Jones merely smiled. Turning away from her, he walked over to where Blancanales stood with his hands cuffed behind his back and a goon hanging off each arm.

"Just who the fuck are you, mate?"

"Leave him alone, Dingo," Carter said without turning. "He doesn't know anything about you and me."

"I don't believe I asked you to speak for him,

Anne." He kept his eyes on Blancanales. "Do it again and you'll be sorry."

When she remained silent, he spoke to Blancanales again. "I asked you a question, mate."

"My name is Ros—"

Jones's blow to his belly took Blancanales by surprise, knocking the wind out of him.

"I don't want to know your bloody name. I want to know what you think you're doing with her and what the two of you are doing in Miami."

Blancanales fought for his breath. "I met her…in California…and asked if she wanted to come…here with me to buy a boat."

"There aren't any bloody boats in California?"

"None that I want to buy."

Jones backed away to take Blancanales in from head to foot. "You don't look like the yacht club type to me, mate. You look more like a player, a dealer of some kind. What is it, drugs, guns, or—" he glanced over at Sarah "—girls."

"She isn't part of my business," Blancanales put bite into his reply. "She doesn't know anything about what I do for a living."

Jones sneered. "I'll bet she doesn't. She's just your woman for the week, and you don't want her to get in the way of doing business, right?"

"Something like that."

"Then you won't mind if I reclaim her, will you?"

Carter shot him a frightened glance, but Blancanales had to ignore it. This was no time for him to stand up to Jones. "Not at all," he replied calmly. "Like I said, I don't have any claim on her."

Jones studied him for a long moment, his eyes drilling into him. "You're a right bastard, aren't you? Pick up another man's woman like she was some kind of street whore, and then have the balls to bring her back to her hometown. You're a real piece of work."

"I didn't ask her any questions about her life before I met her," Blancanales replied. "I figured that was her personal business."

"My business, you mean."

"I didn't know that."

"Well, you do now."

Jones walked back to Carter and, locking eyes with Blancanales, ran his hand up under the curve of her breast, cupping its fullness. "Get him out of here," he told his two henchmen.

"What do you want us to do with him?" Caldwell asked.

"Just see that he leaves town."

The last thing Blancanales saw as he was being led out was Jones standing in front of Carter, both of his hands roaming over her body. She stood unmoving as if she were frozen in place. It was a thoroughly sickening scene.

"SHOULDN'T WE HAVE HEARD from Pol by now, Gadgets?" Carl Lyons asked Hermann Schwarz.

"He's late, yes," Schwarz replied. "But, then, he didn't give us an exact ETA when he expected to be back. You gave him a long list of places to check out, and maybe he and Sarah stopped off for dinner or something.''

"That damned woman.''

Schwarz was very much aware that Lyons wasn't a charter member of the Sarah Carter fan club. Lyons had made it perfectly clear that he felt she was getting in the way of Able Team's doing business. How much of that was simply because the drop-dead gorgeous Sarah was hooked up with Blancanales instead of him, he couldn't tell. But something about her was biting Lyons's butt big time. And it wasn't like him to be so down on a woman, particularly one who looked like she did.

But whatever it was, as far as Schwarz was concerned, the only problem Sarah Carter presented to the operation was Lyons's reaction to her. "Give it a rest, Ironman,'' he said. "She's not any worse than a dozen other blondes you used to hang with.''

"The difference, dammit,'' Lyons almost spit, "is that Pol's acting like she's part of the team now. He doesn't go anywhere without her.''

"Come on.'' Schwarz sighed and shook his head. "She's part of his cover this time. He needs her hanging around so that no one will wonder what he's doing. One look at her and they'll know what's going down, namely her.''

"That's what I mean,'' Lyons said. "We're supposed to be on the job down here, not screwing around.''

"This isn't the first time the job has called for a little screwing around, Ironman. So like I said, give the guy a break.''

"I still don't like it."

"Your opinion has been duly noted and recorded."

Even though he had tried to put a good face on it, Schwarz was also worried about Blancanales. If he was going to run over, he would have called to let them know. "You want me to call the car phone?"

"Do it."

Punching the buttons, Schwarz placed the call to the mobile phone in the Caddy. He let it ring a dozen times before switching off. "Nada."

"Can you trace the car?"

"Actually, I should be able to," Schwarz said. "All I have to do is to dial it up on the GPS network."

Going to his laptop, he rang a local cellular phone number and punched in a code to remotely access the onboard GPS unit in the car. Quite a few top-of-the-line cars were now equipped with the devices, which doubled as a theft deterrent as well as a navigator. He was able to activate the GPS, but when he tried to locate the car, he couldn't get a reading.

"Something's wrong," he said, frowning. "I activated it and I should be getting a reading, but nothing's coming through. Maybe it's parked in an underground parking structure or something like that. The damned thing won't transmit through concrete."

"No sweat," Lyons said. "I'm going after him anyway."

"Exactly what did you have in mind?" Schwarz started to get alarmed. When Lyons got in that mood, all too often anything could, and did, happen.

"It's simple." Lyons shrugged. "I'm going to go to Jones's headquarters and ask him if he's seen Pol and Sarah."

"Subtle. Very subtle. Faced with your righteous wrath, he'll just 'fess up and hold his hands out for the cuffs."

"I don't need any smart mouth from you right now, Gadgets. I want Pol back, and Jones can keep that damned woman for all I care."

"But she's the key to all of this," Schwarz pointed out. "She's the one who knows where the cyberbodies are buried. If we're going to make any headway against this thing, we have to have her."

"You know something? I really don't give a damn what happens to the banks when the world ends. The whole planet is going to go tits up, and I really don't care. Maybe it will clean out some of the human garbage polluting the earth and we'll all be better off for it."

Schwarz wanted to laugh, but since he didn't want to go in for extensive dental work in the morning, he refrained. He was a bit surprised, though, to see the coldly logical Carl Lyons buying into the Millennium Madness thing. His hope that the millennium would bring on some kind of general cleansing of the planet was more of a New Age scenario than the traditional Christian take on it, but it was no more logical, nor more likely to happen.

When the first day of the year 2000 rolled around,

the planet was still going to be populated with an overly large number of two-legged animals who were no damned good to anyone and never would be. That was simply the human condition, and nothing short of total destruction of the planet was ever going to change that. The only thing that any man or woman could do to make the world a better place was to see that they didn't fall into that group.

"Why don't we try something a little stealthier?" Schwarz suggested carefully. "We might be able to gain access to Jones's empire through the back door, hack our way in. I know you feel like busting someone's head right now, but let's try and find out which head will do us the most good to bust. After that, we can go around smacking anyone we feel like, but that might be counterproductive right now."

"With you or without you," Lyons said, "I'm going in there tonight."

"Okay, okay." Schwarz held up his hands in mock surrender. "Just let me get my breaking-and-entering kit. We might need it to pick locks and such."

"Don' t take too long."

WHEN BLANCANALES and his captors left the Rainbow Cybertech parking structure, Roy Bogs was at the wheel of the Caddy and Gunner Caldwell was in the passenger seat turned to keep an eye on his prisoner. He didn't have a weapon in sight, but Blancanales knew that a gun muzzle was pointed at him and the back of the car seat wasn't much protection. He also knew that he had only the slimmest chance of surviving the next hour or so.

It would have helped a lot if Sarah Carter had told him that Dingo Jones wasn't only a power-hungry maniac, but a killer as well. Had he known that bit of information, Able Team might have planned its Miami operation a little differently. For instance, Schwarz could have worked up a couple of his subminiature locators and a panic button, or Lyons could have rode shotgun with him. As it was, his partners wouldn't know that anything had gone wrong for several more hours and by that time, he'd be biodegrading in a nearby swamp.

He now realized that Carter had left a great deal out of the story of her life before San Diego. He had understood her reticence about going into the intimate details of living with Jones. She hinted just enough about his sexual proclivities for him to know that she had been abused physically as well as mentally. She hadn't, however, mentioned that Jones was psychotically jealous as well.

He was still a little taken back by her completely passive behavior since they had been carjacked. He had forgotten about the Stockholm Syndrome, as it was now called. Captives, particularly women, often underwent a complete loss of will when abused and ended up identifying strongly with their captors. This also occurred in many domestic abuse cases. Intellectually, he understood that this gave a woman a better chance of personal survival in a bad situation. But as a man, he didn't understand how anyone could surrender to a life of degradation and not fight to stay free.

During the time Carter had been with him, it had looked as if she hadn't been able to shake her mental bondage to Jones. Almost the instant that she was back with him, she had meekly submitted to him.

All that background information was good to know, but it wasn't going to help him get out of his current situation. Rather than analyze what had happened, he needed to make something work right now. The only thing he had going for him was that Jones's two thugs were using his rental car to drive him to wherever they planned to dump his body. The fact that the Caddy was a ragtop might give him an opening.

When they headed back into Little Havana, he realized that they weren't going to dispose of his body in a swamp as he had figured. They were going to leave him in a back alley with his throat cut and make it look like another Greater Miami tourist murder. The fact that they had stripped him of his wallet, ID and watch would lend credence to that story.

ROY BOGS WAS ROUNDING a corner onto a side street when he slammed on the brakes and started honking his horn. Ahead was some kind of procession blocking the street. It looked like there were a hundred people all carrying candles converging on a small church.

"Try to get around them," Caldwell ordered. "We need to get to that warehouse."

When Bogs turned in the front seat and looked over his shoulder to back up, Blancanales made his move. With his hands cuffed behind his back, his options were limited, but he took the opening. Throwing himself forward, he twisted and drove his shoulder into Bogs's face as he dived for the open side of the car.

With Caldwell watching the procession, it took him a split second to turn back and, by that time, Blancanales had thrown himself over the side of the Caddy. With his hands bound behind him, he had no choice but to land on his face. Even so, he'd fared better than Bogs. He'd caught the gunman square in the face and put him out of action with a smashed nose.

Knowing that he'd be shot in the back if he stood and tried to run, Blancanales got to his knees and crawled behind the car.

Cursing at the top of his voice, Caldwell leaped out of the car, his 9 mm pistol in his hand. Showing the gun was a bad move. Several young Hispanic toughs on the sidewalk had witnessed this action and started moving in, pulling their pistols as they came.

"Help me!" Blancanales shouted in Spanish. "He's trying to kidnap me!"

Not wanting to get involved in a gun battle he couldn't win, Caldwell jumped back in the car. "Get the hell out of here!" he yelled.

Nose bleeding profusely, Bogs slammed the car into gear, cranked the wheel hard and did a one-eighty, peeling rubber as he sped away.

Blancanales was trying to get to his feet when one of the gangbangers kicked him in the ribs. "Where do you think you are going, amigo?"

With his hands bound, Blancanales couldn't defend himself. He looked up at the thugs surrounding him and said. "I can pay if you help me."

A blow to the side of his head sent him into darkness.

CHAPTER EIGHT

Stony Man Farm, Virginia

Since Hal Brognola was sitting in as the Farm's mission controller, he took Katzenelenbogen's report about the foiled attack on the villa in Beirut. That was a good sign because it was further confirmation that the Vedik tip was valid. If the Bosnian doctor wasn't in Beirut, the team wouldn't have been targeted twice. The first attempt could have been a fluke, but a fifteen-man attack on the villa could only mean that they were on the right track.

Katzenelenbogen's theory that the attackers had been from some kind of born-again version of the medieval Assassin cult, though, wasn't good news. If it was true, it added another dimension to an already complicated situation. Picking up his notepad, he headed downstairs to the Computer Room to brief Kurtzman on this new twist.

"Assassins?" Aaron Kurtzman sat back in his wheelchair and clasped his hands behind his neck. "Real Assassins of the Brotherhood? This is getting more and more interesting as it goes along."

"But what does it mean?"

Kurtzman turned and his fingers flashed over the keyboard as he went into an infrequently used database. "I haven't thought about those fanatics in quite awhile. Man, they make the Hezbollah and Hamas thugs look like a Catholic schoolboy's choir. They were probably the best terrorists the world has ever seen. At least they were the most successful."

"Wonderful." Brognola reached into his jacket pocket for his ever-present roll of antacid tablets. Another drawback to Price's absence was that the medical supply closet was running out of his favorite medication. He had just broken open his last roll, and when they were gone he'd be reduced to drinking baking soda in water.

Kurtzman looked up from his monitor. "Katz and the boys might have tripped over a serious hornet's nest there. I had forgotten the religious underpinnings of the Brotherhood of Assassins."

"But they were hashish-addicted killers, right?"

"They reportedly used hash, yes." Kurtzman nodded. "But it wasn't quite as simple as that. If doing hashish was the answer, every street punk in the inner cities of America would be a superman. The Assassins were dedicated holy warriors following a very unusual Islamic splinter group."

"I'll bite," Brognola said to keep Kurtzman talking.

"They were Nizari, which was an offshoot of the Ismaili, a sect of the Shiite branch of Islam. And, as with Christians, the more times you break away from the mainstream, the more unorthodox you become. The Nizari weren't content just to break away and be different, they created a synthesis of damned near every religion that had ever existed in the area. They mixed elements of Christianity, Judaism, Mithrism and Persian pagan beliefs, the whole nine yards.

"Among other things, the Nizari were into the millennium scenario just like the Christians of the time were. Since they were picking and choosing their beliefs as they went along, they accepted Jesus as a major prophet and counted his birth as a significant event. Even though they were nominally Muslim, if they're back, I would expect them to be on hand for the millennium party."

Brognola shook his head. "You're telling be that an ancient sect of killers has been reborn so they can help bring about the end of the world?"

Kurtzman shrugged. "Stranger things have happened and, as far as that goes, we've got a lot of strangeness happening right now. Just look at the daily Millennium Madness report Hunt's tracking. Supposedly perfectly sane citizens of the world's most advanced nation are relapsing into a completely medieval mind-set and have taken to worshiping water stains on stop signs and patterns on tree bark. And we're the nation that invented the computer and sent men to the moon."

He shook his head in disgust. "You have to remember, Hal, that civilization is a very thin veneer. Bosnia is a good case in point as well as every nation in the Middle East for the past fifty years."

"India, Northern Ireland," Brognola continued

the litany of religiously inspired brutality that was haunting the modern world. The century had started with nationalism and political ideology being the major threats to civilization. But after almost a hundred years of that, religious lunacy seemed to be taking the world's center stage as the new excuse to slaughter your fellow man.

"Now that I stop to think about it," Kurtzman said, "I'm not surprised to hear that the Brotherhood of Assassins has been resurrected. Needless to say, we Christians don't have a patent on lapsing into religious insanity every thousand years or so. With the strong Nizari tie to the millennium, someone could have used that to recruit fanatic followers. All we need now is to have another Mahdi show up and all of the pieces of the puzzle will fall in place."

"What puzzle is that?"

"The one that pictures the end of the world," Kurtzman replied calmly. "The real Armageddon that the Bible-thumpers and doom-criers have been wailing about for the last couple of years. Since the appearance of the Mahdi signals the end of the world, the Muslims would get into it as well, big time. They really take their religion seriously."

Brognola closed his eyes as if to shut out the world. Not all that many months ago the world had been a much more rational place to live. Not that it had been less dangerous, but the maniacs who were trying to blow up the world back then had all been motivated by greed or a lust for power. Both of which could be considered rational motives. Religious mania, however, followed neither reason or logic.

"I'll need a white paper to send to the Man."

"On what, the Assassins or the Mahdi?"

"Both."

"I have the Mahdi paper in the can. All it'll take is a quick update. The Assassin study will take at least twenty-four hours."

"Do it in twelve."

THE OLD MAN of the Mountain hadn't heard from Naji Nahas yet, but he was fully aware of what had happened at the villa in Beirut. The watchers had reported to him as soon as the last silenced shot had been fired.

He didn't regret having sent fifteen brothers to their deaths. He never regretted sending his followers to paradise. And their deaths hadn't been without value to him. He was now certain that the mysterious foreigners were the shadowy commando force led by al-Askari. It was obvious that they had been fully prepared for such an attack. In fact, it looked as if they had invited it to happen. They, too, wanted to know who they were up against and taking prisoners would have been high on their agenda.

The bodies of the fifteen Assassins who had made the assault had been found laying in a row on the sidewalk around the corner from the main gate of the UN compound. All of them had borne bullet wounds, but one's throat had been slit as well. Knowing what he did of al-Askari, he was certain that the American hadn't mutilated the corpse. True to his vows, the Assassin had killed himself to keep from being captured.

Al-Ismaili's concern now was to keep the Americans bottled in Beirut until he could make his appearance as the Mahdi. He didn't think that the commandos were after him per se. No matter how good they were, he would have been astonished if they had heard of him at all. Beyond the men of the Brotherhood itself, no one knew that Malik al-Ismaili had brought the Assassins back to life. It was more than apparent, though, that the Americans were looking for Insmir Vedik.

Naji Nahas had acted properly in silencing the Bosnian nurse immediately. But he might have overreacted when he ordered the first UN man killed as well. It was true that he'd been told that protecting Vedik was of the utmost priority, but carrying out those orders had had unseen effects. Al-Ismaili could see now that the commandos had come to Beirut because of those two deaths. How they had learned about them was of no importance. They had, and they had moved on the information. This, too, was a sign that he wasn't facing the CIA or some other normal American intelligence agency. The CIA could never have moved that fast.

Al-Ismaili had wanted to keep Vedik on hand until the Mahdi had the East firmly under his control. The threat of the millennium plague would be a good counter to have against Western reaction to the appearance of the Mahdi. It could be used to divert attention from the Islamic upheaval that would result. But those were merely contingency missions. Now that the disease had done its main job of clearing the unbelievers out of the Middle East, it didn't have the importance that it had once had.

Vedik's manufactured plague had worked well in conjunction with the Islamic prophecies. It had showed the faithful that God was watching over them and that He was punishing the infidels. While the hysteria about the disease had leveled off in the Western World, Muslims still buzzed with talk about it. After so many decades of being dominated and humiliated by the West, the Faithful were rejoicing to see the Infidels run in panic. They could see now that God was still with them and was taking His vengeance on the heathens.

The return of the Mahdi would be the last step in this process of revitalizing a beaten people. For one thing, it would put an end to the endless wars that had torn the Arab world for so long. One of the biggest reasons that the West had been able to dominate the Middle East was that the Islamic nations didn't present a united front. Petty tribal and nationalistic differences still divided God's people.

In the post-World War II era, the old United Arab Republic had been a good attempt to unify the region, but it had been torn apart by greedy men and the internal conflicts continued. The more recent Iranian-Iraqi war, the invasion of Kuwait, the seemingly endless torment of Afghanistan and the bloodletting in Algeria were all examples of the Muslim world devouring itself. The Mahdi would put an end to all of that. He and he alone had the power to bring the peace to Islam that it hadn't known since the death of the prophet.

Maybe he could afford to sacrifice Vedik if it would keep the Americans from interfering with the appearance of the Mahdi. Leaving the doctor in Beirut would guarantee that he would be spotted again. Al-Ismaili would insure that he would be well protected, and if the Yankees got too close to him, he would simply be killed to prevent his capture.

Going to his communications room, he quickly issued new orders.

NAJI NAHAS HAD SPENT the night praying that the merciful God of his fathers would show him mercy yet one more time. He knew, though, that his life was forfeit for the debacle at the villa. Fifteen brother Assassins had died there without even as much as a sound. Had it not been for the muzzle-flashes he had seen from his vantage point, he wouldn't have believed that a firefight had taken place. It was almost as if the earth had opened and demons had swallowed them.

Nahas didn't believe in demons, but he did believe that a demon in the form of an American had come to Beirut. Al-Askari had killed the five men in the car-ambush team, and now he had taken fifteen more lives.

He hadn't reported his failure to the Old Man of the Mountain yet. He knew that he was honor-bound to do so and to accept whatever punishment he was given. But there was something he had to do first. In hopes of partially redeeming himself, he was going to eliminate the last link to the sighting of Insmir Vedik in Beirut. As long as René Clostermann was alive, the secret of the Bosnian's whereabouts wasn't a secret.

Gathering the three men of his remaining cell, he drove across town to the apartment building where Clostermann lived. After instructing his brothers, he climbed the steps of the stairwell leading to Clostermann's third-floor apartment. His watchers had told him that the UN man was at home instead of at his office, but he hadn't called to announce his visit. This wasn't going to be a social call.

Pausing on the second-floor landing, he took a sound suppressor out of a side pocket and threaded it on the end of the barrel of his 9 mm Makarov. The pistol fired a subsonic cartridge and was perfect as a silenced weapon. The puff of explosive gases could hardly be heard across a room, much less through an apartment wall. Stuffing the pistol into the back of his belt, he climbed the last flight of stairs.

Nahas had to knock twice before an obviously agitated Clostermann opened his door a crack. "What are you doing he—"

Nahas shouldered his way through the door and closed it behind him. Seeing the half-packed luggage scattered around the room, the Lebanese smiled. "You are thinking of leaving Beirut, René?"

"Something has suddenly come up." Clostermann tried hard to keep his voice level as he backed away from the Lebanese man. "My...my wife has taken sick. The call came in right as I was leaving the office yesterday. I'm going back to Paris for a week or so."

"That's a lot of luggage for a week's trip," Nahas commented dryly as his eyes inventoried the suitcases. "If I didn't know better, René, I'd say that you were planning to run out on me."

The flicker of anxiety that crossed the UN officer's face told Nahas all he needed to know. "You know I can't let that happen, René. Those two men you talked to yesterday turned out to be the wrong people for you to have talked to."

"How was I to know that?" Clostermann pleaded. "They walked into my office and started asking me questions about Wendelmann. I already told you everything they said and the answers I gave them. I did not tell them anything about my connections with you, and I told them that they would have to talk to the police if they wanted to know more about Wendelmann and the nurse. I swear—"

Hearing Clostermann mention the nurse, Nahas drew the Makarov from the back of his belt and, bringing it up in one smooth move, fired once. "Go with God."

The 9 mm slug entered Clostermann's head directly under his right eye and continued into his brain. Like a puppet with its strings cut, the UN officer crumpled to the floor. Blood pumped out of the entry wound like a fountain as his heart pumped its last beats.

Stepping over the body, Nahas went to the table under the window where Clostermann's passport and wallet were laying beside an open briefcase. To give the impression of a robbery, he pocketed both items before glancing through the paperwork in the briefcase. There was nothing of importance but his copy of a canceled apartment lease showed that he had been planning to leave Beirut permanently.

God had been good to him. He had been just in time to prevent that from happening. Another hour and he might have missed him. He was turning from the table when he saw a car pull up to the curb below and four men step out. Though he had never seen any of them before, he instantly knew who they were. Al-Askari had come to visit René Clostermann.

God was indeed being good to him today. Now he had a chance to completely redeem his life. The Old Man of the Mountain would honor him above all men if he could kill the legendary Yankee demon.

In his rush to catch Clostermann, Nahas hadn't brought a radio, but he had his cellular phone. Flipping it open, he dialed the number of the leader of the three Assassins he had left guarding the building. After issuing his orders, he dropped the magazine out of the butt of the Makarov and inserted a fresh one.

It was only one short round, but many gunfights were won by the last shot fired.

CHAPTER NINE

Beirut, Lebanon

When Jack Grimaldi stopped the Alfa Romeo sedan at the curb in front of René Clostermann's apartment, Bolan and Katzenelenbogen quickly stepped out followed by Rafael Encizo and J. R. Rust. Grimaldi would wait behind the wheel while Encizo and Rust guarded the building and Bolan and Katz went upstairs for another chat with the UN man. The attack on the villa the previous night could mean that he hadn't gotten the message.

Katz and Bolan had barely gotten inside the door when Encizo's voice broke in on the com link. "I've got two bandits lurking by the back of the building," he said. "They look to be armed."

The presence of the gunmen put Bolan on full alert. It could only mean that Clostermann was of interest to someone besides him, and that could only be the opposition. "Just watch them," he replied. "But make sure they don't follow us."

"No sweat."

"And if they do, try to keep from killing both of

them. If they're who we think they are, I'd like to talk to one of them.''

''I'll try.''

Bolan paused in the entryway to slip his Beretta 93-R from his shoulder leather and thread its custom sound suppressor in place. Beirut was well accustomed to the sounds of gunfire, but the locals also tended to shoot back. If it came down to a firefight, silent kills were definitely in order.

Katz swung his mini-Uzi from under his jacket and slipped it off safety. It, too, was silenced and well suited to a midmorning confrontation in a building.

As Bolan started for the stairs, he caught a moving shadow thrown on the wall by the light at the top of the stairs. Someone was on the landing above. Considering that they were in an apartment building, it might be one of the residents going across the hall to borrow something from a neighbor. But his instincts told him that it wasn't. They had come too late to talk to Clostermann.

Signalling to Katz, he paused while he tried to scope out the stairwell. The landing above looked clear, which meant that the shadow's source was on the third floor. Before he moved out again, Bolan triple clicked his com link to let Encizo know that he was going into action. A double-click answer told him that the Cuban and Rust were holding the back door.

Motioning to Katz, Bolan took the wall side of the stairs while Katz stayed to the right. Their rubber-soled boots made no noise on the concrete steps as they slowly advanced. Bolan hung back to let Katz get one step ahead of him. With them spread out, an attacker would have to choose who to take on first.

NAJI NAHAS CROUCHED by the banister on the third-floor landing, his Makarov ready. Holding the high ground at the top of the stairs would give him certain victory over the men who were coming to visit Clostermann. After hearing the front door close, though, he hadn't heard any movement. It didn't sound like anyone was coming up the stairs.

Carefully peering around the banister, he caught the shadow of a man slowly coming up the stairs with his back to the wall. Crouching again, he waited to let him get a little closer. When he thought that the target was close enough, he sprang, Makarov lowered.

Too late he saw the other man on the inside of the stairs. Snapping a shot at the big man, he was bringing his pistol to fire on the other target when a burst of silenced 9 mm lead tore through his upper body.

Bolan took the last two steps in a single bound, but their would-be ambusher was dead. A glance down the hallway showed that he had been alone. He signaled to Katz that they were clear.

"Rafe?" Bolan called over the com link.

"We're secure down here," Encizo answered. "They got excited when they heard the shot and tried to get past us. I'm sorry that I couldn't save one for you to talk to."

"Get ready to pull out. We'll be down in a minute."

While Katz ran a check on the body, Bolan stepped inside Clostermann's apartment. All it took was a glance to tell the story. The UN man had been heeding their advice to get out of town, but apparently he hadn't seen the need for urgency. From the consistency of the blood on the floor, Clostermann hadn't been dead for more than a few minutes, ten or fifteen at the most. A quick search of the apartment turned up nothing of value, and he closed the door behind him as he left.

In the hall, Katz was also finished. "He's completely sterile," he said. "But see that scar by his mouth? Remember what Clostermann said? That's his Assassin contact."

"Another dead end."

"At least another dead body. And speaking of which, we'd better be moving on before the police arrive. Someone is bound to have called them by now."

AS FAR AS Katzenelenbogen was concerned, he, Bolan and Phoenix Force were in a state of war. The only problem was that since he still didn't know exactly who was attacking them, he didn't know who they should target for reprisal. But there were ways to bring the rats out of the rubble. As a first step, he called a meeting as soon as they returned from Clostermann's apartment.

After recounting the thwarted ambush at the apartment and the UN man's death, he made an announcement. "We're going to change tactics," he told the commandos. "We're going to start trolling."

"For what?" Rust asked.

"For anyone who wants to mess with us, and that includes Hawkins's Assassins. I'd like to be able to narrow it down a little better than that, but as yet, I can't."

"What about Vedik?" James asked.

"We're still looking for him, but since we just lost our last link to the original sighting, we're going to have to try to develop another lead. And that is what's behind this new program. By going out and looking for them instead of sitting here and letting them come to us, we should have a larger haul to look at."

"When do we start?" Hawkins asked.

"Tomorrow. I want you guys to spend the rest of the day familiarizing yourselves with the maps and intel reports on suspected factions."

Bolan sat through Katz's briefing without adding much. He knew that their mission to find the creator of the millennium plague had been a long shot at best. Playing long odds was a Stony Man specialty, but even the best players had to come up short every now and then. He also knew that every day they didn't find Vedik was one more day that Barbara Price and the rest of the victims of the plague would suffer.

When the briefing broke up, he joined Katz. "I'm going to go out tonight, alone."

The Israeli looked at his old friend and comradein-arms. "Do you really think that you can develop something that way? We don't even know what the guy looks like, and we have no reason to think that he's still in the city."

"I know," Bolan replied. "But the Assassins know where Vedik is, and maybe I can get my hands on one of them before he can put his knife in his throat."

"Take one of us with you."

"I'd rather do this one solo."

"At least let us provide backup for you," Katz offered. "We don't know how many of the bastards are watching the villa, and you don't want to pick up a tail."

Bolan smiled. "At least not too soon."

Katz couldn't help but smile back. Beirut was known to be a dangerous city after dark, but as soon as the sun went down that night, it was really going to become dangerous.

MANNING WAS ON THE SNIPER RIFLE again as Bolan waited by the south corner of the west wall. It was well past dark, and the locals were all safely behind doors. After one last sweep of the vicinity with his scope, the Canadian keyed his com link. "It looks clear, Striker. Good hunting."

A click in Manning's earphone told him that Bolan rogered. He would track him with the rifle scope as long as he could to watch his back.

After cutting the razor wire and pulling it apart, Bolan went over the wall. He left the wire gaping in case he needed to come back by that route. Once he was on the street, he started trolling for Assassins.

He started with the streets bordering the villa's walls and planned to work his way out. He kept his movements stealthy, but exposed himself as often as possible. It would take a good man to pick him up, but he didn't want to attract street thugs. Even though it might make life more liveable in Beirut if he took out a few, he only wanted to deal with the pros.

"Striker," Manning's voice said over the com link, "you've got one on your six, about twenty feet out."

"Thanks," Bolan replied. "I heard him."

The Executioner was of two minds about what to do with the tail he had picked up. On the one hand, he wanted to capture one of the born-again Assassins to question. On the other, though, he wanted to conduct psychological warfare on their leader, whomever he was. He and Katz had already started that process by delivering the casualties of the assault on the villa to the sidewalk beside the UN compound. Taking out the Assassins who had killed Clostermann had been another gambit. As opening moves, they had been well delivered. Now, though, he wanted to really bring it home to them.

Pulling the Cold Steel Tanto fighting knife from his assault harness, Bolan pulled back into a deep shadow cast by a kiosk. Slowing his breathing, he heard his tail stop as if to look around. After a faint muttered curse, the man hurried forward again.

As he passed Bolan's hiding place, the Executioner stepped out behind him. His left hand clamped over the man's mouth and jerked his head to the side as his right hand drove the point of the Tanto into the hollow of his neck above the collar bone. The razor-sharp blade entered the side of the Assassin's neck and sliced through his jugular vein, carotid artery and trachea with one swipe.

Bolan held the Assassin in a deadly embrace as his feet kicked. The hot, coppery smell of blood was strong in the cool sea air. When he was dead, Bolan eased the Assassin's body to the ground face up.

After patting him down and finding another dagger, Bolan folded the man's arms across his chest in repose. He planted the distinctive dagger hilt in his dead hands with the blade pointing toward his feet. He didn't know if that meant anything to the Brotherhood, but it would show them that he knew the significance of the dagger and was on to them.

Back on the street, Bolan went looking for his victim's partner. To do a proper night surveillance, more than one man would be watching each sector. He hadn't found a radio on the corpse, but that didn't mean that the Assassin wasn't expected to report every so often. It just meant that the second man was probably close by.

He was approaching the end of the block, when a dark shape suddenly blocked his path. The man who had stepped in front of him was dressed like an Islamic terrorist in a made-for-TV movie. He was in black from head to foot and even had a black kaffiyeh wrapped around his face. His AK-47 was slung over his back and, drawing the curved dagger from his waist, he assumed a crouched fighting stance. The knife's hilt was against the butt of his hand instead of the thumb against the hilt grip, which was favored in Western steel techniques.

Bolan hadn't expected this, but he would go along with the program. Taking this guy down with his knife would only add to the message he wanted to send to his masters. Drawing his Tanto fighting knife, he assumed the classic low blade stance of most Western knife-fighting styles.

The Assassin's jambiya was a couple of inches longer than Bolan's weapon, but while the curved blade was good for slashing attacks, it was no good as a stabbing weapon. Bolan's straight, chisel-pointed Japanese blade was probably a much better all-round fighting knife. The next few seconds, though, would determine that.

For a moment, the Assassin stood his ground, his dagger moving in a complicated blocking pattern that spoke of extensive training. Bolan knew that when he struck, he wouldn't make the mistake of trying a high, chopping attack. Only untrained men and women ever tried that one. It was too easy to block, and it left the attacker's body completely exposed for a counterthrust.

When it came, the slashing attack was blindingly fast. Bolan was barely able to deflect the curved blade fast enough to keep it from gutting him. The back-slash follow-through was equally fast. This affair was going to have to be concluded quickly if he wanted to keep from getting hurt. He couldn't afford to go into a give away defense where he allowed his opponent to score a cut in order to momentarily occupy his blade while he struck a killing blow in return.

The Assassin stepped back and went into the moving blade defense again. From his body posture, Bolan saw that the Assassin was confident, maybe a little too confident. He also sensed that the next attack wouldn't be the same as the first. Since the slash had failed, the Assassin would try something different. In the dark, Bolan couldn't see his opponent's eyes, so he focused on the set of his shoulders, watching for the change that would signal the attack.

Again, the Assassin struck swiftly, his blade flashing through the space between them. This time, Bolan let it come. In his mind's eye he tracked its path, instinctively turning and stepping into the arc instead of pulling back.

Caught off guard, the Assassin tried to change his attack, but it was too late. Bolan's forearm blocked the man's wrist while he stabbed the Tanto straight into his belly. A twist of the blade severed his aorta, bringing death in an instant. As with most knife fights, the deadly contest had taken only a few seconds. Two attacks and it was over.

When Bolan stepped back, he realized that he had taken a slash across the top of his left forearm when he'd blocked the Assassin's knife. It wasn't serious, but it was enough to put an end to his evening stroll.

First, though, he laid the corpse on his back with his knife in his hand. The message was going out that messing with this particular group of Yankees carried a price.

Stony Man Farm, Virginia

WITH EVERYTHING ELSE that was going on at the Farm, Aaron Kurtzman had almost forgotten about his search to find a photograph of Insmir Vedik. After the initial search had come up with nothing, he'd been forced to put it on the back burner to take care of more pressing matters. He was pleasantly surprised when he clicked onto an E-mail from the UNPROFOR Mission in Sarajevo and found a message asking if he was still looking for a photo of the Bosnian doctor. He was on the phone to Bosnia before he even finished reading the message.

Fortunately, the UNPROFOR Headquarters had a quality fax at its disposal, and the photo came through beautifully a few minutes later. According to the report that came with it, the group shot had been taken at a reception that had been held at the Sarajevo Medical University a few years before the war and was the only image of Vedik they had found so far.

In the photo of some two dozen people, an unremarkable looking man had his head turned away from the camera as if he were talking to the woman next to him. Fortunately, he was tall enough that his face wasn't obscured by the man in front of him. Kurtzman would have preferred to have had a full-face mug shot, but the three-quarters profile was better than nothing and it would certainly do.

Placing the photo on the tray of his chair, he wheeled himself to Akira Tokaido's workstation to let him have a go at it. Tokaido was a genius at manipulating photographic images. Give him a badly blurred snapshot, and he could make it look almost like a studio shot.

"Here's our man Vedik." Kurtzman held out the photo.

"Not much to look at, is he?" Tokaido studied the shot. "But guys like him rarely look like maniacs, do they?"

"Can you rotate this and give me a full-face view?"

"No sweat," Tokaido said. "But remember that it will be fully symmetrical instead of showing what the other side of his face really looks like. But I can make a real good profile shot from this side if you want."

"How long will it take?"

Tokaido glanced at the digital clock display on his screen. "I should have the profile done before dinner. But the frontal view will take a little longer."

"I also need it with glasses and facial hair versions, at least one with a Middle Eastern-style mustache."

"Piece of cake." Tokaido grinned. "I have all the hair templates I need already in the program."

CHAPTER TEN

Rainbow Cybertech Headquarters, Miami, Florida

Towering against the night sky, the glass and chrome towers of Dingo Jones's Rainbow Cybertech headquarters complex looked like it was straight out of a Star Trek movie. From a distance, they looked like a computer-enhanced set design. The slender skybridges connecting the towers and glittering glass domes were lit up to further enhance the futuristic look, but were jarring against the backdrop of the neighborhood they bordered.

The landscaped campus around the buildings was carefully manicured, but it hadn't been designed with the aim of keeping out intruders. The dips and hollows combined with decorative plants gave Carl Lyons and Hermann Schwarz a well-concealed approach almost all the way from the street to the main structure. A final dash across fifty yards of darkened open ground put them in the deep shadows at the base of the building.

WHEN THE INTERCOM in his bedroom suite buzzed, Dingo Jones stopped what he was doing and rolled over in his oversized bed to answer it. "What is it?" he growled.

"Mr. Jones, we have intruders on the grounds," the security duty officer reported.

Jones sat up and punched a code into the keyboard of his bedside workstation. The monitor instantly snapped to a multiple-screen image showing two dozen scenes of the grounds. He clicked on four of them, and the screen switched to show four views of two men making a cautious approach toward the side of the main building.

Looking over Jones's shoulder, Sarah Carter immediately recognized Carl as one of the two men. There couldn't be two big blond men in Miami who had balls enough to try to break into Dingo Jones's complex. Apparently, they had realized that something had happened to her and Blancanales and had come looking for them.

She suppressed a gasp as she watched them race to the side of the building and duck into the shadow. There was no way that they were going to be able to get in and even if they did, they'd be captured. Jones had a twenty-man internal guard force on duty at night, and she knew that they were well armed.

ONCE SAFELY HIDDEN in the deep shadows of the Cybertech building, Schwarz took out one of his gadgets to check the electronic environment they had entered. "We're being video-scanned," he said. "They know we're here, and I recommend that we get the hell out of this place ASAP."

"Do you have that laser zapper of yours with you?" Lyons asked calmly.

Schwarz's video camera killer had proved so successful on its first outing that he had modified it a bit and made it a part of his standard break-in kit. The laser now looked more like a pistol, albeit a futuristic one, and the battery pack had been incorporated into the pistol itself like an ammunition magazine.

It still fired line of sight, and Schwarz had no trouble taking out the first video camera he found mounted on the wall. Once he had it in his sights, the thin, red laser beam streaked out to disappear into the camera lens. There was no visible effect of the weapon's effectiveness, but he knew that was one electronic eye that could no longer see them.

Looking around, he located another camera and lined up to take it out as well.

WHEN DINGO JONES SAW the first video screen blink out, he knew what was happening. Even the best video surveillance could be defeated by using the right weapon. "Get some men down there quick," he ordered the duty officer. "I want those guys caught."

"Do you want me to notify the police?"

"No! Use our own people."

"Right away, sir."

"Where are you going?" Carter asked when Jones started dressing.

"Down to greet my visitors," he replied. "And

I won't be surprised if they turn out to be friends of yours, too."

"I'm scared," she said, sitting up and letting the sheet fall. "Please stay here."

Jones took one look and decided to let his hired hands handle the problem. Usually, he preferred to do his own dirty work, and he was certainly not the kind of man who listened to anything a woman had to say. But this was a special case. She had been gone a long time, and he hadn't had his fill of her yet.

"They had better not get away," he said as he turned back to her. "And they'd better not be anyone you know."

"I THINK WE CAN MOVE out now," Schwarz said after zapping three more video cameras. "But we're going to have to keep a sharp eye out. Someone has to notice that their security system has gone tits-up."

Just then, they heard a shout and the glare of a flashlight beam cut across the manicured lawn right in front of them. The two crouched low in the shadows against the wall, weapons ready, to see if it would pass.

WHEN ROSARIO BLANCANALES woke up, he saw that he was lying on a table in some kind of Cuban gang hangout or local social club. The Cuban flag hanging over the pool table was a dead giveaway, so was the music blaring from several boom boxes around the room. At least, though, he had woken up and wasn't facing a chat with Saint Peter.

"Amigo," a young tough said when he saw that Blancanales's eyes were open. "You are with us again. That is good. Now you can tell me what you will give me for saving you from those two bad guys."

Blancanales felt like he had gone ten rounds with Mike Tyson, but nothing seemed to be broken or seriously damaged. Apparently, he'd been battered after the blow to the head. "What happened to those two men who were after me?" he asked in Spanish.

"I usually get paid for information. And that kind of information is worth even more than what you owe me for having saved your life."

Blancanales sat up and looked around. With the average age of the room's occupants looking to be around eighteen, he had to be in a street-gang hangout. A social club would have had older Cubans in it as well. Talk about jumping from the frying pan into the fire. Holding people for ransom had become a popular sport with the gangs in Little Havana recently. Usually the victims were locals who had managed to do well and whose family had money to buy back loved ones. But the occasional tourist had been grabbed as well.

"I don't have my wallet with me," he pointed out. "But I can make a call and get some money here."

"Now you are talking," the kid said with a smile. "Let me get you a phone."

"Ramon," he called across the room, "your phone, if you don't mind."

Ramon walked over with a cellular phone and handed it to Blancanales's captor. "What is the number?"

Blancanales held out his hand for the phone.

"Oh no. You might dial the wrong number and we don't want that to happen."

"You mean that I might call the cops?"

The kid dropped the smile. "You are very smart, mister."

"Look," Blancanales said, "I don't know where I'm at and I don't know who you are and I don't want to know. I also don't think that you want the trouble that you're going to get if I don't walk out of here before too long."

A 9 mm Glock appeared in the kid's hand as if by magic. "I have some trouble right here, pal, all the trouble that I need. If you want to talk about trouble, this will do the talking for me."

Blancanales wanted to wipe the floor with the kid, he didn't have time for bullshit macho games. Why was it that every street punk who got his hands on a gun thought that he was a god?

"Put the gun away. I'm not worth a damned thing to you dead, and you know it."

"It might be fun to kill you."

Blancanales locked eyes with the gunman. "Do it or shut up."

The young Cuban was puzzled. This wasn't the way this scenario was supposed to go down. This Spanish-speaking man wasn't afraid of him, and he didn't understand why he wasn't. Everyone else he had pulled the gun on had begged for their lives.

"You'd better listen to the man, Paco." The voice came from the other side of the room. "He sounds like he might eat you if you don't stop bothering him."

When the room erupted in laughter, Blancanales turned and saw an older gangbanger, a man in his late twenties, sitting at a table by himself drinking a beer and smoking a fat Cuban-style cigar.

"If you can get this kid to wise up," Blancanales said, "I might be able to make a contribution to your club here." He shrugged with great emphasis. "If not, my associates are likely to become annoyed at my loss. And I don't think you want to talk to them about why I was killed."

"You spoke of a contribution," the other man said, getting to his feet. "What would this be for?"

"Your friend here said that you deal in information, no?"

The man nodded. "It is a valuable commodity in a place like this, yes."

"My associates and I pay well for information of the right kind." Blancanales turned back to the kid with the Glock. "We do not, however, pay ransom. In fact—" he looked the kid straight in the eyes "—we take pleasure in killing kidnappers, great pleasure."

"I am Gutierrez," the man said as he walked in front of the kid with the pistol.

Blancanales held out his hand. "Rosario Perez."

"What kind of information do you seek, Mr. Perez?"

"Before we talk about that, I need to call my associates so they do not waste their valuable time looking for me. Believe me, it will be much easier on your neighborhood if I make this call."

Gutierrez studied Blancanales for a long moment. "Call them, and then we will talk."

Blancanales took the phone and punched in the mobile phone number they were using for this operation. When it was not immediately picked up, he punched in a three-number code followed by the number on the phone.

"I can't seem to reach them right now, but they'll be calling back soon."

"Can I get you something while you wait?"

"Coffee would be fine."

SCHWARZ FELT the vibrating silent ring of his cellular phone. Pulling it from its pocket inside his night suit, he read the three-number code displayed on the digital readout. "Pol's okay," he whispered to Lyons.

"Where is he?"

"I don't know, but he left a number to call back."

"Let's get the hell out of here and find him."

"Sounds good to me."

Getting clear of Rainbow Cybertech, however, wasn't going to be as easy as their approach had been. Not when the ground was crawling with guards. The two guards with the flashlights had gone around the side of the building, but there were others scattered around the grounds.

"Wait a minute." Schwarz said. Digging into his carryall, he took out two minicharges with remote detonators, pulled the tape off the adhesive strips and slapped the devices on the wall. "Okay, let's go."

A short dash took them to the first clump of decorative shrubbery. No sooner had they gotten under cover than Schwarz triggered the first charge.

The small explosion was followed by shouting as the flashlights converged on the smoke-cloud.

"Get ready," he told Lyons, finger poised on the remote. "Go!"

The second explosion sent the guards scurrying for cover, and in the confusion, Lyons and Schwarz disappeared into the darkness.

DINGO JONES WASN'T surprised when his security patrols reported that the intruders hadn't been able to break in and had run away. His headquarters was a fortress with every kind of security safeguard known to man built into it. Short of blowing a hole in the wall, there was no possible way to break in. And even if an intruder did get inside, he would face an arsenal of sensors, automatic locks and the armed guard force. He wasn't pleased, however, to learn that they had eluded the search. He'd have a new security supervisor in the morning.

He turned back to Sarah Carter. "It looks like your friends have gone. They must not have wanted to get in here too badly. They ran at the first sign of trouble.''

''They weren't my friends,'' she replied wearily. ''I told you. I came here alone with Rosario and no one else knows that I'm here.''

Jones carefully studied her for a moment. Now that he had been with her for a couple of hours, he saw that she had changed. She was still the most beautiful woman he had ever known and her erotic skills hadn't diminished, but something about her had changed, and he wasn't sure that he liked the changes.

When he had first met her, she had been the most wanton thing he had ever known. She had revelled in sex as if she were addicted, placing no limits on what she would do with her body or let be done to her. She had also been completely devoid of the routine lies and deceits that passed as normal behavior for most women. Unlike every other woman he had known, she had never once said no when she really meant yes.

Now, though, he had sensed reluctance in her, and he could smell the lies she was telling. There was more to her being back in Miami than she was telling him, much more. Why she had come back was going to be interesting, and he would find out. After having stolen the microchip, only a completely insane person would have ever come back. And he knew that whatever else she might be, Anne Keegan wasn't crazy. Rosario Perez had to play a role in this.

He had intended to wait until morning to ask her

about the stolen microchip. But since this had happened, he might as well get started on it now. How long it would take for him to learn the truth would depend on her. If she was stubborn, it might take all night, but he had always done his best work at night.

He was again interrupted by the intercom. "This had better be good," he said, picking up the handset.

Jones's slitted eyes flicked over to Carter. "I'll be right down."

"What is it?" she asked, alarmed at the look he'd given her.

"Your new boyfriend has nine lives. He escaped from Bogs and Caldwell."

Carter knew that she couldn't let the relief she felt show on her face, but she was glad to hear that Rosario was safe. He had been good to her, and it wasn't really his fault that she was back in a hell of her own making. He had tried, but she was weaker than she had thought.

"I'm going down to talk to the boys," he said. "But you and I are going to continue this when I get back."

CHAPTER ELEVEN

Miami, Florida

The mood in the Cuban social club lightened while Rosario Blancanales waited for his call from Schwarz and Lyons. The punk who had tried to shake him down had put away his gun and faded into the woodwork. Along with the coffee he had asked for, Gutierrez offered Cuban rum, but Blancanales declined.

The conversation stayed light and inconsequential until the borrowed cellular phone rang. "Perez," he answered with his code name.

"Where are you?" Lyons asked.

"What's the address here?" Blancanales asked. When Gutierrez told him, he passed it on.

"We'll be there in fifteen minutes," Lyons said. "Do we need to bring the artillery?"

Blancanales looked up at Gutierrez. "No, everything's okay here, but watch the neighborhood."

"Got it."

Blancanales handed back the phone. "It is good that I made that call. My associates were already looking for me and no one will have to be hurt now."

Gutierrez was burning to ask about these "associates," but he knew better. This was looking like one of those instances where he didn't want to know. "You mentioned needing information earlier," he said. "What information are you looking for?"

"Do you know of a man named Dingo Jones? He runs Rainbow Cybertech."

A dark look came over Gutierrez's face. "The Wild Dog."

"That's what his nickname means, yes."

"We know him, and I will tell you everything we know about him and his men for free."

"Why is that?"

"He comes into the barrios at night and looks for those who do not know about him. Particularly the younger men like Paco here, who think that they are dangerous and want to prove that they are men. He always gives them the first move and then he hurts them."

"What do you mean?"

"I mean that he doesn't always kill them, but he makes them wish that they were dead. He cripples them in a way that they are no longer good for anything. The lucky ones are the ones he kills."

"The police have not been told of this?"

Gutierrez laughed. "The police are not our friends here. If they knew of this, they would think that we had only gotten what we deserved. They would not hunt a man who is doing what they wish they could do to us themselves.''

Though he didn't agree with it, Blancanales understood that sentiment completely. Many police officers thought about Able Team the same way. The difference was that Able Team usually operated under a sanction from legal authority and their targets were more than simply street punks.

''My associates and I are interested in Jones for more than his street crimes. He's far more dangerous than anything he has done to your people in the barrios. I can't go into it in any detail, but we intend to take him out of action as soon as we can.''

''You are not Mafia,'' Gutierrez said, studying him carefully, ''and I do not think that you are from the cartels. Are you connected with the government?''

''In a way,'' Blancanales answered honestly. ''But we're not from any government agency you have ever heard of. And,'' he added quickly, ''we're not interested in the kind of crimes most agencies work on. We have no interest in drugs, illegals, smuggling, betting or others like that. We are only interested in putting Jones out of operation.''

''I hope you have many associates,'' Gutierrez said, ''because Jones is not just any rich businessman. He has used his money to buy a private army.''

''What does he need them for?''

Gutierrez shrugged. ''For anything he wants. Why else would he spend the money?''

''But what do his people do?''

"For the most part, nothing much," Gutierrez admitted. "They spy for him and collect information. That's about all we ever see them do."

"But you think that they do more for him?"

"We hear things."

"Like what?"

"I have heard that they make sure that his buildings and warehouses are not bothered even by homeless people trying to find a place to sleep. We think that a lot of the deaths among the drunks and addicts in the area are his work."

"Try to get as much information as you can about his activities," Blancanales said. "And, seriously, we'll pay you for your time."

"I can do that."

USUALLY DINGO JONES didn't get mad, he got even. This time, though, he was raging. Caldwell and Bogs stood and took it like men. When he was done, he phoned his security office and issued orders for increased security at all of Rainbow's facilities.

When he went back into his suite, Carter appeared to be asleep. Reaching over, he grabbed her shoulder and jerked her awake. "Your boyfriend has caused me a lot of trouble tonight," he said.

"What do you mean?"

"Bogs and Caldwell were driving through Little Havana when they got blocked off by some kind of Mexican procession. Anyway, when a bunch of street punks came up to the car, Mr. Perez managed to jump out. The last they saw, the punks were trying to kick him to death, so maybe I'm rid of him anyway.''

Carter blinked once, but that was all the emotion she could afford to show. If she survived this, whatever her survival would look like, then she'd mourn Rosario. Right now, she had to concentrate on staying alive.

"YOU LOOK LIKE SHIT," Schwarz commented when he saw Blancanales.

"I'm glad you like it. It took all evening for me to pull this look together."

"What happened?" Lyons asked.

"Well," Blancanales said, "it's a long story."

Gutierrez stood back while the strangers had their reunion. He hadn't quite known what to expect of Perez's so-called associates and, now that they were in the club, he still didn't. The tall blond guy had "cop" stamped all over him. His hard eyes swept the room like the muzzle of a .45, not missing a thing. Were it not for the way he carried himself, the other one could have passed as some kind of businessman.

He could see the three of them as a team, but what they really did was still unclear. He could buy that they weren't run-of-the-mill Feds. There was nothing of the government about them. Their confidence and bearing was more like some kind of military strike force. Gutierrez had done a brief stint packing an M-16 for the contra back when he had been too young to know better, and he knew the look of true professionals.

"Where's the guy who found my partner?" Lyons asked when Blancanales had finished his recitation. "I have a little something for him."

"Paco," Gutierrez called across the room, "the señor wants to reward you."

The kid swaggered over, his Glock stuck in the front of his pants.

"This is for helping my friend," Lyons said, handing over two one-hundred dollar bills.

When Paco reached for them, Lyons slammed a left hook into his belly, lifting him off of the ground. By the time the Cuban hit the floor, Lyons had his Colt Python in his hand and was standing over him. "And that was for threatening him," he said calmly. *"¿Comprende?"*

Staring into the black muzzle of the .357 aimed at his face, Paco nodded slowly.

"And let me give you a little advice, amigo. If I ever hear of you shaking anyone else down, I'm going to kill you. As far as I am concerned, kidnapping is a capital offence and I don't screw around with courts and lawyers. When I find a kidnapper, I kill him, so you might want to find another hobby. Got that?"

"Sí, señor."

Slipping the pistol back into his shoulder leather, Lyons stepped back.

Throughout this little demonstration, Gutierrez had kept his hands carefully at his sides. He was certain that he was dealing with mercenaries. No one else had the balls to walk into a place like this and pull a gun on one of the homeboys. It was either that or he was completely loco, but either way, he didn't want any part of this man.

When Lyons turned back to Gutierrez, he was all business. "I want to thank you." He stuck out his hand. "We may be getting in touch with you later if we need more information about Jones."

"Like I told your partner, anything I can do to put that man down, I will gladly do."

"Good, because I intend to put him down."

"I TOLD YOU she was no damned good," Lyons snapped as Blancanales recounted his visit to Dingo Jones's headquarters as they were driving back to their motel.

"She didn't give me up, though," Blancanales reminded him. "If she had told him what she knows about us, I don't think I would have gotten out of his office alive. She was just doing what she had to do to keep herself alive."

Lyons shook his head. "She sure can pick 'em."

"I'm not going to leave her there, Carl," Blancanales said calmly. "I owe it to her. Hell, we all owe her for the San Diego operation, and you know it."

"If I can butt in," Schwarz spoke up, "Pol has a point, Ironman. And if you'll remember, we were looking for a criminal act to use as leverage to get at our man Dingo? Well, he just kidnapped Sarah Carter and, if I remember correctly, even in Florida that's a federal crime."

"What are you saying?" Lyons asked.

"I'm saying that if we put on our Fed suits, we

can go in there and have a little chat with Mr. Jones in broad daylight. It might be helpful to eyeball him, as it were. For one, I'd like to get a look at his defenses so if I have to go in there again, I can be a little better prepared. We almost got our asses handed to us tonight, and I don't like that feeling.''

Lyons thought for a moment. Once again, Schwarz had a point. Regardless of what the woman had done, this could be their way in. If nothing else, it would be easy for Brognola to get them a federal warrant. ''Let me think about it.''

BACK IN THEIR MOTEL-ROOM command post, Schwarz clicked on the big-screen TV in the corner of the room. The set was tuned to CNN and was showing scenes of destruction and chaos from the Middle East. Interspersed were scenes from Italy, Spain and Latin America where religious riots were also taking their toll. But the damage wasn't anything like what was going on in the Muslim nations.

''I feel like we've been left out,'' Schwarz said. ''It's much too quiet on this side of the world.''

''We should be thanking God that we're not in Beirut with Phoenix,'' Blancanales said. ''There's only one bad guy and a couple of goons for us to deal with here.''

''That's a good point.'' Schwarz turned to Lyons. ''So, what are we going to do about him?''

''I don't know yet,'' Lyons said thoughtfully. ''The kidnapping rap is a good idea, but all we really have is an aggravated domestic-violence beef that we might be able to stretch to a kidnapping.

Considering how so many of those things go down, we really can't count on the woman backing our play."

"What do you mean?"

"Just read any newspaper or watch LAPD. Some woman calls the cops on her boyfriend because he's been slapping her around, so they come and tow him away. But when it comes to pressing charges, she uses some lame excuse and backs down. If Sarah runs true to form in these cases and begs off the kidnapping rap, it'll leave us with our thumbs up our asses and looking stupid."

"There's still the killer chip," Schwarz reminded him. "Brognola's really wound up about that."

"You know," Lyons said, "I don't even think that there's a law against blowing up a bank's records with a computer. At least if there is, I've never heard of it. The most we could pin on him would be some bullshit obstruction-of-trade charge and he'd get a walk on that one for sure. And even if there was a law against what he might be planning to do, it'd be a bitch to prove until he actually does it. It's not like he's stockpiling nuclear matériel or anthrax that we can use to prove intent and have an excuse to get serious with him."

Blancanales couldn't believe what he was hearing. "So you're saying that we're going to sit on our asses and do nothing?"

"Not quite," Lyons said. "All I'm doing is running through what we actually have to work with here. Since we don't have a hell of a lot to pin on him, we're going to have to fall back on the good old payback mode. Jones pulled Pol off the street, roughed him up and was intending to kill him. That's a big no-no in my book. Then, he also snatched Sarah. And, regardless of what I've said about her in the past, no one deserves to be kidnapped and mistreated. That's also a no-no.''

Schwarz sighed. Lyons's thinking out loud could go on all night if someone didn't interrupt. ''So what's the bottom line, Ironman?''

''We're still going to use your kidnapping idea, but we're going to go in there to look for Pol.''

''If you haven't noticed, Carl, I'm not missing.''

''But,'' Lyons said with a grin, ''Jones doesn't know that. Since his side boys took off rather than go head-to-head with a street full of Cuban gangbangers, they don't know how that incident turned out. You could be dead for all they know.''

Schwarz grinned. ''That's almost as low-down and sneaky as something I'd come up with, Ironman. I love it.''

WITH THE PRIMARY FOCUS on Phoenix Force's Beirut operation, Able Team's Miami mission had been relegated to being a sideshow. Hal Brognola had been working on a ''no-news-is-good-news'' basis and had put it completely from his mind. The call from Carl Lyons, though, made him shift gears.

When Lyons finished updating him, he laid out the next move. ''We'd like to do a Fed number on this asshole, complete with a valid warrant.''

Brognola had set up both Able Team and Phoenix Force with valid federal documents many times before. Usually, they were arranged well in advance as part of mission prep because it was easier to build a cover that way. These emergency requests always carried a risk of not being backed up in depth, but it was doable. The Justice Department had a federal judge whose sole duty was to sign off on stuff like that.

"How do you want to work it?"

"We're thinking of hitting Jones on the kidnapping angle, but telling him that we're looking for 'Perez' instead of the girl. Maybe we can tag him as a protected witness, or something like that, who was last seen in the building before he went missing."

Brognola liked that idea. The Witness Protection Program had enough cutouts in it that they wouldn't run too great a risk of coming across a real federal agent who might break their cover. "Go for it," he said. "I'll have the WPP paperwork to you in the morning."

"With the warrant?"

"No problem."

CHAPTER TWELVE

Beirut, Lebanon

The com-room in Phoenix Force's villa wasn't set up as a full-blown command center, but they had most of the necessities: a Satcom radio, a computer with a modem and a fax machine. With that minimal equipment, they could stay in full communication with Stony Man Farm and have any paperwork they needed sent to them electronically.

Katzenelenbogen smiled when he looked at the Vedik mug shots he had just received from Kurtzman. "I finally got you, you bastard.

"Striker," he called out, "Aaron just sent us a present—photos of Insmir Vedik."

When Bolan took the photo, he stared at the face of the man who had engineered and unleashed the millennium plague that had infected so many, including Barbara Price. It wasn't a remarkable face in any way, but it took only a moment for him to fix the image in his mind.

"What's the fastest way to get these out on the street?" he asked Katz.

"I think I'm going to try to enlist my Druze contacts," the Israeli answered. "They lost a good friend when the nurse was killed, and they might be interested in helping us as a way to get payback for her death."

In a land where vendettas stretched back to the dawn of recorded history, blood vengeance was a far greater motivator than mere money. Everyone wanted payback.

"Will it help to post a reward, maybe grease a few palms at the UN, for instance?"

"Considering that the last two UN officers who knew about him were on the take, it might not hurt. The problem there is that if we try it with an honest man, he might want to see Vedik turned over to the UN so he can be sent to the War Crimes Tribunal for trial."

Bolan saw Katz's point. Though some UN officials weren't above taking a payoff under the table, they couldn't afford to allow Vedik to fall into the hands of the UN until they'd had a chance to talk to him first.

"While you're getting your Druze contacts on board," Bolan said. "I can have David send the guys out to cruise the more popular areas of the city, pass out the posters and offer a reward."

"Good idea," Katz said. "Since Vedik's a European Muslim, have them concentrate on the more Western parts of the city and particularly around the beaches. The upper class Lebanese women are inclined to show more skin than anyone this side of

Rio. After living in a place like Bosnia, he might want to know what a woman looks like.''

Bolan smiled grimly. Using the honey-pot ploy worked even if the women didn't know that they were part of it and had nothing to do with setting it up.

AHMED HAMMAD WAS was very proud to have been given his new assignment, but he was acutely aware that he couldn't allow himself to fail. Naji Nahas had failed, and fortunately for him, the commandos had killed him instead of his being ordered to report to Mount Alamut for his punishment. Hammad had once witnessed the punishment of a failed Assassin and the message had been clear: do not fail the Master. Those who did died in great pain. The instrument of the Greater Punishment was something he never wanted to feel on his body. Far better the clean kiss of the blade across the throat.

The Old Man of the Mountain had ordered the Brotherhood cells in Beirut to set a trap to eliminate the commandos once and for all. Fortunately, Hammad had been given the perfect bait to draw the infidels out of their urban fortress—Dr. Insmir Vedik. He didn't know why the Bosnian, who had once been considered so valuable, was now being used as a target. He didn't need to know why this was so. He only had to carry out his orders without fail.

Vedik was to be given the run of the city, particularly in the UN strongholds. He would be given a sizeable bodyguard, of course, but they would take no measures to keep him from being spotted. In fact, although the Bosnian didn't know it, they would be showing him off like a prize bull. The plan was that once he was spotted, the foreign commandos would follow him and learn that he was staying in the villa. Then when they attempted to either kill or capture him, they would be annihilated.

It was a simple plan and Hammad had confidence that it would work. To believe otherwise was unthinkable.

INSMIR VEDIK WAS beginning to like Beirut a lot. He still wasn't quite sure why Malik al-Ismaili had suddenly decided to give him more freedom, but he didn't want to ask. For a man who had gone through the destruction of Bosnia, Beirut was paradise. And for a man of his tastes, it was a bountiful paradise at that. He had never seen so many beautiful women in his life or so much of them.

While there were still many women who draped themselves in the head-to-ankle chador of strict Muslims, hundreds more wore Western clothes, even pants. Even more stunning, though, were the young women who frequented the Cornich, sunning themselves on the beach. Their bathing costumes, if they could be called that, were skimpy. Even the German women who had come to the Dalmatian coast in the summers before the war hadn't been so audacious about revealing their bodies.

And these women were more attractive to him than the Germans and Scandinavians had been. Even though they had been fairly free with their favors, there was something unnatural about blond women with their pale hair. The women of Beirut were as beautiful as Houris, the virgins God promised the faithful would find in paradise. Vedik felt that he had already been sent there.

The Beirutis also didn't strictly follow the prophet's admonition against strong drink. Like most Bosnians, Vedik liked his wine and arrak, and it was easy to find in Beirut.

BY THE END of the first day, the Stony Man Team had been able to place several dozen of the wanted posters in the right hands and, before the sun went down, they started getting reports. Two informants placed him at the café of the Hotel Saint Georges in the afternoon and another at a fashionable restaurant in the Hamra district later in the day. The best informant, though, found Vedik in a bar, then had followed him to a villa in the western sector of the city. The address placed it close to the old Green Line that had separated the Muslim sector from Christian sector during the war.

"This is almost too easy," Katz said as he discussed the reports with Bolan and David McCarter. "If I were a suspicious man, I'd think that someone was trying to set us up. Whoever Vedik's working for can't be that stupid as to let him out like that."

"They're not stupid," McCarter said. "They're just trying to get us to commit our forces by following up on these sightings."

"That's what I said. We're being sucked into a trap."

"It's only a trap," Bolan said, "if we don't know

that it is. Since we do know, it's an opportunity for us to make our move and wrap this thing up once and for all."

"That's all fine and good," McCarter replied. "But we need to do a little counterreconning before we get too enthusiastic here. We have to make sure that Vedik is actually where we think he is."

"I wouldn't think of doing anything else."

"Good. Let's take a drive."

"You get Rafe and I'll pull Jack away from his card game."

JACK GRIMALDI FIRST DID a normal drive-by past the Assassins' villa in West Beirut. It was built like a fortress and was old enough to have actually been one. Situated on a high knoll, the flat ground that surrounded it for a hundred yards provided clear fields of fire. A scattered grove of young orange trees had been planted, but they provided no cover and barely any concealment. Storming that place during daylight hours would be virtual suicide. Attacking at night wouldn't be much better, particularly if the Assassins had anything in the line of modern night-vision optics.

"Find a place to park," Katz said as soon as they were a few blocks away.

After paying a couple of older street kids to keep an eye on their locked car, the commandos made their way to a deserted, shell ravaged building. Climbing onto the flat roof, they had a commanding view of the compound inside the villa's walls.

The main house was built against the north wall

with the auxiliary buildings spotted against the other walls. There was only one gate, facing south, and it had ground-level bunkers on either side and what appeared to be a guardhouse right inside. The wall itself had bunkers built at each corner and a firing step all the way around. Twenty men with modern weapons could hold it against an infantry attack by three times that number.

"I want to do a daytime assault," Bolan said after he had studied the defenses.

"You must be crazy, Striker." McCarter couldn't believe his ears. "They'll chop us to bits before we get even halfway there."

"If they see us coming," he agreed.

"How can they not? The damned place's wide open."

"For one thing," Bolan pointed out, "I don't think they're going to be expecting a daytime assault. Remember, they're primarily night fighters and they know they're protected by open ground that no one wants to cross."

"And secondly?"

"They won't see the main attack because they'll be too busy trying to keep their asses under cover from the secondary attack."

"How many people are you talking about here?"

"I was thinking that if we can get a couple dozen good men from Katz's Druze, they can be the diversion and fire support while we do the real work. We'll have to get to Vedik before someone kills him, and that means keeping him safe from his keepers, so they don't kill him as soon as the attack starts.''

''You really think they're finished with him?''

Bolan nodded. ''If they're parading him the way they are, I think his usefulness to them is over. His plague has done its job, and I don't think whoever he was working for has anything more for him to do right now. Plus, he's not an Arab, he's Bosnian, and many of the Islamic radicals don't accept them as being real Muslims. In short, he's expendable, particularly if he can draw us into a kill zone.''

''Which is exactly what he's doing.''

''Remember, though, the best defense is a strong offense.''

''Right.''

''YOU ARE THE ONE known as al-Askari.'' The old Druze looked over at Bolan after Katz explained his request for fighters.

Bolan nodded. ''I have been called that.''

''Good,'' the old man replied, showing a gap-toothed smile. ''My young men will be glad to go with you.''

''Do they know who they will be fighting?''

The Druze spit on the ground in front of him. ''The black killers, the ones who think they are the ancient warriors but who are not. They are just common scum who think too much of themselves and who follow a madman.''

''What do you know about their leader?''

''He is a Nizari fanatic who calls himself the Old Man of the Mountain, but his real name is Malik al-Ismaili. When the war started here in Beirut, he had a small band of fanatics and thought that he could create a union of the Islamic factions. When he was driven out, it is believed that he went into hiding in Syria.''

The old man shrugged. "From there, who knows? But his killers started showing up right after the Syrian army came in to end the war.''

"You're saying that he is allied with the Syrians?''

"Not officially,'' the old man said. "But he has been protected by someone in their government.''

"Do you know where his headquarters is?''

"They say it is in a hidden mountain fortress, but I do not know where it is. No one does.''

"We will look for that later, but now we need to do this first.''

"When do you want to do this thing?''

"Tomorrow about noon.''

"In the daytime, al-Askari? That is dangerous.''

"If you want to catch a night animal, you should go to his lair when the sun is shining. The Assassins like to fight at night, and they will expect us to do the same. Forcing them to fight during the day will be to our advantage. Plus, we will be able to see our targets better, and there is one man in there who must not be killed.''

"Who is that, al-Askari?''

"The Bosnian.''

"The man the French nurse saw?''

Bolan nodded. "I must have him alive.''

"My men will not kill him,'' the Druze promised,

"but you will have to protect him from the black killers. If they think he will be captured, they will surely kill him."

"We will try," Bolan said.

KATZ MADE A QUICK CALL to Stony Man Farm and had enough money transferred into the Druze's Beirut bank account to pay for what they needed. As always in Beirut, money talked, and one of the nice things about the Middle East was that there was no shortage of weaponry. After many years of warfare, there were probably more weapons per capita than in any other region of the world. And much of it wasn't in the hands of any of the governments.

Even with their Syrian overlords, Beirut was the premier arms market of the Middle East. Along with small arms, fire support weapons were also readily available.

The Russians made a very nice 82 mm mortar and like all of their small arms, it was foolproof.

The Druze buyers scored two of the Russian weapons with the full base plate and bipod necessary to aim them properly. In a pinch, the 82 mm mortar could be fired by placing the ball on the end of the tube in an upside-down steel helmet, but accuracy suffered. With the standard base plate, bipod and sight, it was a very good area fire weapon, accurate to within ten yards at a range of three thousand yards.

The other item readily available in Beirut was the Russian RPG-7. This rocket launcher and the AK-47 had become the signature weapons of nearly every non-Western fighting force of the past forty years. The 85 mm rocket it fired was not only good against light armored vehicles and bunkers, it was often used as fast-moving, light artillery. In that role, it was more accurate than any mortar. Taking out the villa's guard towers and machine-gun emplacements would be simple for a couple of decent RPG gunners.

Best of all was that there was no shortage of RPG rockets in the city. Since the RPG was a standard weapon in almost every Middle Eastern army, most Muslim nations made ammunition for it. The best rockets, though, were the ones that had been imported from East Germany and Czechoslovakia before the collapse of communism. Even though several years old, they were preferred to the locally manufactured rounds.

LATER THAT EVENING, Bolan and McCarter inspected the weapons their money had purchased and found them to be in excellent condition.

"These are good," Bolan told the Druze leader. "But I also need to use a truck that you don't want anymore, and several kilos of plastique."

"Ah, a truck bomb."

"A heavy truck, at least a two-tonner. I want to drive it into the main gate."

"I will get you a Syrian army truck. They use one just the right size."

"Isn't that dangerous?" Bolan asked.

The Druze smiled. "Not as dangerous as driving it will be."

CHAPTER THIRTEEN

Miami, Florida

Not surprisingly, the receptionist at the main entrance to Rainbow Cybertech was a man. Australians rarely used women for serious work, and the guy certainly looked serious. So did the two uniformed security guards in the lobby.

As they always did when they were working this particular scam, Lyons took the lead role. Not only did he look the part of a steel-eyed Fed, his days with the LAPD had permanently marked him as being "on the job."

"Ian Jones's office?" Lyons asked as he flipped open his badge case to display the gold Justice Department special investigator badge.

"Is he expecting you?" The receptionist wasn't about to wilt at the sign of a badge. Ian Jones had a way of making badges disappear whenever he felt that they were getting in the way of business.

Reaching inside his coat pocket, Schwarz produced the federal warrant and smiled as he handed it over. "He'll see us."

Brushing off a badge was one thing, but going down on a federal rap for obstruction of justice wasn't in the receptionist's job description. Keying his headset, he rang through to his boss. "You have two federal agents here to see you, sir... No, sir, but they have a warrant."

After a brief moment, the receptionist looked up. "One of the guards will escort you to Mr. Jones's office."

"Thank you." Schwarz smiled.

Jones met them alone in his outer office. "What can I do for you gentlemen?"

"We're looking for this man," Lyons showed him a mug shot of Blancanales. "Rosario Perez."

"I can't say that I've ever seen him," Jones said a little too quickly. "What is he wanted for?"

"He's a protected person," Lyons replied cryptically. "And it's not necessary that you know anything more about him."

Jones tried to look confused. "But I don't understand what this is all about, gentlemen. Why are you asking me about this man?"

Lyons produced the federal warrant and handed it to him. "We have reason to believe that he was last seen coming into this building, and we want to have a look around."

"That's preposterous," Jones protested. "I don't know anything about this man, and I'm confident that no one in my employ has had anything to do with him, either."

"Are you saying that you aren't going to cooperate with this warrant, Mr. Jones?" Lyons said. "If that's the case, let me inform you that I can have a fifty-man federal Emergency Reaction Team on the premises within five minutes of making the call. We are going to look for this man. The only question is how much help we will have doing it. And if I make the call to the ERT, I will also call the INS, the AFT, the EPA and the IRS. I'm sure that I'll be able to keep you out of business for several weeks if it comes to that.''

''I don't bloody believe this,'' Jones exploded. ''I'm a well-known and respected businessman in this country, and I'm not accustomed to being threatened this way.''

''To be precise,'' Schwarz said, flipping open his notebook, ''you are a naturalized citizen who has been filing tax returns since 1981. You are also currently servicing several federal defense contracts, any or all of which can be canceled with cause if it is determined that you are engaged in illegal activities. Refusing a federal warrant can be construed as de facto evidence of illegal activities.''

Finding himself between a rock and a very hard place, Jones had no choice but to capitulate. ''Okay, gentlemen, I get the message.''

''I'm glad that you decided to cooperate, Mr. Jones,'' Schwarz smiled widely. ''That'll make it go a lot easier for all of us.''

''What do you want to see?'' Jones asked Lyons.

The Ironman locked eyes with him. ''Everything.''

Jones didn't blink. ''Follow me.''

IT WAS OVER FOUR HOURS before Schwarz and Lyons walked out of Jones's establishment. With Jones leading the way, they had been taken through the entire Rainbow Cybertech complex from the executive penthouse suites to the maintenance tunnels and storage rooms. They had even put on Clean Suits to tour the microchip making facilities. Nowhere, of course, did they find a trace of Rosario Blancanales. Neither, though, did they see anything that might lead them to Sarah Carter.

"Are you satisfied?" Jones asked when they were back in the lobby.

"For now," Lyons said, the threat to come back implicit in his answer.

"This is completely unwarranted," Jones said. "My legal staff will be in contact with your superiors about this harassment."

Lyons smiled. "That is your legal right." The number on the card he had given Jones was a cutout directly to Hal Brognola.

Out in the parking lot, the two didn't speak until Schwarz ran a bug detector over their rental car.

"When we go back there," he said after sweeping the car, "we're going to need that ERT you threatened him with to get into that place."

"You noticed."

"I also noticed that our man Jones pulled a number on us."

"What do you mean?"

"We didn't see everything. He was holding back on us."

"What did we miss?"

"I'm not sure." Schwarz frowned. "But one of those towers was two floors shorter than the other. Or at least the elevator ride was."

"What do you think he's hiding in there?"

"No idea, but that's enough area to hide damned near anything he wants. Plus, there was another area that we didn't get to see at all. According to the floor plans Kurtzman came up with, there are two large areas off his office that he didn't show us."

"Do you think it's worth going back for?"

"No. Let's just let him think that he put one over on us this time. I like the bad guys to think that we're dumb shits. It makes our job just that much easier."

"He's going to be sorry," Lyons vowed.

"That he will." Schwarz grinned. "But we'll let him have this one for now."

"Only for now, partner."

As soon as Lyons and Schwarz cleared the parking lot, Jones hurried to the suite off his inner office. Carter was lounging on the bed in a nightgown watching TV. Since Jones had taken her street clothes away and there was nothing to read, there wasn't much else for her to do when he wasn't there.

"You didn't tell me that your new boyfriend was a Fed," he snapped at her.

Carter blinked. "He didn't say any—"

Jones's hand streaked out and pounded the side of her face. Caught off guard, she fell back dazed.

Suddenly, Jones stepped back. "You told him about the chip, didn't you?"

Now fear showed in her eyes. "No, Dingo. I—"

"You bitch!" he spit. "You bloody bitch. You told them about it and put them onto me, didn't you?"

He stood over her and screamed, "Didn't you?"

When she didn't answer, he started beating her with his open hands. She curled into a fetal position to protect herself as best she could.

"WE FOUND THAT YOU weren't being held in that place against your will," Schwarz reported to Blancanales when they got back to the motel room.

"How about that?" Blancanales grinned.

"But we didn't see Sarah, either."

Blancanales dropped the grin. "I don't think he's had his side boys drop her body in Little Havana. He's into her a little too heavy to do something like that."

"He might change his mind after our visit," Schwarz suggested.

"No, I still don't think so. He might slap her around for a while, but I don't think he'll kill her."

"I sure hope not, because it's not going to be easy to get into that place to pull a rescue. I'd rather try to break into the war room at Langley."

"Langley's a snap," Blancanales replied. "All we have to do is flash our metal and they wave us on through."

"The badges got us in there this time," Schwarz said, "but they're not going to work again. If he's even half as smart as everyone says he is, he's going to figure it out. I don't think we're going to be able to use any more of our Stony Man scams on this guy."

"Which is fine with me," Lyons stated. "Now we can go off-book and do what we want about our Mr. Dingo problem. If Hal gets upset about it later, we can tell him we had to make our move when we saw an opening. If we should just happen to take care of Hal's business while we're taking care of ours, so be it. One way or the other, though, Dingo Jones is going down."

Schwarz applauded. "That's the Ironman I know and love. Now, how're we going to do it?"

"How about an aerial assault?"

"Too noisy." Schwarz grinned. "Particularly with the loudspeakers blaring 'The Ride of the Valkyries.' How about going into a harassment mode instead. He accused us of harassment, so why don't we try a little of it on him? Let's see how the man handles pressure."

"But what about Sarah?" Blancanales asked. "The longer she's in there with him, the more he's going to slap her around. I don't think her life's in danger, but if we go into a harassment mode, it's going to take time before we can force him into making a mistake."

"Since we can't get at him with anything short of a strike force," Schwarz said bluntly, "I don't see anything we can do for her right now. I hate to say it, but she's going to have to be on her own for a while."

Blancanales realized the truth of what Schwarz was saying. As much as he wanted to help her, he knew that going off half cocked would only make matters worse. Rather than repeat the mistakes that had resulted in him and Sarah being carjacked, they were going to have to work this like it was any other case.

"What are you suggesting?" he asked.

"You know," Schwarz said, "I'll bet the last thing Dingo needs right now is to have a lot of public attention focused on him."

"What do you mean?"

"Look, if our information is correct, he should be pretty busy right now getting ready to take over the world's finances. I mean that when the banks go down, if he intends to move in and take over, he needs to do a lot of groundwork first. He's going to be concentrating on that and is not going to want to have to deal with outside problems."

"Such as?"

"Well, since Jones's establishment is in the middle of a Hispanic district, I was thinking that we could maybe have a miracle appear on the side of one of those towers and see how he handles the crowds and the media. Considering the population demographics, I don't think that Miami's had its full share of Millennium Madness yet. They're due, and I'm the man who can make it happen."

"How do you want to work it?"

Schwarz smiled. "I need to pick up one of those plaster figures of the Holy Virgin. You know, the one with her smiling holding her hands out."

WHEN DINGO JONES LEFT the suite, Sarah Carter didn't even try to get up. She didn't think anything was broken. Dingo was too skilled to make that kind of mistake. She was bleeding, though. Dingo was very thorough about his punishments.

For the first time since she had run away from Miami, she didn't have the slightest idea what she was going to do next. It was almost as if she had gone back in time to when Dingo had first taken her out of the dance club and installed her in his suite as his newest mistress.

At first, it had been fun to be a rich man's sex toy. She had always been into sex the way some women are into shopping. It was how she measured herself against the world. That attitude and her stunning looks had gotten her everything she had ever had, including the lavish life Dingo had bestowed upon her. Dingo's psychotic jealousy hadn't shown up for several months, and by the time that it did, she had been trapped.

Now she was trapped again and she wasn't sure that Dingo's twisted desire for her was going to be enough to keep her alive. He accurately suspected that she had passed on his secrets, and there was nothing he hated worse than disloyalty. There was also nothing he liked better than to have her ask his forgiveness for having crossed him.

As much as she hated to grovel on her knees in front of the bastard, she was going to have to play the role of her life if she wanted to stay alive. And as long as there was any chance of Rosario and his friends breaking in to rescue her, she did.

GUTIERREZ HAD BEEN as good as his word. When Blancanales contacted him, he had a lot of intelligence on Dingo Jones to pass on.

"I have learned that Rainbow Cybertech has been hiring a lot of security guards recently. And they're not taking just anyone like those rent-a-cop agencies. They're paying good money for good men who have military or police backgrounds. Even better, they're doing background checks on them and only picking the ones with combat skills."

"You've done some time in uniform yourself, haven't you?" Blancanales asked.

Gutierrez nodded. "I signed on with the contras when I was eighteen. I thought it would be an adventure. As it was, I got shot at, got sick and went a long time without a bath. It was not too adventurous, but we won, or it looked like we did then. The bastard Sandanistas are still down there, so nothing has really changed in Nicaragua."

"That happens a lot," Blancanales said. "It's called politics. But let me assure you that when my associates and I have finished our business with Dingo Jones, he will not bother anyone again."

Gutierrez smiled. "You know, for some reason I believe you. It has a lot to do with that big blond friend of yours. He looks like he is a very serious man."

"Believe me. He is."

"Then," Gutierrez said, getting back to his briefing, "Jones is sending these new men to stand guard on his warehouses and buildings."

"What does he have in there?"

"That I do not know. It is very difficult to get near them, and I have never had a need to know what was there before. But now, I am going to make the effort."

"Be careful."

CHAPTER FOURTEEN

Beirut, Lebanon

It was first light when Bolan led Phoenix Force to their jump-off points around the Assassins' villa. Had it not been for the roving Syrian street patrols, they would have moved in before dawn. As it was, when the local residents saw the commandos getting out of their borrowed truck wearing battle dress, they went back into their homes and locked their doors. They had been through this before and knew enough to keep low. They also knew not to contact the authorities or they might be next on someone's hit list. It was best to ignore the doings of the powerful factions in Beirut, particularly when they were conducting their little war games.

On the high ground overlooking the main gate of the Assassins' villa, the Druze leader moved his fighters into position at the same time. They, too, had been forced to wait until the Syrian troops went back to their barracks. Now, they made sure to keep out of sight as they set up their mortar tubes and moved the RPG gunners into position ready to open the attack.

The young man who had volunteered to drive the truck bomb was standing by in his Syrian army uniform with its red beret. He was chain-smoking while he joked with his friends to hide his nervousness, but his pride was evident. Now that the cease-fire had been imposed, the chance for a young man to prove his bravery didn't come very often. If he lived through this, he would be a hero.

When Katz had proposed letting the truck bomb simply roll down the hill into the main gate, the old Druze protested. There was too great a chance of something going wrong, and explosives were too expensive to be wasted. He suggested that one of his men would dress as a Syrian, drive down the road past the villa and fake a breakdown in front of the gate. Katz didn't want to risk a man's life, but the Druze chief insisted, saying that he would have more than enough volunteers to choose from.

"We are ready," the Druze called over the hand-held radio Katz had supplied.

"Go for it," Katz sent back.

McCarter and Bolan watched as the two-ton Russian truck with Syrian army markings drove down the street that passed in front of the villa. Steam was boiling out of the grille, and they could hear the engine running roughly. The young Druze driver stopped the truck in front of the gate, stepped out of the cab and yelled something to the gate guard before walking down the road.

All that time, Manning had his sniper scope zeroed in on the guard. If something went wrong, he would put a bullet in his head and give the driver a better chance to escape. He kept his rifle on the target until the Druze was a hundred yards away and had ducked around the first corner.

McCarter swore when he saw a man come out of the villa and go around to the back of the canvas-covered truck.

"Not to worry," Manning said with a grin. "I put an antitamper switch on it as well."

To prove the point, the bomb detonated a few seconds after the man climbed into the bed. The explosion echoed off the surrounding buildings and threw a pall of smoke and dust into the air as it blasted the gate and one of the flanking machine-gun bunkers to rubble.

The Druze gunners were a little put off by the premature explosion of the bomb, but they quickly recovered. The dust hadn't completely settled before the first of the 82 mm mortar shells were on their way to the compound. The rounds hit inside the open ground, and the gunners quickly shifted their aim to the bunkers and fighting positions along the walls. The buildings weren't to be targeted so as not to risk killing Vedik.

The RPG gunners had to wait a little longer until they could see their targets more clearly. But when they could, the first two rockets took out the remaining bunker on the left side of the gate. Then they shifted their fire to the four corner bunkers on top of the walls.

The Assassins responded to the attack as if they

were reading a copy of Katz's script. They ran for the walls facing the direction of the Druze attack, expecting to have to repulse a ground assault. Instead, they were punished by the rain of explosive-laden steel falling out of the sky.

With the two watchtowers on their side of the compound blasted to rubble and the Assassins massing on the front wall to hold off the Druze, it was time for Phoenix Force to join the party.

At Bolan's order, the commandos took off across the open ground at a trot, their eyes seeking targets for their ready weapons. They were spread out in a loose line, taking advantage of what little cover the orange trees offered.

When they had closed to within twenty yards of the wall, a shout of alarm sounded over the crash of falling mortar rounds. The shout was answered and followed by a long burst of AK fire aimed in their direction.

"Go! Go! Go!" McCarter shouted as he sent a long burst sweeping the top of the wall.

The other commandos also fired as they ran. There was no cover, and going to ground would only give the Assassins time to call for reinforcements to pick them off one by one. Their only chance was to go for it.

Bolan scored first when an Assassin spotted him and turned to fire. A 3-round burst dropped the man behind the wall. James and Hawkins teamed up on the other one from ten yards away, and the wall was swept clean.

Sprinting the last few yards, McCarter and Encizo

both tossed flash-bang grenades over the top. Fragmentation grenades would have been a better choice, but since they didn't know if Vedik would be among the defenders, they couldn't risk killing anyone they couldn't first identify.

Kneeling against the base of the wall, James became a stepping-stone for Hawkins who climbed onto him to gain the top of the wall. Ignoring the broken glass embedded in the concrete, Hawkins crouched on the top of the wall for a last look before jumping down.

When an AK round ricocheted off of the concrete below his feet, Hawkins snapped a short burst at an Assassin running toward him. The man folded in midstride and went down.

"Watch it," he reported. "It's cooking down there."

"I'm coming up to cover you," Encizo said.

When he and McCarter reached the top of the wall, Hawkins dropped inside the compound. For a moment, he remained unnoticed. But when Encizo jumped down to join him, someone spotted the intrusion. A shout went up, and several Assassins rushed to try to close their back door. McCarter leaped down to join his comrades and, for a moment, the three commandos had it all to themselves.

Going flat on the ground to present as small a target as possible, they put up a barrage of automatic fire as AK bullets blazed over their heads. Running into a solid wall of steel, the Assassins were swept off their feet.

"It's clear," James radioed and then came over the top of the wall to join them.

Now that Phoenix Force had breached the compound, the Druze stopped firing their mortars and RPGs and raced down the hill to get in on the kill. From their positions along the front wall, the Assassins poured fire into them, but the Druze RPG gunners had brought their rocket launchers to the charge and were stopping to fire them at every target they saw. The antitank rockets easily penetrated the stone wall, creating havoc among the defenders.

Phoenix Force did its best to keep the Assassins pinned down from behind as the Druze stormed the ruined front gate. Once the gate was forced, it became a dogfight. The Druze and the Assassins were traditional enemies and, in their mutual hatred, no quarter was asked and none was offered. When magazines ran empty, the fighters turned to knives and daggers rather than stop to reload.

With the Druze fighters holding their own, Phoenix Force could now start looking for Insmir Vedik.

"Calvin, T.J.," McCarter called over the com link. "You take the main house."

James raced for the villa with Hawkins covering his back. Halting beside the open door, James pulled a flash-bang grenade and lobbed it inside. No sooner had it detonated than he was going through the door with Hawkins on his heels.

A grenade-dazed Assassin fumbled with his AK as James put him down with a short burst.

"Down here!" Hawkins called as he looked to his right and saw several doors leading off a central hallway. Tossing another grenade down the hall to his left, James turned and ducked to shield his face before following the ex-Ranger.

Working as a team, Hawkins kicked open the first door while James stood ready with his subgun. The room was empty, but from the bedrolls and equipment on the floor, it looked like it was a bare-bones barracks room. The next two barracks rooms were also empty. With the compound under attack, that was to be expected. The only people left in the building would be noncombatants or the wounded.

There was another door at the end of the hall that could open into another room. They quietly moved forward to cover it and stood for a moment listening for movement inside. Nothing could be heard over the roar of gunfire outside, so James gave the signal.

When Hawkins booted the door, James tossed in a flash-bang grenade before they both rushed in. This room was more than a bare cell. A man was on his hands and knees in front of a desk, feeling around blindly.

James didn't have to check the photo in his jacket pocket to know that this was their man. When Vedik came up with a pistol in his hand, the Phoenix Force commando stepped up and kicked him in the armpit.

The gun went flying out of his nerveless hand, and the two commandos rushed him. Slamming his face into the floor, they jerked his arms behind his back and secured his wrists with plastic riot restraints.

''We've got him,'' James called over the com

link as Hawkins pulled their prisoner to his feet and slammed him against the wall.

"Where are you?" McCarter asked.

"The back room on the north side of the main building."

"Keep him there until we finish out here."

"Will do."

Now that Vedik had been found, the Phoenix Force warriors fought their way to take up positions around the main house. This was no time to let an Assassin get in to try to kill him.

By now, though, the battle of the villa was quickly coming to an end. With both the Druze fighters and Phoenix Force inside the walls, the Assassins still on their feet had no place to run. A lucky few of them made it over the wall and managed to get away. The rest fought frantically without thinking of surrender as they knew the Druze weren't taking prisoners.

WHEN THE LAST SHOT echoed away, the ruins of the Assassin villa had the look and smell of a slaughter house. The acrid reek of cordite, the sweetish smell of blood and the sour stench of voided bowels and bladders filled the air.

The battle hadn't been all one-sided, however. Khaki-clad Druze bodies were mixed in with the black-clad Assassin casualties. A couple more hadn't made it to the main gate, and several men were seriously wounded. Druze medics were treating the wounded and starting the evacuation process. An ambulance from the French medical mission arrived to take the most serious cases

When McCarter sent the all clear, James and Hawkins came out of the main house dragging a man between them—Dr. Insmir Vedik, the sole reason the Stony Man team had come to the Middle East.

As the photo had shown, the Bosnian wasn't remarkable in any way. He could easily lose himself in almost any crowd in the region. He didn't look too much the worse for having been captured, but his face was almost unreadable. There was a slight sign of fear and a trace of defiance, but his emotions were as tightly guarded as the plastic riot cuffs that bound his wrists behind his back.

"Where are you taking me?" he asked Katz in French, the second language of Lebanon.

"Gag him," Katz told James and Hawkins, "and get him out of here."

James whipped a field bandage out of the first-aid pack on his assault harness and tied it across Vedik's mouth. The doctor's dark eyes glared as he was hustled off.

"I don't know what I was expecting," Manning said, "but he doesn't look like a guy who figured out how to kill millions of people."

"Those kind never do," Katz replied. "If you're manufacturing death in a laboratory, you don't have to be a leader of men or even look like one. All you have to do is have murder in your heart."

AFTER QUICKLY TREATING their wounded fighters, the Druze evacuated them along with the bodies of their dead. Then came the second most important job—looting the Assassins' villa of anything that might be useful to them. The stockpiles of weapons and ammunition were high on their priority list. A second stolen truck had been driven into the compound to transport the expected loot.

When the Phoenix Force commandos drove back to their CP with Vedik in custody, Katzenelenbogen stayed behind to thank the Druze leader for his help.

"How long do you think it will take for the Syrians to get here?" he asked him.

"They always wait until after the shooting has ended," the old Druze said with a laugh, "so they don't get caught up in the battle. When they're sure it's over, they sweep down and collect anyone left standing. I would say that we have another half-hour or so."

"Make sure that you get all of your people out of here before that," Katz said. "I don't want any more of them to get hurt."

"We took our losses, true," the Druze said matter-of-factly, "but this has been a great victory for us. The Assassins have always been our enemies, and we have not always been able to kill as many of them as we did today. I want to thank you for inviting us to this great killing."

"It is we who have to thank you," Katz replied. "Your fighters made this possible."

"It was our pleasure. We will sing about this raid for generations to come."

Katz laughed. "Just make sure that you tell it as it actually happened and get my name right."

"Oh, yes, the one-armed Jew who is the friend of the Druze will have his name remembered for this day as will the famous al-Askari and his warriors. My young men will never let me get that part of it wrong. They will want everyone to know that they fought beside you this day."

"Thank you again old friend," Katz said.

"No. As I said before, it is we who should thank you. If that man you came for is the one who was responsible for the nurse's death, the price was cheap enough. She was good to us and we repay our debts to our friends. And this was a great opportunity to show the factions that we Druze are not toothless. When the Syrians finally leave, this will do much to show that we too should have a seat at the table of power. A people who can kill so many of the dreaded Assassins have to be listened to."

As it was in Asia, fate was a powerful force in the Middle East, as powerful as vengeance.

CHAPTER FIFTEEN

Beirut, Lebanon

Back at the villa, Katzenelenbogen put Phoenix Force on full alert. He didn't think that they had left enough Assassins alive in the city to have to worry about them for a while. But dropping their guard after a successful firefight was a good way to get their heads handed to them on a platter. He didn't know what contacts or alliances the Brotherhood had made with other armed groups in the city. Crazed fighters out of history weren't the only people in Beirut they had to keep watch for.

Phoenix Force had kept Vedik under guard, waiting for Katz's return before interrogating their prisoner. James and Hawkins were with him in one of the back rooms, and he looked up when Katz and Bolan walked in.

"I don't know who you people are," he said in French when he recognized Katz, "or why you have brought me here, but I demand that you set me free immediately."

"Forget it," Katz answered in the same language.

"You are Dr. Insmir Vedik and you invented the mutated anthrax plague that struck down so many people here."

As expected, Vedik was defiant and unrepentant. "You have the wrong man," he said. "I know nothing of this plague of yours beyond what I have heard on the television. I am not to blame if you unclean infidels have picked up another deadly disease."

"Another one?"

"First you have the AIDS and now you have this so-called millennium plague. It is God's revenge for the evil you Americans have done throughout the world."

"So you are not Dr. Insmir Vedik of the Sarajevo Medical University?"

Vedik shook his head. "I am a Bosnian Muslim, yes, but I am not the man you seek. I am no doctor. I am a civil engineer."

"That's interesting." Bolan held out a small metal case with a combination lock. "We found this medical case in your room at the Assassins' villa."

"Be careful!" Vedik snapped in heavily accented English. "You do not know what is in there."

"I do now," Bolan replied as he opened the case. "It's what I thought it was, and I know what to do with it."

"Hold his arm," he told James.

Vedik tried to come out of his chair. "Keep that away from me!" he shouted.

James and Hawkins held the man in place while Bolan filled the syringe he had taken from the Phoenix Force medic's bag. After carefully tapping all the air out of the needle, he pushed it under the skin of Vedik's forearm and injected the fluid.

"Now," Bolan said as he pulled the needle out of the arm, "as I understand it, you have about twelve hours before the anthrax starts to affect you. In twenty-four hours, you'll slip into a coma, and you will die in another twelve or so. You might be interested in knowing that we discovered a way to keep the disease at bay for a few days. But as you know, we don't have a way to kill it. So you can either talk to me now, or you can die. And to make sure that you don't die too quickly, we'll give you the treatment that will prolong the process. My understanding is that it's very painful."

Vedik's eyes blazed as he screamed obscenities in Serbo-Croatian.

"He's calling you a motherless bastard, among other things," Katz announced. "And he's saying that we will all die with him."

Bolan smiled coldly. "Empty words aren't going to help you, Vedik. When you decide that you want to live a little longer, let me know and we'll talk.

"And," Bolan said, as he held the syringe in front of Vedik's face, "don't forget that we know how to make it take a long time for you to die. I'm not going to let you get away by dying on me."

The Bosnian was still screaming when Bolan left the room.

When Katz turned to go, Vedik started talking. "I will tell you what you want to know. The treatment is simple."

Katz turned back. "I think we'll wait a while

longer, Vedik. I'm not sure that you're ready to tell us the truth yet."

"No, please. I will not lie to you. The treatment is not difficult. I spliced a viral gene to the anthrax, but it is vulnerable to an enzyme found in another vaccine. Believe me, it is a simple process to stop the disease."

Taking out a notebook and pen, Katz handed it to him. "Write it down and don't leave anything out."

Vedik quickly wrote out a treatment schedule and the medications to use. "Here," he said as he handed it back. "Make sure that you follow it exactly."

"We will, and this had better be right because this is what we will be giving you. Any mistakes in this, and you die." He turned and left the room.

"We got it," Katz said as he joined Bolan outside.

"That was quick. Do you think he's telling the truth?"

"He's scared to death. He's worked with anthrax long enough to know what it can do to a person. I think he's telling the truth."

"We'll send it, then."

"What do you want to do with him?" Katz asked.

"I'm not sure yet," Bolan replied. "We'll keep him here for now. I'll tell Hal we have him and see what the President wants done with him."

"WE GOT VEDIK," Katzenelenbogen triumphantly told Hal Brognola, "and he cracked like a plaster saint."

"Thank God."

"Thank Striker." Katz laughed. "He found a small stash of the plague toxin and gave Vedik a shot."

"That was taking a real risk, wasn't it?" Brognola said. "That stuff's contagious."

"Not really," Katz said. "The shot we gave him was water. He thought it was the real stuff, though."

"That's cold."

"Not as cold as what that bastard did. I'd as soon give him the real stuff and watch him die."

"What's the treatment?"

Reading from what Vedik had written in French, Katz translated it into English.

"That's all?" Brognola asked as he read over the short note he had taken.

"I'll fax the original, but that's all there is to it."

"I'll get this out ASAP."

Atlanta, Georgia

"HENDRICKSON," said the harassed director of the Atlanta CDC Wildfire Unit as he picked up his phone.

"This is Kurtzman," the now familiar voice said. "I'm happy to say that we've had a breakthrough on the millennium plague. A commando unit has captured the man who cooked it up and he was persuaded to talk."

Hendrickson was stunned, he hadn't heard anything about this development. Now that the once stabilized plague cases had started dying in wholesale numbers, the disease was headline news again, and he should have heard about something that important.

As if Kurtzman could read his mind he said, "You're not going to read about this in the papers, Hendrickson, and it's not going to make it on CNN, either. In fact, you're going to have to keep that bit of information entirely to yourself. Anyway, the man, Insmir Vedik, says that using pertussis vaccine will destroy the viral gene he grafted to the anthrax bacillus and make it vulnerable to antibiotics again. He suggests using it at twice the normal dosage per kilogram of body weight with the standard antibiotic regimen for anthrax and says that you should see results within twelve to eighteen hours."

"But pertussis is a childhood disease, for God's sake." Hendrickson frowned. "It's whooping cough."

"I know, Doctor." Kurtzman had looked it up in his handy Merck before he made the call. "But that's what Vedik told us, and I'm inclined to believe him. He said that the vaccine contains an enzyme that will weaken the gene splice and let the antibiotic do its job."

"How sure of this are you?"

"Very sure," Kurtzman replied. He would have liked to tell Hendrickson why he was so sure, but he was afraid of offending his Hippocratic sensibilities.

"If this works, can I share the information?"

"Certainly," Kurtzman replied. "I just need you to keep the source of the information secret."

"Who do you work for anyway, the CIA?"

"No, not the Company. Let's just say that I advise the President on national security matters, and all information about the source of this treatment falls under that blanket."

"If this works," Hendrickson said, "I can keep a secret."

"Good, because you're going to have to. And," Kurtzman added, "you can consider this to be your official notification that the National Medical Emergency Protocols are in effect. You have presidential authority to bypass normal informed consent procedures to make these tests."

That stunned Hendrickson. The National Medical Emergency Protocols were known only to a handful of people, and they were to be implemented only under the most extreme circumstances.

Originally designed by NASA and the National Security Council in the early days of space exploration, they were to be put into effect if an alien infection was brought back to Earth by a returning spacecraft, an Andromeda Strain scenario. Once it had been learned that the moon was sterile, the protocols had been put in a file somewhere and locked away. He hadn't heard them mentioned in years.

"You are sure about that?"

"Do you want me to have the President call you to confirm?"

"Oh no," Hendrickson replied quickly. "I'll take your word for it."

"Good. Now if there are no more questions, I'll leave this in your hands."

"I'll get right on it and call you as soon as I have a result."

When Kurtzman hung up, Hendrickson reached for his Merck Manual. He wasn't a pediatric specialist and wanted to refresh his memory on whooping cough. That done, he called up pertussis on the on-line Mednet and saw that the British military had used it as an accelerator for an anthrax vaccine they had given to their troops during the Gulf War. In that usage, though, it had apparently reacted with something in the mix and was suspected in weight-loss problems some of the troops claimed to have suffered as part of the wider Gulf War Syndrome.

That might still be a problem as the vaccine hadn't been tested and cleared for use on adults, but at this point in time, he really didn't have any other choice but to try it. More and more of his patients were relapsing and dying every day. He had lost four of them yesterday and one already that morning.

As he wondered how to administer this therapy, he remembered Barbara Price telling him that he could test anything that came up on her. To be sure, that was less than a formal informed consent, but it was more than he would get from any of his other patients. She wasn't on the deathwatch yet, but he knew that she was close. Others who had been in-house less time than she had were already dead.

It took a couple of hours before he could get a supply of pertussis vaccine delivered, as it wasn't something they kept in stock at CDC. When it arrived, he took a vial along with the antibiotic to Price's room.

Checking her monitors, he saw that she, too, was starting to go into what he had learned to recognize as the long slide into oblivion. Judging from his other patients, she probably had only another twelve hours or so left before she went critical. At that point, nothing could bring her back. With that fueling his final decision, he prepared his medicines and syringes.

After swabbing her arm, he injected the pertussis followed by the first injection of the antibiotic. She showed no immediate reaction to the injections, but he stayed with her, writing his notes on her chart for a few more minutes to make sure there was no delayed reaction. When he was done, he rang for a nurse. The next antibiotic injection was due in two hours, but he didn't want Price to be left unattended for a minute during this test.

BARBARA PRICE LOOKED deathly ill, but she was awake when Dr. William Hendrickson entered her room. Her honey-blond hair was matted and tangled, her face was almost skeletal, there were dark circles under her eyes and she was sickly pale. But considering that she had been near death twenty-four hours earlier, it was a vast improvement.

"How do you feel?" he asked as he put his fingers on her wrist to take her pulse. The bio-monitor was already doing that and its results were plainly visible on the digital readout, but he liked the personal touch.

"I feel much better. What happened?" she asked.

Hendrickson smiled. "I gave you whooping cough."

"You did what?"

"As strange as it may sound, it appears that pertussis, the bacteria that causes whooping cough, has an adverse effect on the mutated anthrax you picked up. In fact, it gets into the organism and forces it to shed the viral gene that was spliced onto it. After that's happened, a strong antibiotic regimen is all it takes to kill it."

She shook her head. "How in the world did you ever come up with that one?"

"I'd love to take the credit," he said. "But a fellow by the name of Kurtzman passed that treatment on to me. He said that it came from some kind of government intelligence source."

She smiled broadly knowing that the source was a big man named Mack Bolan, "A guy named Kurtzman, you said?"

"Yes, do you know him?"

"Oh, yes," she replied. "And I'll be sure to thank him when I see him."

She tried to sit up in the bed. "Speaking of that, when do I get out of here?"

"Not so fast," he said. "We have to make sure you're out of the woods completely, then we have to help you get your strength back."

"You've got two days," she said flatly.

He frowned. "What do you mean by that? You

almost died, and you're not going to be in any kind of shape to do anything for a couple of weeks."

She leveled a gaze at him and didn't blink. "I'm walking out of here on the third day, Doctor. And if I can't walk, I'll crawl, so you'd better make sure that I'm able to get to my feet."

Hendrickson sighed. From what little he knew about this patient, and he realized that he really didn't know diddly, he did know that she was strong-willed. Maybe a little too much for her own good. But he didn't feel like trying to cross her on this, she had friends in high places.

"Ms. Price," he said, "I'll do what I can, but I can't work miracles."

"You already did, Doctor. I'm still alive. And you'll do another one when I walk out of here on schedule."

Knowing when he'd been bested, he got to his feet. "Well, if you're going to walk out of here, I'd better see about getting you something to eat."

"I'm partial to red meat." She grinned. "Lots of it, usually in the form of two-inch-thick sirloin with a fully loaded baked potato and a fresh spinach salad on the side. Something with chocolate for dessert would be nice too. And, bread, lots of bread, with real butter."

He smiled. "I might have to send out for that order. Our kitchen runs more to tuna casserole, diced carrots, watery mashed potatoes and tapioca."

"Put it on my bill, Doctor. The government's good for it."

As soon as the door closed behind Hendrickson,

Price reached for the secure phone she had insisted be installed. She'd not been able to use it before, but she'd had about all that she could enjoy of being sick. It was time for her to get back to work.

CHAPTER SIXTEEN

Miami, Florida

It was midmorning, and Dingo Jones was in his private command center updating his financial database when a call from the security command center was routed to him. "Jones," he answered.

"Sir, we have a problem," the newly promoted security chief said. "I don't know what's going on yet, but we've got several hundred locals gathered on the south grounds and more are coming every minute."

"Clear them out of there immediately," Jones ordered.

"We might have a slight problem with that, sir." This was the chief's first day at his highly paid new job, and he didn't want to do anything rash. "Apparently, the local police have the street blocked off to automobile traffic and they are letting these people through."

"But what are they doing?"

"It looks like they're praying."

"They're what!"

"Praying, sir."

Jones was in no mood to listen to crap like that. "Get the chief of police on the phone. I'm coming down."

When Jones reached his security command center, the security chief pointed to the TV set tuned to one of the local stations. "You'll want to see this, sir."

On the screen, a young Hispanic female reporter was speaking into the camera. "…phenomena was first reported during the early-morning commute. Several people phoned into Channel 8 about seeing a vision of the Virgin Mary on the south tower of the Rainbow Cybertech complex. The vision isn't visible right now, but the faithful have gathered to pray in hopes that they, too, will be blessed when it returns. In a time of great anxiety like this, signs from—"

"Jesus!" Jones shook his head. "That's all I need right now, a mob of bloody religious fanatics camped out on my bloody lawn."

"We have a TV crew in the lobby, sir," the receptionist called up. "They want to talk to you about the vision of the Virgin."

"Get down there and clear them out," Jones ordered the security chief.

"We might want to be careful about doing that, sir," the security chief said cautiously. "They are the press."

"I don't care if they're the bloody reincarnation of Christ and all the Apostles! Get down there and get the bastards out of the building now!"

"Yes, sir."

On the lobby security monitor, Jones watched the security chief tell the camera crew that they couldn't set up their equipment in the lobby. The monitor didn't show, however, that a handheld camera was recording the confrontation. When the crew refused to leave without speaking with Jones, the chief called up to the command center and passed on their demand to Jones.

"Not now, not ever!" Jones thundered. "Get those bloody people out of my building, or you're fired!"

The handheld camera was still taping when the Cybertech security force moved in to remove the TV crew. Some of them walked out on their own, but most of them had to be carried out the doors. The footage looked great on the six-o'clock news. It looked even better on CNN Headline News.

BY EARLY AFTERNOON, the Rainbow Cybertech-Virgin Mary story was top-of-the-hour news in most of the United States. By the time night came to Miami, an estimated eight to ten thousand people had gathered at Jones's compound in hopes of seeing Schwarz's projection of the Virgin Mary on the mirrored glass of the towers.

After taping dozens of tearful women clutching rosaries and praying, since there was nothing else to talk about, the reporters started commenting on the reclusive man who had built his company into one of America's microchip giants. A few still shots of him from his California days and some taped clips from local charity and civic events he had attended over the years were aired. They were followed by the tape of the security guards clearing the camera crew from the lobby of his building.

For Able Team, set up in a second-story hotel room right down the street from Jones's complex, the best thing the TV showed was a shot of the man's personal yacht, *Digger,* moored at one of the city's more expensive marinas.

"That's a real nice piece of naval architecture," Schwarz said. "I wonder what would happen if the Virgin Mary showed up on board her."

"How could you work that?"

"The same way that I did with the towers except I'd use a hologram projector instead of the video. Hell, with that I could even put her on deck in a red bikini with a piña colada in her hand and have her waving to the crowd."

"We're trying to cause him a little grief, not start a riot."

"Why not start a riot?" Schwarz asked. "Anything we can do to put him off his pace works to our advantage. In fact, I could switch images on our Mr. Jones and really turn up the heat on the bastard. Instead of the Holy Virgin, the next time I fire up my little projector, I can show the crowd an image of Satan smiling down on them. They'd really go bat shit at that."

"Use the one of that Persian idol, or whatever it was, that they used in the opening scenes of *The Exorcist,* Blancanales suggested. "I always thought that was the best satanic image I'd ever seen."

"What do you think, Carl?" Schwarz asked.

"I don't know," he said. "What we're doing is effective, but I'm not sure that we want to unleash a full-blown millennium freak-out session here. It might make it impossible for us to get to him at all."

"It might also cause him to break and run for some place where we can get to him easier than in those towers. Remember, all he needs for what he is planning to do is a computer and a modem. That can be set up anywhere."

"You've got a point there," Lyons said. "But let's keep doing this tonight, and we'll take another look at it in the morning."

"Nothing to it." Schwarz glanced down at his watch. "Speaking of which, it's about time for another miraculous appearance."

"You're going to go to hell for this, Gadgets." Blancanales laughed.

"For what, flashing the Virgin Mary on the side of a building?"

"No, for having so much fun doing it."

WHEN JONES'S CALLS to the mayor and chief of police did nothing to effectively control the gathering crowds, he called Florida's governor. Rainbow Cybertech and Jones himself were important contributors to both the governor and his party. In fact, his money had made it possible for him to win the important Metro Miami-Dade County vote in the last election. The governor's campaign people had flooded the region with TV spots and daily coverage of the candidates' appearances.

Right before midnight, Miami units of the Florida National Guard had started moving in to take up a cordon around the Rainbow Cybertech complex.

The minute the military vehicles started off-loading troops, the TV crews, both local and national, converged on them. With the network's satellite uplink vans humming, the images were sent out and broadcast almost instantly. What had started as just another Millennium Madness story immediately turned into an abuse-of-power story. And there was nothing that a TV reporter loved more than a visible abuse of power, anyone's power.

"Those bloody bastards," Jones muttered as he watched CNN take him and the governor to task for having called in the National Guard to control a peaceful religious gathering. A heavyset female reporter was saying that this excessive use of force might have been prevented if the mysterious Mr. Jones had simply granted an interview with the media to put the people's minds at rest.

"As it is," the reporter continued, "Jones's repeated refusal to speak to the press is puzzling. There are those who think that this might be some kind of sick hoax perpetrated by Mr. Jones himself or someone in his company. A few minutes ago, the Florida State attorney general announced that his office would undertake a full investigation of this incident. He assured CNN that Mr. Jones would talk to him. He decried the fact that he hadn't been consulted before the troops were sent in and said that if he had been, he would have advised against it.''

When the phone rang in the Cybertech command center, Jones picked it up to find that the governor was on the line. He lit into him before the man even had a chance to speak.

''For Christ's sake, Dick,'' Jones bellowed, ''why the hell can't you control your own attorney general? I assure you that if you can't get the bastard in-line, you can kiss my financial support goodbye. I didn't pay good money to put a gutless wonder in the State House.''

When the governor tried to protest, Jones cut him off. ''I can talk to you any damned way I want, Dick, and you know it. You screw this up, and I'll put your opponent in your chair so bloody fast your head will spin off your neck. Now, get on the bloody phone and get this taken care of.''

Jones slammed down the phone. ''If there's anything I hate, it's a politician who won't stay bought.''

''But we don't have to worry,'' Caldwell said, trying to calm his boss. ''This isn't any of our doing.''

''I don't want anyone snooping around here,'' Jones said. ''Not now, not ever.''

To keep the pressure on Dingo Jones, Schwarz turned on his TV projector a couple more times during the late night and early morning. Each time the image of Mary glowed from the tower, the crowd surged forward and the National Guard had their hands full trying to keep them from storming the building.

"I can't help but feel sorry for those poor bastards down there," Schwarz said as he watched the crowds. "This is one of the dirtiest tricks I've ever pulled on someone who didn't richly deserve it."

"You've got a point," Blancanales said. "But we're doing it for all of them. Even the guy who just stepped off the boat needs a bank account, and they all need work. If Dingo pulls off his coup, the riots down there are going to be a lot worse than this."

"I know, but it feels like we're using those people."

"We are," Blancanales agreed. "There's no doubt about that. And the only thing I can say is that sometimes we have to do it. Believe me, if the financial markets collapse, they'll really be screwed. People like that are always the first to take it in the shorts when times are tough."

"That's why they're out there," Lyons said. "They're vulnerable because they think they can pray their way out of whatever mess they're in instead of working to change things. But if prayer was an effective way to deal with the world, it wouldn't be the way it is."

"I still feel sorry for them."

BY DAYBREAK, the Rainbow Cybertech campus looked like the location for the greatest outdoor rock festival of all times. The TV stations had quit even trying to estimate the crowds, but over a million

people had gathered and there were no signs of anyone leaving. The city had turned out to try to provide services for the people, but it was a drop in the
bucket compared to what they needed. Medical aid
stations had been set up, portable toilets were
brought in and food vendors were cleaning up. City
cops had barricaded a ten-block area bringing traffic
almost to a standstill.

Gunner Caldwell and Roy Bogs were still with
Dingo Jones in the command center watching the
situation on the video monitors. "I swear I'm going
to sue the city for damages," Jones said. "It's going
to take weeks to get this place cleaned up."

"It looks to me like it's going to take a couple
of days for all those people to just get out of here,"
Caldwell grimly observed.

With the complex blocked off the way it was,
there was also no way that Jones's employees could
report for work. In fact, except for the night shift,
the complex was completely shut down, and that
would cost him millions in lost revenue.

Jones made a decision. "Call the airport," he
said, "and have the copter brought up. I'm flying
out to the *Digger* and I want you two to come with
me."

"No problem," Caldwell answered. "Do you
want me to bring along a few of the lads as well?"

Having some of his security guards on board
might not be a bad idea. "Get two more good
men."

"I know just the right two blokes."

SARAH CARTER HAD BEEN watching the TV coverage of the crowds. Even before her stint in San Diego with the Temple of Zion, she hadn't been religiously gullible and that experience had done nothing to make her believe that the Virgin Mary had really come to Miami. Knowing the talents of Rosario and his friends, she was certain that they'd had something to do with making the image appear.

She had no idea, however, how the mob outside was going to help her. Beyond giving Dingo something to do that didn't involve slapping her around, she couldn't figure out what they had in mind. All she could do was trust that they had a plan to free her from Jones. If they didn't, she wasn't sure how much longer she could keep her silence.

She had never been good with pain, and her earlier life with Dingo had shown her that he was. The only reason she had been able to escape the first time was that she had play-acted well enough to lull him into relaxing his vigilance. There was no way that she'd be able to do that again. If Rosario didn't get her out of here, she'd die in Dingo's towers.

IN THE HOTEL ROOM down the street from the Rainbow Cybertech compound, Able Team continued to watch events unfold via the local TV stations.

"We've got him," Hermann Schwarz crowed. "He's got a chopper coming in, and I'll bet you that he's headed for that boat of his."

"Lock this place up," Lyons said. "I want to follow him."

Knowing what would happen when they started

projecting their image, Lyons had parked Blancanales's Caddy several blocks away on a side street. Had it not been for that, they'd have never been able to get out of the hotel. A jog of several blocks brought them to the Caddy and with Blancanales driving and Schwarz reading the map, they raced for the marina. When they reached the Miami Beach marina they had seen on TV, they didn't have to ask which boat they wanted. They weren't the only ones who had figured out that Dingo Jones was fleeing to his yacht. The TV crews had beat them to the punch and were already on hand taping as the red-and-white helicopter bearing the colorful Rainbow Cybertech logo on the side flared out for a landing on the aft deck of the ship.

"We're just in time," Lyons said. "Now we'll see what the bastard does next."

Schwarz had no doubts about what was going to happen next. Any fool could see that Jones had a ship and the oceans were wide. In just a few days, he could be anywhere he chose, even Asia.

CHAPTER SEVENTEEN

Miami, Florida

When the Rainbow Cybertech chopper landed on the *Digger*'s afterdeck, Jones had Caldwell and Bogs escort Sarah Carter directly to the master suite. "And make sure she stays there until we get out to sea," he snapped.

"No problem."

Jones then went up to the bridge where his captain was preparing to get underway. "How long till you can cast off?" he asked.

"We're ready now, Mr. Jones," Captain Johnson replied. "If you tell me where we're going, I can file with the Coast Guard as soon as we cast off."

"It's none of their bloody business where I'm going," Jones snapped. "Just get me out of here."

"Yes, sir."

As the powerful twin marine diesels fired up, Jones went below to the main cabin to check on his captive. Everything had been going just fine until she turned up again, and he couldn't help but think that she and that Perez bastard were somehow involved with this. He wasn't a man to believe in coincidences any more than he believed in visions of the Holy Virgin.

One way or the other, he'd get to the bottom of this. And how much damage it caused Anne Keegan would be completely up to her. She should know better than to try to cause him grief.

"GODDAMMIT!" Carl Lyons exploded when he saw the yacht's deckhands cast off the lines and get underway. "He's putting out to sea."

"Well, it is a boat," Schwarz observed. "And that's what boats do."

"Why don't I follow him?" Blancanales suggested. "I should be able to rent a boat somewhere along here. I can shadow him and keep you updated on where he's going."

"What if he takes off for Grand Cayman or someplace like that?" Lyons asked.

Blancanales shrugged. "I can rent a boat with a big fuel tank and work on my tan while I follow him."

"Get on it. At least keep him in sight until I can get the Farm locked on to his ass. In fact," he said, as he slid out from under the wheel of the Caddy, "take this and get going. We'll retrieve it later."

Blancanales fired up the Cadillac and dropped the gearshift lever into reverse. "I'll be in touch."

"Now what are we going to do?" Schwarz said. "Walk back to the hotel?"

Lyons looked over to the Hertz rental office right

outside the marina fence. "We're going to rent another Caddy ragtop."

Stony Man Farm, Virginia

AARON KURTZMAN and the Stony Man crew had picked up on the Miami Virgin Mary incident. Not knowing that Able Team was behind it, they had simply logged it and filed it in the Millennium Madness file for future reference. When Lyons called in, though, it suddenly came clear.

"Tell Gadgets that was a nice piece of work." Kurtzman chuckled. "Using a popular religious belief to isolate a bad guy is a first, I think. I don't know, however, how Hal's going to take it. Manipulating religious mania is a touchy topic with the Man right now."

"Tell Hal to stuff it," Lyons said in his usual fashion. "And the President too. Everyone else's doing it, and at least we weren't doing it for personal profit. We did it to try to keep that guy from ruining everyone's New Year's celebration. If they don't like it, they can come up with a better idea and we'll try it.

"Anyway," Lyons said, getting back to business, "Jones just put out to sea in his boat, the *Digger*. I sent Rosario after him to try to shadow him, but Gadgets suggested that you try to get a lock on him as well. The boat should be in the marine registry, and the Coast Guard will probably have it in its data bank too. If you can get the DEA's blue boy satellite to track it, we'll know where he's going in case Blancanales loses him tonight.''

The DEA satellite was an ex-Air Force recon bird that had been refueled and rededicated to tracking the surface and air traffic in the Caribbean and Central America as part of the expanded drug interdiction program. It had a full spectra sensor bank and could track multiple targets on land, sea and in the air.

''I'll get someone on that ASAP.''

Miami, Florida

ROSARIO BLANCANALES lucked out at the first boat rental place he came to. He found a powerful sixty-five-foot cabin cruiser fully equipped with navigation aids, including GPS and radar, a full radio suite, long-range fuel tanks, autopilot and, best of all, a fully stocked galley ready to be taken out to sea. The customer who had ordered it had called off at the last minute.

Plunking down the ''company'' plastic, he was able to sign off and get underway in less than half an hour. Knowing that the *Digger* would probably keep to the shipping lane until it reached international waters, Blancanales shoved the throttles all the way to the wall and took off after him. Flipping on the GPS, he found his position before radioing back to Lyons and Schwarz.

''I'm underway, Ironman,'' he said as he gave his current position. ''I'm heading south-southeast in the shipping lane, and I'll call again as soon as I make visual. Over.''

"Roger," Lyons came back. "Gadgets called the Bear and we're trying to get the DEA bird on him. Once you have him, make sure you keep well back out of range. There's no telling what he's packing on that thing, and I don't want you to get blown out of the water. I'm also going to have Hal alert the Coast Guard to your mission and have a rescue chopper on alert if you need it. Over.''

"That's a good idea. But I don't think I'll need it. Call you later. Out.''

ONCE IN INTERNATIONAL waters, Dingo Jones went up to the bridge and relieved Captain Johnson. A check of his powerful radar screens showed that he had picked up a tail out of Miami. A smaller boat, sixty-five feet, according to the readout, appeared to be following him. What made it suspicious was that it was scanning with radar and that could let it follow him unseen.

He had no idea who the guy was, but he knew what to do about him. He immediately went into stealth mode and changed course. As a designer and supplier of Defense Department electronics, he had installed a full battery of devices, both experimental and well tested, on his vessel. Only the most advanced warships had the kind of protection the *Digger* carried. That protection included radar jammers, all-frequency scanners, decoy projectors and IR shielding.

He had also incorporated a few offensive measures during the last rebuild. Since he knew that the best defense was a good offense, he had a select sample of weaponry to defend himself against anything short of a full military attack. And even then, the *Digger* could hold her own against most coastal craft and patrol planes. The usual criminal garbage one encountered on the Caribbean—drug smugglers, pleasure-boat hijackers, petty pirates and just plain thieves—wouldn't stand a chance against him.

This nautical shadow could be a media boat or it could be Anne's mysterious friend or friends. Whatever, if it became too much of a problem for him, he'd simply blast it out of the water. First, though, he'd try to lose it.

Stony Man Farm, Virginia

AARON KURTZMAN HAD GIVEN the Able Team support mission to Akira Tokaido to handle. He was good at satellite surveillance and, since the DEA bird was already on station in the region, it was easy to tap into it and direct its attention to the area in question.

"Aaron," Tokaido called out after a few minutes, "I've got an anomaly here."

"How's that?"

"I've got Rosario in sight. I checked with him, and he confirmed his position with the GPS. But, the boat he's following doesn't read what it's supposed to be. According to the marine register, the *Digger* is 110 feet, but the Coast Guard says it's 180. Blancanales says the boat he's following reads out at 145. I think this Dingo guy is trying to pull some kind of scam on someone.''

"Sounds like the old smuggler's trick. Pretend to be a different boat than the one the authorities are looking for. Tag the one that Blancanales's following, and we'll sort out the facts about it later.''

"I've got the *Digger* as Track Two and Rosario as Track One. We're coming up on BENT, so I'll have to switch over to radar and IR before too long.''

"Just don't lose them.''

"Not as long as the satellite's up there I won't.''

Florida coast

BLANCANALES HAD BEEN keeping his hull below the horizon so Jones wouldn't spot him and was following the *Digger* on his boat's radar. Now that night was falling, he considered getting in closer and trying to do a little visual recon with the night-vision goggles. He had purposefully left his running lights off and would again depend on his radar to warn him of any approaching craft. It wasn't the best marine radar in the world, but it seemed to be powerful enough for his purposes.

It still wasn't apparent where Jones was going. After reaching international waters, he had changed course to the east, but was keeping a straight line right now. After checking the course, Blancanales engaged the autopilot and went below to inspect the galley. The marina had said the galley was fully stocked, and he hoped there was something in the freezer he could microwave quickly and bring topside to eat as he continued the pursuit.

Finding a frozen shrimp jambalaya and rice packet, he put it in the microwave and hit the timer. While his meal was cooking, he went to the medical cabinet to see if there might be something in it to help him get through the night. As he expected, he found a bottle of caffeine tablets. They weren't as powerful as what he was used to, but they'd help take the edge off those cold hours right before dawn when the body said that it had had enough and needed to recharge the batteries.

When the timer dinged, he took out the steaming plastic dish and, finding eating utensils, went back topside. When he glanced over at his radar screen, he was shocked. The *Digger* was nowhere in sight.

He hadn't been below more than a few minutes and there was no way that Jones could have slipped away in that short period of time. Reaching for the radio, he changed to one of the Stony Man frequencies and put in a call to the Farm.

"What happened, Rosario?" Akira Tokaido asked as soon as he came on the line. "My radar track on him just disappeared. Did he sink?"

"I'll be damned if I know," Blancanales replied. "I left my boat on autopilot and went below to fix myself a quick dinner and a cup of coffee. When I came back up, he was gone. Have you checked your IR?"

"The IR's giving me a faint trace off to the south, but it doesn't look big enough to be your target."

"Give it to me," Blancanales said. "I'll try it anyway."

When Tokaido gave him the plot, Blancanales changed course and advanced his throttles to full. The powerful twin gasoline engines sent him plowing through the waves.

"Have you got me?" he asked Tokaido.

"You're showing up clearly, but he's getting fainter."

Blancanales started out into the dark at a blank expanse of water. "Damn!"

This was where he needed Gadgets and a couple of his lash-ups to get more power out of the radar. Determined to regain contact, he continued on course at high speed.

ON THE BRIDGE of the *Digger,* Dingo Jones smiled as he looked at the screen of his powerful radar. For the first time since leaving American waters, the blip that had been following him was gone. He had no idea who it had been, but he was gone now. This was the first time that he had really tested the countermeasures he'd had installed in his boat, and they had worked as advertised. The IR cloaking had been a recent addition, but apparently it had worked as well. With night-vision goggles so cheap now, it had seemed a worthwhile thing to do.

Now that he was alone on the Caribbean water, he rang for the captain to come back and take the helm. He had business to take care of in his suite below.

"What course, sir?" Johnson asked.

"The course is set," Jones replied. "Keep running with the lights off and if anything else shows up on the radar, give me a call. I'll be in my cabin."

"Yes, sir."

WHEN JONES WENT into his cabin, he found Sarah Carter asleep. He stood for a moment, marvelling in her beauty and letting it sink into him. She was his, all his, and he'd see her dead before he'd let her get away from him again. He'd also see that Perez bastard dead as soon as he could take the time to see that it was done properly. This time, he'd take care of it himself to make sure it was done right.

First, though, he had to have another talk with her. These talks hurt him as much as they did her, but he had to know what she wasn't telling him so he could keep her partners from ruining his carefully laid plans. When the future of the world, his world, was at stake, a little pain was nothing. Not when compared to the life she'd live later. She'd thank him when this was all over and she was with the most powerful man in the world.

Reaching down, he touched the side of her face. "Anne, darling? Wake up. We have to talk."

Miami, Florida

BACK IN MIAMI, Hermann Schwarz and Carl Lyons had been monitoring the radio traffic between Blancanales and the Farm from their hotel room CP.

"Dammit," Schwarz said. "It looks like Jones stealthed out on us. I should have expected something like this. The bastard's been supplying microships to defense contracts for years, and I'll bet the contractors gave him prototypes for all sorts of military goodies. If a couple of them kind of got lost, so what?''

''What in the hell are you talking about Gadgets?'' Lyons frowned. ''Pol lost him. It happens all the time.''

''The satellite lost him, as well,'' Schwarz reminded him. ''And that takes stealth technology.''

''But I've never heard of any stealth that could do this.''

''Actually, the Navy has some in development, and they've been working on radar and IR countermeasures for a long time. Mostly it's been done to confuse targeting radar and IR guidance systems, but there's nothing to say that it wouldn't work against a satellite as well.''

''Now what do we do?''

''We wait till daybreak and see if Akira can pick him up optically again. There's nothing he can do to mask that.''

CHAPTER EIGHTEEN

Mount Alamut, Syria

When Malik al-Ismaili got word of the assault on the Beirut stronghold and the capture of Insmir Vedik, he realized that he had seriously underestimated al-Askari. One of the major tenets of the Brotherhood's Book of War was to know the enemy, and he hadn't known him well at all. He was guilty of the dual sins of ignorance and pride. And for those sins, he would have to pay the same price that any of the Brotherhood would pay for making the same mistakes.

He was the undisputed Master of the Brotherhood, but only because he was bound to the same order of discipline as were the lesser brothers.

The instrument of the lesser punishment lay in its bed in the Hall of Rectitude. To someone of the Western world, it would have been called a cat-o'-nine-tails, a scourge. This lash had thirteen long leather strands, each one tipped with a flesh-tearing five-point iron barb. Any way it hit, it would draw blood.

Pulling his robe over his head and laying it aside, he stood in his loincloth and reached for the instrument of his punishment. Kneeling upright on the floor, he shook the strands in front of him so they weren't tangled and would fly straight and true.

It had been a long time since he had last felt the touch of the lash, but he didn't hold back as he administered the prescribed number of strokes to his naked flesh. Pain was a necessary ingredient of learning. Pain focused knowledge and fixed it firmly in one's mind. As the blood flew from each stroke he laid on himself, he vowed never to underestimate an enemy again, particularly an enemy like al-Askari.

In the days of the original Brotherhood, the foreigners had been mighty warriors worthy of respect, and the Soldier was a man in that heroic tradition. To have underestimated him because most modern Westerners were weak and worthless had been stupid.

When al-Ismaili was done, he cleaned the blood and small strips of flesh and skin from each of the strands. The cleansing of the instrument was as the cleansing of the soul and was the final act of the ritual.

Now that he had fully awakened his senses, he knew that he still had to deal with al-Askari and his men. But this time he wouldn't underestimate this band of commandos. With the heavy losses he had taken in Beirut, he would have to call in the Assassin cells from other cities to deal with this lingering threat. And a threat it clearly was. For al-Ismaili's plan to be implemented, al-Askari had to be destroyed. Also, this setback meant that he would have to move up the date of the Mahdi's appearance.

He had intended to wait until October for the Mahdi to show himself to the people. By that time, the Western nations would be completely embroiled in their own millennium crises and wouldn't be so eager to meddle in Middle Eastern affairs. But with al-Askari and his commandos poised to strike God only knew where next, the uprising had to come now. The Mahdi had to free his people and show them the way to greatness once again.

LATER THAT DAY, Malik al-Ismaili stepped in front of the video camera in the communications room of his mountain fortress. He was wearing the seamless white robe prescribed by the Koran as the proper dress for a pilgrimage to Mecca. On his head, he had the green turban of a hajji, a man who had made the holy pilgrimage. At his side was a curved Persian sword, a classic shamshir, with a jade hilt and resting in a jeweled scabbard. Tradition had it that the sword had once been owned by Hasan ibn-Sabbah, the founder of the Assassins.

His dress was that of the cultural icon, a holy warrior who had come to free his people. In this garb, he was the personification of the Mahdi, the savior who would unite all Muslims against the infidel and bring the Golden Age of Islam that had been prophesied for so long. This was a role he had always longed to play and he had prepared carefully for it. Since it was told that the Mahdi would be known by his deeds, he had reformed the Brother-hood to be his mighty hands and had spent years working on the prophecies that had been so widely distributed. The time had come for him to put his plans into action.

To keep his transmission from being traced, the video signal would be tight-beamed to one of the Saudi communications satellites in geosynchronous orbit over the Middle East. From there, it would be retransmitted to millions of TV sets on every chan-nel. The signal was so strong that it would override all local programming, and everyone would hear the apocalyptic message at the same time.

The fact that the electronic technology that was making all of this possible came from the Christian West was one of the ironies of this history-making moment. The Islamic world had once been the world's leader in science and technology, but the division of Islam into warring factions had let that lead pass to Christian Europe. Now, to bring back the Golden Age meant having to use the machines of the infidel, but al-Ismaili didn't mind at all. He was a practical man who used whatever tool was the best for the job.

When the production man signaled him, he was ready. *"Allah akbar!"* he said, his deep voice elec-tronically altered to make it more resonant. "God is Great!

"I, the hidden imam, the Mahdi, have returned," he continued. "The time has come for the world to fear God's retribution. His world must be cleansed of unbelievers. Their stench must be removed from

His nostrils and their faces from His sight. The ancient prophecies foretold my return, and I have come as was promised. Now justice can prevail and the world will turn its face to God.

"The fight against the unbelievers will not be easy and not all of the enemies of God are foreigners. Many are the doers of evil and many of them hide behind God's name, but they do not preach His word. Do not listen to them and their false preaching, heed only God's word in His holy Koran.

"Go from your homes and praise God. Go forth and take your lives back from those who would hold you in chains of false belief. The time is here to take your rightful place in God's glory. Go now.

"Allah akbar!"

When the Assassin technician signaled that the cameras were shut off, al-Ismaili stiffly stepped down from the stage. It was done. The dream of centuries had been accomplished. The Mahdi had returned, and now the Muslim world could get back on the path of greatness. With the Brotherhood acting as his eyes and ears, he would be able to oversee the process from his mountain fortress and guide the faithful back to the glory they had known in the days of the prophet.

"THAT'S ALL WE NEED right now," J. R. Rust growled as the TV in their Beirut villa went back to the regular programming. "Another damned Mahdi to show up."

"What's the story on this Mahdi business?" David McCarter asked. "I remember reading about a

Mahdi leading the Sudan uprising of the 1880s, Gordon of Khartoum and all that. But I didn't think that was still going on today.''

''Believe me,'' the CIA man said, sounding thoroughly disgusted, ''it's still going on. In fact, if it wasn't for the legend of the twelfth imam, or the Mahdi as he's usually called, the Middle East would be a much quieter place for everyone to live.''

''How's that?''

''Well, it goes like this. As you know, there are two main branches of Islam, the Sunnis and the Shiites, kind of like our protestants and Catholics. The break came in the ninth century and, as it usually does with that kind of thing, it had to do with who was going to be top dog in the Muslim world. Anyway, eleven successive imams who were descended from the Prophet Muhammad through his daughter Fatima had ruled the Shiite branch of Islam.

''When the last one suddenly died, his juvenile son was in line to become the twelfth imam. But the kid was only ten or eleven and questions about his age were raised, particularly about who would be calling the shots until he came of age himself. Anyway, while the in-fighting about who was going to actually be in charge was going on, this kid disappears one night and is never seen again.''

McCarter shrugged as if to say ''What's new?''

''The best bet,'' Rust continued, ''is that the kid walked down the wrong dark alley and got himself stuffed down a well or something like that, but he disappeared without a trace. And ever since then, the Shiites have been looking for him to come back and take over their brand of Islam. He's called Muhammad al-Mahdi or the hidden imam. Mahdi means savior, and according to them, when he returns he will usher in a golden age of pure Islam by wiping out all the evil infidels in the world and starting over clean.''

''But what's he doing getting involved with the Christian millennium?'' Manning asked.

''That's a good question,'' Rust replied. ''Like the Christians, they, too, have a calendar of when their savior might come back, but with them it's every hundred years rather than a thousand. And, if I remember correctly, the Mahdi isn't due for another eighty years in the year of the Hijra 1500. The last guy who tried to play Mahdi showed up in 1979 and attacked the holy city of Mecca. The Saudis were forced into taking military action in the sacred precinct, and they took a great deal of flak from the other Islamic countries for doing it, but they put him down.''

''But if there was a Mahdi in 1979,'' Hawkins asked, ''what are we doing with another one now? And I don't remember any kind of fanfare like this back then.''

''With the Muslims, the Mahdi won't appear in a cloud of light accompanied by singing angels or anything like that. He'll be known only by his deeds and that's why anyone can play. If you proclaim yourself the Mahdi and keep from getting killed, you're him. If you die, though,'' Rust said with a shrug, ''you were an imposter and no one cares.''

"Doesn't this guy coming at the wrong time automatically make him an imposter?"

"One would think so. But with the imams preaching the millennium thing now, no one's looking too closely at the calendar. And whoever this guy is, if he can pull this off, he'll own most of Islam. The Muslim national governments will collapse, the people will raise the green flags of jihad and this whole part of the world will be in deep shit."

"But won't anyone try to dispute his claim?" Manning asked.

"Of course," Rust replied. "In fact, damned near every Islamic leader will. None of them will want to take a backseat to some newcomer. But all it'll take is for a few of them to die suddenly and you'll see the others cave in. Around here, nothing succeeds like success. If this Mahdi can bring a few major figures into his camp, it'll be a done deal."

"And you think that he'll be able to overthrow the region's civilian governments?"

"Right now, I'd say that he has a real good chance," Rust stated. "And if he can pull it off, he'll have accomplished what no other Muslim leader has been able to do since the days of the Ottoman Empire—bring this place under one rule. He'll be calling the shots, and those who don't go along with him won't last very long. This is the beginning of a whole new ball game."

"What a way to start the new millennium."

"I think that's the idea."

As Rust had predicted, the appearance of the Mahdi, even on television, sent the Middle East into spasms. In the West, Millennium Madness affected only a small, albeit vocal, minority, and mostly female. In the Middle East, the majority of the population joined in this Islamic version of what was sweeping the West. Where it was Christian women who were mostly affected by the hysteria, Islam was a religion of men. There was no Virgin Mary in Islamic thought, and women existed only to give pleasure and children to men. And in the Middle East, it was the men who had the guns. In the urban centers of the region, it was the poor and the dispossessed who reacted the strongest to the Mahdi's message. They had the least and wanted what he promised the most.

No one was surprised when Egypt became the first Muslim nation to fall to the followers of the Mahdi. The millennium prophecies that had been spread earlier had already caused great civil unrest and riots that took days to control. In a population already primed for religious unrest, the Mahdi found fertile ground for his words. He told them to go forth and take their place in the grand scheme of things.

The Egyptian capital of Cairo had already experienced several serious incidents where large numbers of slum poor had attacked the homes of the rich. Calling in the army to put down the unrest had brought an end to this orgy of rioting and looting. It had also exposed the great weakness of the Egyptian forces. The troops of police and military also came from the poorer classes, and the message of the prophecies affected them as well.

What was surprising, though, was how quickly the Egyptian military and police collapsed. Desertions began almost immediately after the Mahdi's message was broadcast. When moderate officers tried to restore order, they were deposed and Mahdist imams were installed in their place. The first thing the clerics did was to close Egypt to foreign traffic from the West of all kinds, including air.

When a German government-chartered Lufthansa 757 didn't follow instructions to turn around as it approached the Egyptian coast, two MiG-29 fighters were launched to intercept it. The instant that the airliner entered Egyptian airspace, both of the MiGs fired on it. Heat-seeking air-to-air missiles homed in on the plane's huge fan jet engines and detonated. The wreckage rained over the desert.

FROM CAIRO, the Mahdi-inspired insurrection spread like a plague. Its first stop was the Gaza Strip. The disruptions started out small and were easily controlled by the police of the Palestinian Authority. As with the police forces of most Islamic nations, the Palestinian officers weren't hampered with Western-style concerns about breaking heads. Heads were broken and their owners imprisoned.

The Israeli units guarding the Strip wisely kept out of what they saw as a purely internal affair. If the Palestinians were breaking their own people's heads, it was not their place to interfere. While it was never said in so many words, many Israeli officials really didn't care if the Palestinians fought among themselves. The more they fought each other, the less strength they would have to kill Israelis.

From the Gaza Strip, though, it was only a short trip to the Arab Quarter of East Jerusalem. Thus far, the holy city had escaped most of the Millennium Madness, including the so-called Muslim prophecies. Since Jerusalem was holy to three religions, no one wanted to see it trashed. But Millennium Madness wasn't under anyone's control, least of all the religious authorities in the city. It was true that certain Muslim and Christian groups were promoting irrational behavior in the name of the millennium, but so far the damage had been minimal. Then came the Mahdi.

Within hours of the news of open warfare in Cairo and the Gaza Strip hitting TV screens, Jerusalem erupted, and most of the victims were Christian.

For years, the Christian population of Jerusalem had been in decline. In the decades-long unofficial war between the Palestinians and the Israelis, the Christians had been the unspoken enemy of both sides, particularly in East Jerusalem. The rising influence of the Ultra Orthodox Jewish factions in Jerusalem had also increased the pressure on them. Now, though, the age-old conflicts raged anew, and their ancient Muslim enemies took vengeance for ancient wrongs dating back to the Crusades.

Stony Man Farm, Virginia

THE APPEARANCE of the Mahdi had done little to improve the mood around Stony Man Farm, but Aaron Kurtzman welcomed the distraction to keep his mind off of Barbara Price.

Not only was the Mahdi causing unrest in the Middle East, there was also fallout from his appearance in the Christian nations. The image of the Mahdi had no sooner faded from the TV screens than Christian cult leaders were denouncing him as the antichrist foretold in the Book of Revelations.

The New Agers also got into the game and started reciting the prophecies of Nostradamas who had predicted that the greatest tyrant of all times would appear in the Middle East. According to most readings of the coded quatrains the prophet was famous for, the tyrant had been due to show up last year. But being only one year off was no big deal. Particularly when the real beginning of the millennium wasn't until the year two thousand and one

As with everything else about the millennium, though, reason and logic weren't top priorities when it came to the Mahdi. No one bothered to ask how a resurrected twelfth century religious figure had managed to show up on a twentieth century medium—satellite television. No one tried to find out who he really was and what he was up to. Everyone, Christian and Muslim, just jumped on the bandwagon.

CHAPTER NINETEEN

Beirut, Lebanon

David McCarter found Mack Bolan on the top of the tower above the villa, looking north to the sea. For once, the soldier looked at peace with himself and the world. Peace for him was so fleeting that McCarter hesitated to break it, but he had good news for a change.

"We've just been told that Barbara's okay," McCarter told him. "Vedik's cure worked, and Hal says that she's going to recover completely."

"I know." Bolan looked up.

After a pause, he looked back out to sea. "I was afraid that I wasn't going to be able to help her this time, David. There's only so much that we or anyone can do when something like that happens."

"But we were able to help her," McCarter said. "We came here, and we were able to find the key to saving her and a lot of other people as well. I say that it's been a job very well done."

"So far," Bolan said ominously. "But the mission here isn't over yet."

"I didn't think so." The ex-SAS commando smiled grimly. "But I wanted to check with you first. Sometimes Hal wants to haul us up short before we've reached the goal line, and he was talking about our withdrawal before the unrest gets too much worse."

"Hal only passes the word down from the Wonderland," Bolan said in defense of his long-time friend. He and Brognola went all the way back to the earliest days of the Executioner's Mafia War. Even though the big Fed was no longer active in the field, they knew each other's minds about as well as any two men ever could.

"If he'd been calling the shots himself," Bolan reminded him, "a lot of what we've had to do over the years wouldn't have gone down the way it did because we'd have been able to stop it before it got out of hand."

"There is a lot of truth to that," McCarter agreed. "Politics is usually the worst thing that can happen to any situation and that's sure as hell the case here. The people of Beirut have suffered for years from too much politics and too little common sense, and it's not over yet."

"It isn't over for them or for us," Bolan said. "There's a stain on the planet that needs to be erased. Any man who thinks that he can unleash a deadly plague on the world and get away with it needs to be dealt with."

"But don't forget that he's a major religious figure now, a messiah," McCarter pointed out. "You know how politicians feel about getting involved with religious leaders."

Bolan leveled his cold blue eyes on McCarter. "I don't care if he's the Pope. He needs to be brought to account for this, David. Too many of the greatest crimes in history have been excused in the name of religion, and that's not going to happen this time. Mahdi or not, he's responsible and he's going to go down for it."

"That's my take on it," McCarter said. "But I just wanted to make sure that we were in agreement. So, how do you want to work it?"

"That's the problem, isn't it?" Bolan said. "If what Vedik told us is true, we're not going to be able to take care of it with a quick raid and a couple of pounds of C-4 in the right place. This is going to be a major operation."

The soldier looked out to sea again. "But doing more than that is going to be difficult without sanction and support from the Man. He's in control of all the things we really need to do the job."

"Why don't you talk this over with Hal?" McCarter suggested. "And you might want to remind him that while we have Vedik in custody, this Mahdi has the lab and stockpiles of the mutated anthrax, and he can use it again whenever he wants. So, it might not be a bad idea to take care of it now before this part of the world gets too much crazier and we can't get to him."

"That's a good point," Bolan said. "Let's go have a chat with Katz first. I want his input on this before I suggest anything."

WHEN McCARTER AND Bolan got down to the main house, Katzenelenbogen told them that Hal Brognola was on the line. In the communication room, the two-way video link was up, and the big Fed's face was on the monitor.

"The President extends his thanks to all of you," he said. "The millennium plague treatment is reported as successful everywhere it's being used. This Armageddon, at least, has been defused."

Bolan smiled grimly. "We would like to send a little Armageddon of our own to this Old Man of the Mountain, so he won't think of trying something like that again."

"I totally agree with the sentiment," Brognola said carefully. "But with the situation in the Middle East the way it is right now, I don't think that the Man will go along with something like that."

"What do you mean?"

"If you haven't been watching CNN, the Islamic world is a mess from top to bottom, and the appearance of this Mahdi was the last straw, so to speak. What few Westerners were in the region are being evicted, and even their own governments are under siege. No matter how deserving, any action by the United States will only make a very bad situation worse. The political fallout would take years to settle."

"We'd like you to talk to him about it anyway," Bolan said. "And you can remind the Man that if the Mahdi would plan something as criminal like that plague, he won't stop at anything. Plus, he still may have stockpiles of the plague and would be able to attack us again with it. Even though we know how to stop it now, there would still be those who couldn't be treated in time and would die. Particularly in a mass casualty situation.''

Brognola looked thoughtful for a moment. ''What do you think it would take to completely eliminate the threat that guy represents?'' he asked. ''If the President decided to make a move on your recommendation, he'll want to make sure that it's effective.''

''Tell the Man that he has only two options. The first is to declare war on the region and send the entire U.S. military to eradicate it. And I do mean the entirety of America's military strength because every Muslim nation on the face of the earth will declare jihad on us. Short of deploying nuclear weapons, we'll be fighting them well into the next century.''

''What's the second option?'' Brognola knew that the first option was out of the question and had been mentioned only to provide a comparison to what they really wanted to do.

''One small ADM in the right place should do it with a minimum loss of life except to the force that goes in to emplace it. But it will have to be a completely deniable operation. If the United States is connected to it in any way, the first scenario will still apply. And that means that we have to do it.''

ADMs were Atomic Demolition Devices, small nuclear bombs that had originally been developed for deployment in Western Europe as a last-ditch defense against the massive Soviet armies of the sixties and seventies. They were placed in prepared positions in mountain passes and valleys to deny tank armies passage through the terrain.

The Soviets and Chinese had also successfully used ADMs in excavation projects for dams and the like. One had even been used to pulverize oil-bearing shale deep under the earth to create liquid petroleum that could then be pumped to the surface. The resulting oil was faintly radioactive, but most of the contamination was removed during the refining process.

"What yield do you think it would take to bring that mountain down?" Brognola asked.

ADMs were dial-a-yield devices in that the explosive effect could be controlled by varying the degree of the nuclear detonation. That way you could get exactly the right amount of explosive force to do the job and not have to worry about smashing ants with sledgehammers.

"Without looking at the geological reports, I'd say that a 1.5 kiloton bomb in the right place should more than take care of it, but you can have Kurtzman check on that. That's only one-tenth of the Hiroshima bomb, but in an enclosed place like the inside of a mountain, it should be enough. We wouldn't need to obliterate the place from the face of the earth, just bring the roof down on top of it."

"That leaves us with a delivery problem," Brognola pointed out. "All the ADMs are back in the States and it might be tricky getting one to you."

"We don't need an ADM to get the kind of package you want," Grimaldi told Bolan.

"Explain."

"Some of the new aerial tactical nukes are dial-a-yield as well. I know there's one that'll go from 1.5 to 5.5 at the flip of a few switches. And it's small enough that a few men could carry it."

"But that still leaves us with the how-in-the-hell-do-we-get-it-there issue."

"Not really. You can have it flown in and para-chuted to you."

McCarter smiled. "And I suppose that you're go-ing to be the delivery boy in this scenario?"

Grimaldi grinned. "I kind of thought I might."

"And where would we find this particular kind of bomb?"

"How about the carrier task force that's steaming in the Med right now, the *Eisenhower*. I know they'll have them in their war stores. Regardless of all the bullshit that gets into the papers, our carrier task forces are still packing their tactical nukes."

"How would this work?"

"Well, if I can get back to Israel, a Navy COD can come get me and fly me back out to the carrier. Once there, I borrow an F/A-18, load the bomb and deliver it to you guys in the desert. From there, I guess you can drag it to this mountain, set the timer and beat feet out of there. Piece of cake."

"Only if you're not with the ground team," McCarter said. "Why don't you let me do the flying this time, Jack, and you can drag the nuke around the desert?"

"In your dreams, lad." Grimaldi grinned. "I'm

the ace pilot around here. That's why I draw flight pay. You grunts signed on to do all the legwork.''

"That idea might sound a little better to him,'' Brognola said. "You continue to standby in Beirut while I run this past him.''

"And, Hal,'' Katz said, "have Aaron start sending us whatever he has on the site. We need to start working up the details ASAP.''

"Will do.''

Stony Man Farm, Virginia

AARON KURTZMAN WAS SHOCKED when he looked up and saw Barbara Price walk into the Computer Room. She looked like the survivor of a bad embalming job. She had lost so much weight that her fine-boned face looked skeletal, and her skin had an unhealthy, sickbed pallor. Her hair was pulled back in a ponytail, but it didn't have its normal lustre. But seeing her on her own two feet was the best thing he'd seen in too many days.

"Barbara!'' he almost shouted. "What are you doing here? Why didn't you let us know you were coming?''

She smiled wanly. "I didn't want to disrupt your work, so I told Hal not to let anyone know I was being released.''

Before Kurtzman could say anything, Hunt Wethers was hurrying toward her with a chair.

"Thank you,'' she said as she sat next to Kurtzman's wheelchair.

"Can I get you anything?''

"I can really use a cup of coffee," she said, smiling. "That damned doctor wouldn't let me have any."

Kurtzman reached for the intercom. "I'll have the cook make a fresh pot."

"No." She laughed. "I want a cup of your usual stuff, the Bear's Brew."

Backing out of his workstation, Kurtzman wheeled over to the pot and grabbed the first coffee mug that came to hand. "Back in a flash."

"Where are you going?"

"To wash out this thing. Can't have you relapsing."

Price shook her head.

With Kurtzman out of the way, Hunt Wethers, Akira Tokaido and the others gathered to welcome her back.

Kurtzman returned a few minutes later holding the scoured mug in his hand like it was the Holy Grail. After filling it from the Computer Room pot, he wheeled it over to her.

"Thank you, Aaron."

Taking her first sip of the scalding, acid brew, she suppressed a grimace and shuddered. "Now I feel like I'm really home."

Cradling the mug in her hand, Price let the conversation wash over her as the staff tried to bring her up to date on what had happened since she had fallen ill.

"I want to schedule a full briefing as soon as possible so I can get up to speed on what's going down."

"Well," Wethers stated, "go read your Nostradamus and you'll know what's going on in most of the world, particularly in the Middle East."

"I heard about the Mahdi's appearance on the flight back," she replied. "Have we gotten any leads on him yet?"

Wethers shook his head. "We don't have any idea where he is yet. He's using some kind of tight-beam transmission, so we can't pinpoint him. All we know is that he's transmitting from the region, and his message is being rebroadcast from one of the Saudi comsats."

"Can we take the satellite out?"

"We don't have any of the ASAT weapons on station in the Middle East right now. Plus, if we start blasting expensive Saudi hardware out of the sky, they're likely to cut off our oil again. With the Mahdi preaching 'Death to the infidels and all their technology,' we're probably going to have an oil crunch as it is."

"Do we at least know who this Mahdi guy is?"

Wethers and Kurtzman exchanged a quick glance. "Actually, we do," Kurtzman said. "According to Katz, he's the same guy who started the millennium plague."

Price calmly took another drink of her coffee. "What are we doing about taking him out?"

"Nothing as yet," Wethers replied honestly. "Katz and Striker came up with a plan, but the President hasn't acted on it yet."

"Why not?"

"We don't exactly know why," Kurtzman said.

"But the fact that this man is claiming to be the Mahdi probably has a lot to do with it."

"Mahdi my ass," she snapped. "If mutated anthrax is a tool of religious salvation, I'm the Virgin Mary. The bastard's a mass murderer, and the least we can do is drop a nuke on him and see if it will send him to paradise."

"That's one of the options being discussed, but it appears that the President isn't too hot on the idea."

Price drained the last of her coffee and stood. "We'll see about that. Where's Hal?"

"Probably in your office."

She set her coffee mug by the pot and headed for the door.

CHAPTER TWENTY

Stony Man Farm, Virginia

When Hal Brognola saw Barbara Price standing in the open door of her office, he got to his feet. "I thought you were going to rest for a while."

"I've got too much to do," she said as she walked past him and sat in her chair.

"What do you have to do?" he asked. "The mission's over, and I've been taking care of the housekeeping chores for you. You need to rest for a couple more days."

"I find it interesting that you say that the mission's over, Hal," she said. "If I didn't know any better, I'd say that you've been bought off by the peace, love and tie-dye boys of the State Department."

Brognola automatically reached for the roll of antacids in his pocket. A resupply of that vital ingredient to his physical well-being had been picked up when he'd had her flown back from Atlanta. Those who thought that the female gender was somehow the "weaker sex" and that women's heads were stuffed with warm, fuzzy thoughts of peace, love and brotherhood had never met Barbara Price.

"Barbara," he said, "I think you need to come up to speed on the situation in that part of the world before you can understand what went into this decision. Since the appearance of the Mahdi, it's gotten worse than it's ever been. There has never been a worse time for our country to intervene in the region than now. Any move we make is going to ignite a holocaust that will—"

"That's crap!"

Brognola almost smiled. The thing he liked most about Price was that she never said anything other than exactly what was on her mind. And since she loathed politics in any form, every thought she had was a picture of bottom-line clarity.

"If you like, I'll pass your assessment on to the Man."

"Please do," she said. "And while you're at it, tell him that he's a gutless wonder who's going to go down in history as the man who allowed an international mass murderer to go free because he was too afraid to bring him to justice."

"What do you think you can do without getting presidential approval?" he asked.

"Well," she said as she sat back in her chair, "if I remember correctly, the boys on the sharp end of the stick this time were doing what needed to be done a long time before anyone was around to give them permission. I'll grant that it's been a lot easier for them to do their work since Uncle Sam got involved and started providing all the hardware. But I can still remember a time when a small group of men stood their ground and put their lives on the line whenever the situation required it.

And since the world's coming to an end anyway, we might as well go out with it. Why should we escape Armageddon?''

''What do you mean?''

''Well, according to all the millennium blather, there's one of two things coming down the pike in just a few months. The entire world's either going to go up in flames, or we're somehow going to drift into some kind of childlike, liberal dreamworld where everyone loves everyone else and there will be no violence anymore because everyone will be too busy making daisy chains and baking chocolate chip cookies to hate their neighbors.''

Brognola couldn't help but smile.

''No matter which one of those scenarios happens, all of us at Stony Man Farm are going to be out of a job. And if that's the case, what better finale than for us to go out snuffing a monster who decided to loose a plague on the world so he could set himself up as a little tin god?''

''That's part of the problem the President's facing, Barbara, the Mahdi business. Regardless of what the man has done, he has also been accepted as the savior figure of a major religion. There is no way that the President can get any kind of political backing for targeting a religious leader.''

''Religion isn't a hot topic for debate around this place. I don't know what, if any, religious affiliations anyone around here has and I don't really care. All I care about is that people who do abhorrent things pay for them, quid pro quo and posthaste. So, I don't care if this guy is the Pope or the next Dali Lama. It really doesn't matter to me. To put it in religious terms, he excommunicated himself from the human race the day he decided to commit a crime against humanity.

"Now if this Mahdi is, in fact, a reincarnation of some deity, then I assume that he'll have some special power that will prevent him from being killed by any of us mere mortals. But that doesn't mean that we shouldn't try to take him out. Are you with us?"

Maybe she was right, Brognola thought. With the world coming to an end, what did it matter if one madman more or less was alive when it happened? In fact, they might be doing the world a favor if this self-proclaimed Mahdi bit the big one courtesy of Stony Man Farm. Maybe the next Muslim "savior" who showed up would find a different way to save his people that didn't involve killing millions of others.

"Okay," he said, sighing. "I'm in."

"I knew you'd see it my way. Welcome back to the human race."

"Someday I'm going to strangle you."

"Wait till I get my strength back, and I'll go you two out of three falls."

"What do you want me to do?"

"Hang tight until I can talk to Katz and Bolan. I know they've been cooking something up. And I need to see what kind of targeting information Kurtzman has been able to come up with for us."

"Don't wait too long," he cautioned. "The situation over there isn't going to get any better in the next week or so. In fact, it's only going to get worse."

"The only deteriorating situation I'm worried about is in the Oval Office. It's time for a gut check, and I'm not sure the Man is up for it."

"You may be right," Brognola said candidly. "The millennium unrest has him running scared."

"That's what I thought."

WHEN PRICE WENT DOWN to the computer room, Aaron Kurtzman handed her the bad news. Even though Phoenix felt that they had gotten all of the information they could out of Insmir Vedik about the Old Man of the Mountain's hideout, it wasn't enough. The Old Man had made sure that the Bosnian didn't learn where he had been while he had cooked up his deadly mutation. In fact, he had been blindfolded when he had been taken there, and when he had been released finally to go to Beirut. All he knew was that he had been driven west when he left the hideaway.

"The main problem," he told her, "is that the name of the mountain associated with the Brotherhood of Assassins is fictional."

"What do you mean?" she asked.

"If it existed at all, the original Mount Alamut was in Persia, modern Iran, not Syria. And, more properly, Alamut was a fortress on a mountain, not the name of the mountain itself. Actually, it's the name of a river that flowed past the castle. Therefore, I cannot call up my atlas, type in 'Alamut' and come up with a set of coordinates. And when I check the historical references, I get three different locations where the Assassin stronghold might have been. So, as David says, we don't have bugger-all on that avenue of approach.

"But—" he raised a hand before she could reply "—I do have a modern anomaly in a mountainous region of northern Syria that looks interesting. And it ties in with what little Katz was able to get out of Vedik."

He flashed up a map of the region on the screen. Clicking a pointer at the screen, he drew a circle around a small mountain range where the Syrian border joined those of Iraq and Turkey.

"This whole region has been a military zone ever since Syria became a modern nation. As you can see, it's isolated, it's desert with no commercial value and it's too damned close to Iraq and Turkey. It is also a perfect invasion route, and more than one army marched through here during ancient times. Knowing their history, the Syrians took the first chance they had to make that area and access to it a military zone. All that being said, something funny has been going on in those mountains since the Gulf War.

"For instance," Kurtzman said, changing screens, "take a look at this."

The monitor showed an overhead recon satellite shot of a mountain range with a river running along its eastern side. "This was taken in the days right after the Gulf War when we were trying to do something useful for those poor Kurds. As you can see, it's the same as any other shot of Middle Eastern desert desolation. But, when you run through several weeks' worth of shots of the same area, here's what you get."

A freeze-frame montage of shots from the same satellite location showed truck traffic going both toward and away from one of the mountains. Most of these were heavy trucks that one might find at a major construction site.

"It keeps going this way for a few months and then abruptly ends. And on the next shots we see the truck tracks are gone. I ran this through every intelligence agency that would talk to me, and the conclusion is that this wasn't a Syrian military operation."

"Does the Mossad sign off on that?"

Kurtzman nodded. "They do now, but this was the first they'd heard of it and they have very good sources in Damascus."

Knowing that he was about to burst from holding back his conclusion, she let him continue.

"The region's governor turns out to be an Ismaili Muslim," he said. "Now, there aren't too many of them in high positions in the Syrian government, but he's one. Apparently, his family is somehow tied to Assad, and he was given the post for his faithful service."

"So?"

"The 'so' is this," he said, grinning. "If you'll

remember, the Assassins are an offshoot of the Ismaili sect.''

"So you think that this earth-moving job has
something to do with this new Mount Alamut Assassin hangout? Is that what you're saying?''

"I'm saying that I'm supposed to be looking for
a mythological mountain fortress containing a fa-
natical Ismaili sect and its bloodthirsty leader, and
I come across a mountain that appears to have been
tunnelled into a remote region of an area governed
by an Ismaili. It's a stretch, but it does tie in with
what Katz got from Vedik, and it's worth taking a
closer look at.''

"Look more closely," she ordered, "and do it
quickly. We might have to do this one under the
table, and time is running out.''

"Tell me about it," he replied. "You need to
read through the last twenty-four-hours' worth of
Mahdi millennium activities. It's really gone crazy
over there right now.''

"I don't have time to waste on that, so I'll take
your word for it.''

MALIK AL-ISMAILI WENT OVER the reports from all
of his Brotherhood cells in the field. Not only were
they his fists, they were his eyes and his ears. The
reports pouring into his underground fortress headquarters were more than encouraging. Throughout
the Muslim world, the Mahdi's message was being
put into action. Sometimes peacefully, but most often by force, and al-Ismaili didn't care just as long
as it happened.

Not only were the West-leaning governments in trouble, but the Marxist regime of the Sudan had also gone under. Marxism was as much a part of Western decadence as was capitalism, and it, too, had to go.

Best of all was that with the Egyptian downing of that German jetliner, the West had cut off all air traffic to the region. The airlines of the Islamic nations were still flying into the West, but they were only accepting Muslim passengers and only for return flights. This was the great counterdiaspora, the return of the faithful who had, for whatever reason, left their homelands to live in the decadent West. As soon as all those who wanted to return had, that link would be cut as well.

In the Mahdi's plan, there was no place for traffic of any kind with the unbelievers, and that included the traffic in oil. Let the infidels freeze in their northern hells without oil. Let them push their huge cars from place to place if they wanted to flaunt their wealth. And let their ungodly technology grind to a halt. For far too long, the riches of the Middle East had been exploited by the greedy West, but that would soon come to an end.

Like the radicals of any religion, al-Ismaili had no real idea of how the world worked and he felt that he didn't need to know. His eye was on God's world, not on the things of the earth. He was well aware that what technology the Muslim world had it owed completely to the West, and that included the television that made his holy crusade possible.

But he also intended to bring an end to that technology when the time was right.

In the coming world of the Mahdi, the only technology that would be necessary would be that needed to defend the lands of the faithful from foreign invasion. Like in the old days, men would take their needs from the earth as God had intended them to do. Their fields and their flocks would provide a life for them and their families. It had worked that way for thousands of years, and it would work again.

He knew that the Mahdi would have a difficult time getting this message across to the masses. They had been seduced by the West for too long and wanted that which wasn't clean and pure in God's eyes. There were no cars, cellular phones or television sets in paradise, and there would be none in his lands on Earth. There would be no need for so-called Western knowledge when everything that God wanted men to know could be found in the Koran.

Until this perfect time came, though, he would make good use of the Western technology he had acquired. The Mahdi had made an appearance every day at noon, Mecca time, and it was almost time for him to go on the air again. Every time he appeared, the people took strength and renewed their vows to rid God's lands of the infidel and all his works.

CHAPTER TWENTY-ONE

Miami, Florida

The next morning, most of the crowd that had gathered around the Rainbow Cybertech buildings hoping to see the Virgin Mary had dispersed. Schwarz hadn't caused any more visions to appear on the towers, and even the faithful had jobs and homes to go to. The hundred or so people who remained were old men and women who had no other claims to their time. As was usual with this kind of religious event, they'd hang around for the next couple of months and pray for forgiveness of their sins, real or imagined.

The Cybertech compound looked like the aftermath of the world's biggest rock concert. It would take a week to pick up all the trash and several months to restore the grounds. At least, though, the employees could report for work. As with any large corporation, it didn't really matter to them that Dingo Jones wasn't in his office. They had jobs to do, and they did them.

In Able Team's hotel-room CP, Hermann

Schwarz was linked to Stony Man Farm via his modem and was working closely with Akira Tokaido to try to find where Jones had taken the *Digger*. It was a big boat to try to hide, but the Caribbean wasn't a small body of water and it was dotted with hundreds of islands both large and small, with thousands of bays and inlets. It would take high tech diligence and a bit of luck to find him. If, that was, Jones hadn't lit out for the open seas of the South Atlantic.

Schwarz was convinced, however, that Jones was still in the area and that he would return to Miami before much longer. It was true that the man could work his scam from anywhere on Earth courtesy of the wonderful world of cyberspace. All he needed was a phone connection and, with a satlink setup, he could do that from sea. But for something that big to work as Jones intended it to, he needed to be at the controls to react to the unexpected.

As Schwarz knew only too well, it was a law of nature that every plan, no matter how well thought out, ran into the unexpected and needed to be adjusted. Not even a man like Jones would be able to change that.

WHILE SCHWARZ WAS TREKKING through cyberspace with Tokaido seeking the elusive Dingo Jones, Carl Lyons went back into Little Havana. Gutierrez had called to tell him that he had some new information on Jones's operations.

When Lyons walked into the social club, Gutierrez was sitting at the end of the bar smiling broadly.

"I have information about your Dingo Jones, amigo. Now I know why he has always guarded his warehouses so tightly."

Lyons waved away the beer the bartender automatically put in front of him. "What do you have?"

"One of his warehouses is full of weapons and military equipment. It looks like he's planning to invade Cuba or something."

"What do you mean?"

"Not only does he have the arms and ammunition," Gutierrez explained, "he has uniforms, field equipment, combat boots, medical supplies, radios, the whole tamale, and enough to outfit a hundred guys or so. All he has to do is run the men in one end of the building, and they come out the other end armed and ready to go to war."

Lyons smiled to himself. This was what he had hoped to find sooner or later. Jones had just gone beyond the hard-to-trace world of cybercrime and had drifted into hard evidence that would stand in any court. Now he could ratchet up the action several notches and put the bastard away. Dollars to doughnuts, he didn't have a federal arms dealer's licence and the weapons were illegal. On top of that, with all the ancillary military gear, a case could be made for a RICO charge of conspiracy to commit a crime. Outfitting a mercenary force in the United States was a serious offense.

"Who made the entry?" he asked.

"I did." Gutierrez grinned. "When I was working for the contras, I specialized in breaking and entering."

No doubt learned in Miami, Lyons thought. But this was one instance where a life of crime had turned out to be useful in the fight against evil.

"Where is this place?"

After making a note of the address, Lyons checked his watch. "Sit tight on this until I can get back to you," he said.

Gutierrez shrugged. "I don't have anywhere to go, amigo."

WHEN DAY BROKE over the Caribbean, Rosario Blancanales finally decided to call it quits. He had gone throughout the night chasing every blip Akira Tokaido could pick up, but to no avail. Dingo Jones was God only knew where by now. Rather than waste any more time running in circles, he decided to go back to Miami and start all over again. If Tokaido got a fresh sighting on the *Digger,* they'd use an aircraft or a chopper to chase him the next time.

Turning the bow of his boat to the northwest, he set the autopilot before going below to find some breakfast. He had been popping pills all night to stay awake, and the body needed energy if he was to stay awake long enough to get the boat back to Miami in one piece.

He was putting a pack of sausages and biscuits in the microwave when the radio broke into life. "Pol!" Tokaido yelled. "He's back! He's coming up behind you bearing two three zero on a collision course!"

ON THE BRIDGE of the *Digger*, Dingo Jones had the helm. Captain Johnson was standing by with a look of horror on his face. "Turn aside, man! You're going to ram him!"

"Gunner," Jones said without turning his head, "Roy. Take Johnson below. He's breaking my concentration."

The two Australians grabbed the captain's arms and marched him off the bridge.

Now that he was alone, Jones could concentrate on whoever was in the damned boat that had dogged him all night. With his stealthing and his powerful radar, he'd been able to keep from being seen by the smaller boat's radar while still keeping track of his tormentor. Now it was his turn to be the cat and he was about to eat the mouse.

As he approached, he saw that the boat was moving very slowly and there was no one behind the wheel. Suddenly, a man rushed up from below and took the helm. When the man looked back, Jones instantly recognized him. The man who had been trying to follow him all night was Rosario Perez. He didn't know what the bastard's game was and he didn't care. He had vowed that he would kill the man the next time he saw him and that time was now.

Steering in a little more left rudder, he smiled as he aimed the bulk of his yacht directly at the boat in front of him and advanced his throttles.

WHEN BLANCANALES TURNED to look over his shoulder, the yacht looked as if it were doing over forty knots as it bore down on a collision course. He'd had the twin gas engines throttled well back while he had been below, ticking over at a mere 950 rpm, just enough to maintain steerage. With no power, he had no maneuvering ability and he slammed the throttles up against the stop. The engines hiccuped as the fuel injectors flooded the cylinders with raw gas, and that was enough to decide the issue.

Blancanales barely had time to snatch a life vest and head for the side railing before the *Digger*'s bow smashed into his transom. The initial effect was like a cannon shell going off and then it was like a giant buzz saw cutting the boat in two lengthwise.

The initial shock of the impact threw Blancanales clear. But as soon as he hit the water, he was caught in the wake of the bow and dragged under. The smooth hull of the *Digger* slid past his back as it cut his rented boat into two pieces without slowing.

Kicking as hard as he could to keep from being sucked into the yacht's spinning props, Blancanales broke free of the wake and sputtered to the surface. Somehow, he had managed to hold on to the life vest, but he didn't get into it immediately. Being made of fiberglass, most of his boat had instantly slipped beneath the waves. Some of the splintered wooden superstructure, the seat cushions and an empty beer cooler stayed afloat. It wasn't a big debris field, but if Jones returned to check his handiwork, he could try to hide under it.

Fortunately, the yacht continued on course to the north, leaving him behind. With that danger past, he slipped his arms into the life vest. Hopefully, Tokaido had monitored the collision and would get the Coast Guard in the air before he became shark bait.

Stony Man Farm, Virginia

AKIRA TOKAIDO COULDN'T believe his eyes. The *Digger* had blatantly rammed Blancanales's smaller craft and cut it in two. He couldn't tell if Blancanales had been able to jump clear, but there was a small debris field, and he might be floating in the middle of it. Even if he was dead, though, they had to try to recover his body.

Reaching for the phone, he dialed the Coast Guard station in Miami, which was over a hundred miles away, but their chopper could be on the scene in less than half an hour. As soon as he had dispatched the chopper, he called Able Team on the radio.

"Carl's gone right now," Schwarz said when he got the word. "But I'll take the radio and go down to the Coast Guard air field."

"I'll keep looking for him," Tokaido replied.

"You keep a tag on Jones and that damned boat," Schwarz said. "I'll make sure the Coast Guard picks up Rosario."

Neither one of them mentioned that they might be recovering his dead body.

At sea

"WHAT WAS THAT BUMP I felt a few minutes ago?" Sarah Carter asked when Jones walked into his cabin.

"It was nothing." He smiled. "Just some debris in the water the captain didn't see in time. The yacht wasn't damaged."

He sat on the edge of the bed and pulled the sheet down to her waist. "We need to finish our conversation," he said as his eyes wandered over her. "I'm going to go back to Miami today, and I need to know if I can trust you enough to take you back with me."

Even though there was no way out of the cabin, she tried to move over to the edge of the bed. He held her arm and leaned over her. "Show me that I can trust you, Anne."

With the threat of being left behind, she had no choice but to obey.

Miami, Florida

HERMANN SCHWARZ WAS WAITING at the Miami Coast Guard station helipad when the red rescue chopper touched down.

"You look a little the worse for wear again, amigo," he greeted his teammate as Blancanales stepped down from the chopper with an orange thermal blanket draped over his shoulders. "Something about this operation doesn't seem to agree with you."

"The bastard ran me down," Blancanales said as he shrugged out of the blanket and handed it back to one of the Coast Guardsmen. "Jones tried to kill me again."

Schwarz grinned. "You'd better not give him another chance then, old buddy. You know what they say about the third time being a charm."

"I'm tired of dicking around with that guy, and he gets no more chances with me. The next time I see him it's going to be my turn, and I'm sure as hell not going to miss."

"That's the spirit." Schwarz clapped him on the shoulder. "Right now, though, let's get you back to the hotel so you can get into a nice clean set of clothes."

ALL THE WAY BACK to the hotel, Blancanales kept silent while Hermann Schwarz chattered about everything under the sun as he drove. This was the third time since hooking up with Sarah Carter that he had almost been killed. There was something about her that drew danger like ham sandwiches at a picnic drew flies. He could tell himself all he wanted that none of this had been her fault, but the facts remained the facts. The woman was dangerous to be around.

As part of Able Team, danger was his business, but this was above and beyond the usual, even for him. He had known that he was going to have to cut her loose at the end of this gig anyway. But thoughts of trying to find a way to keep her around had been forming in the back of his mind. Now he had decided that when this was over, he was going to leave her behind and he wasn't even going to give her a forwarding address.

Life with Able Team was interesting enough without tempting fate any more than was absolutely necessary. Once more, Lyons had been right, but there was no way he'd ever tell him that.

BY THE TIME Blancanales and Schwarz got back to the hotel, Carl Lyons was waiting for them. After assuring him that he was okay, Blancanales showered, changed and ate the takeout Chinese food they had picked up on the way back. Schwarz took Lyons aside and briefed him on the rescue.

"Akira says that it looks like the *Digger* is coming back," Lyons said. "It should make port sometime early this afternoon."

"Good," Blancanales said. "As soon as the bastard's back in town, I swear I'm going to do him."

Lyons let a slow grin creep across his face. "That's more like it, Pol. Now you're talking."

"Now I'm done talking, you mean."

"But you might want to wait a bit before busting down his door. While you were being rescued, Gutierrez called me down to his 'office' and he had an interesting tale to tell."

"How do you want to work it?" Blancanales asked after Lyons filled him in on the Cuban's report of the weapons in the warehouse. "Call in the Feds?"

"Not yet," Lyons said. "I want to keep it to ourselves for now and see if we can use it to our advantage. I'd rather not get them in on it yet."

"We can always raid it ourselves and try to draw him out that way," Blancanales suggested. "If we bust his weapons stash, he's going to be really pissed. From what I've seen of him, he's not a man to keep his temper under control, and I like going up against morons who can't keep it together."

"That might be a plan," Lyons said. "I can borrow a few of Gutierrez's better homeboys and make it look like it was a local job."

"You don't want that kind of firepower out on the street, do you?"

"No. I'll have them load it and drop it off at the nearest cop shop."

"That's going to look funny," Schwarz cautioned. "If the guns are turned in right away, it'll hit the papers and Jones will know that it wasn't a local raid. He'll smell a Fed."

"You have a point," Lyons agreed. "We'll stash them ourselves and turn them in later."

Blancanales reached for his jacket. "Let's go talk to Gutierrez."

"Geez, Pol," Schwarz said. "We're not in that big a hurry are we? Let me finish my damned coffee."

"Bring it with you."

CHAPTER TWENTY-TWO

Miami, Florida

The Able Team trio found Gutierrez in his barrio hangout, holding court over his homeboys. He looked up and smiled when he saw the three men walk in.

"My friends," he called. "Come inside where it is cool. It is hot out there today. Can I offer you a beer?"

"We have an offer for you instead," Blancanales said, getting right to the point after refusing the beer.

"This sounds like big business," Gutierrez said.

"It's about that warehouse of Jones's you found."

"Let me hear your offer."

"We want you to help us check it out."

"You are going to try to break in?" The Cuban smiled.

"We want to look at it first."

A HALF-HOUR LATER, Hermann Schwarz was inside the Team's van, running a full spectra scan of the concrete warehouse planted in the middle of a run-down area of north Miami. He soon confirmed that Dingo Jones was a typical computer geek who depended more on electronics for his security than he did his people. At the headquarters, his human security forces were mostly employed to monitor the electronics and that appeared to be the case at the warehouse as well. The place was covered with every kind of high-tech security device known to man, but only had three guards on duty.

"How long do you think it'll take us to break into there?" Lyons asked him.

Schwarz looked up from his screen. "It's going to be a bitch, Ironman, and I might need to have the Farm send me some more goodies before I can even try. He's got everything from radar to IR covering that place."

"There is a simpler way," Gutierrez spoke up.

"How's that?"

"Shut the power down. That's how I got in."

"I was meaning to ask you about how you did that."

The man shrugged. "I just had one of my Chicos drive his car into a pole that night and knock it down. That cut the main power and shut down most of the security devices. While the guards were trying to figure out what to do about it, I got in and had a quick look around. By the time the power company arrived to fix it, I was gone."

"I like the way you work," Lyons said.

"It was nada," Gutierrez replied modestly.

"This time though," Lyons said, "we'll do it during the day. This afternoon if we can."

"What if a cop cruises by, Ironman?" Schwarz asked. "We don't want to have to use our get-out-of-jail-free cards unless we have to."

"No one'll notice anything," Lyons said, grinning. "Because there'll be nothing to notice. We'll do a power outage phase two. We drive up to the gate as power company people and say that we have to inspect the lines to make sure that the damage from the crash was repaired properly."

"That would work," Gutierrez said. "I have a cousin who works for the power company and I know I can borrow his truck for a small fee."

"We're going to need a couple more trucks, too, covered vans, to carry the goodies away."

"Do you want to take everything in there?"

"No," Lyons said. "Just the weapons, ammunition and radios."

"How about if I load a few crates of uniforms and combat boots as a bonus?" Gutierrez asked. "We can use them in the neighborhood."

Lyons thought for a moment. "Okay. But if I find out later that you sold them to outfit some mercenary force, I'll come looking for you."

"No sweat. I gave that shit up a long time ago."

"Right," Lyons replied. "And make sure that your people understand that they are to keep their hands off the weapons too. Anyone who tries to dip into the stock is going to be in real trouble."

"Man—" Gutierrez shook his head "—you guys are something else. One minute you're acting like the Mafia and the next the FBI. I'd really like to know which one you are.''

Lyons locked eyes with the man. "No, you wouldn't. All you need to know is that we're not going to bust your butt for whatever you're into. And if your people don't do anything stupid and greedy, we'll leave them alone too. If we were Feds, we'd take the whole bunch of you down just to clean up the neighborhood. And,'' he added, smiling wolfishly, ''if we were from one of the Families, we'd simply waste all of you to cut down on the competition.''

Gutierrez saw the truth in that and decided to back off. It really didn't matter who they were as long as he could do business with them. And since they paid in cash, it was good business.

"Whatever you say, amigo.''

THE RAID WENT OFF without a hitch. Schwarz and Lyons drove up to the front gate in the power company truck. Since they were wearing power company coveralls and hats and had a clipboard on the truck's dashboard, the guard bought their story. He notified his partners in the warehouse that they were coming and signed them in.

Inside the warehouse, Schwarz hooked up a couple of pieces of equipment to the power leads at the junction box, shook his head and called over to the two Rainbow Cybertech guards at their monitoring station.

"Hey, guys! Come over here a minute, will you? I want to show you something.''

The two guards left their station and walked over. "What's the prob—"

"Just stand easy," Lyons said as he pulled the MP-5 subgun from his toolbox.

Facing the silenced muzzle of the subgun, the men froze.

After relieving them of their pistols and radios, Schwarz used plastic riot cuffs to bind their wrists behind their backs, and slapped pieces of duct tape over their mouths.

"You just get comfortable," he told them after sitting them on the floor against the wall. "When this is over, we'll call your boss and tell him to come and get you."

As soon as those two were secured, Schwarz got back in the power company truck and drove the short distance back to the gate. Walking wasn't part of a power company man's job description.

"Hey!" he called out to the guard through the open window. "I need you to come and take a look at something we found."

The guard shook his head. "No can do, buddy. It's my ass if I leave my station."

"Come on," Schwarz said. "This is a major fault and I don't want my ass on the line if your boss gets his knickers in a knot about it. I need all three of you guys to see it for yourselves and sign off on the report."

"My SOP says that I have to stay at my station, and my boss will have my ass if I leave."

"That's fine by me." Schwarz shrugged. "But I'm going to have to shut the power down because you guys have a major safety hazard here. If it shorts out, it's going to take out about a mile of the grid and you guys are going to have to foot the bill if it does.''

"Okay," the guard said. "Let me lock up and log off post first."

The guard climbed onto the truck's running board for the short trip back to the warehouse. When Schwarz stopped, he jumped down and immediately ran into Lyons when the Able Team leader stepped out of the shadows with his subgun in his hand.

After being cuffed and silenced, he joined his two comrades against the wall of the warehouse.

"Pol?" Schwarz called over the com link. "Get 'em rolling."

Blancanales was a couple of miles away on a side street waiting in the cab of the lead furniture van Gutierrez had scored to transport their take. "We're on," he told the Cuban.

Gutierrez hit the ignition. "See, I told you it would work."

AFTER TALKING to his security chief at the Rainbow Cybertech headquarters and learning that the crowds had left the grounds of his buildings, Dingo Jones had brought the yacht back into port. To escape the attention of the media, however, he moored her at Miami Beach instead of his usual upscale Miami marina. And, rather than using his chopper for the short flight to his compound, he called for one of his cars to come and get him. He had work to do, and he didn't want either the media or the authorities to know that he was back in town.

Jones was so wrapped up in his own thoughts as the car turned into the access road to the parking structure that he didn't notice the damage that had been done to his compound. Normally, he would have had someone's job for not having every man and woman on his payroll out there cleaning it up. If there was anything he hated, it was trash.

"This just came in, sir." The Cybertech security chief met Jones in the underground parking structure and handed him a report.

Jones's eyes grew wide as he read about the raid on the warehouse. "When did this happen?"

"Just an hour ago. It took awhile for the guards to free themselves and call me."

"What's missing?"

"I don't know," the security chief replied. "The standing operating procedures for the security of that warehouse say that only you or Mr. Caldwell are authorized to inspect the contents. If you'll remember, sir, you signed off on that yourself."

"Right." Jones grimaced. The problem with people like the security chief was that they didn't have the common sense to do anything on their own. His SOP had nothing to do with an emergency like this, and only a moron would have failed to start the investigation immediately.

"Roy and I will look into it, Dingo," Gunner Caldwell said, stepping up to take the report.

"Call me from the warehouse," Jones said. "I'll be in my office."

Taking Carter by the hand, Jones hurried her into the elevator for the quick trip up to the executive suites. After the interrogation she had gone through on the yacht, she was too mentally and physically exhausted to resist and let herself be led away.

BY THE TIME the two furniture trucks were off-loaded, the storage rental spaces Lyons had leased were full to the top with Dingo Jones's weapons cache, and it was a nice collection of modern fire-power.

"These are brand-new U.S.-issue M-249s," Schwarz said as he opened a wooden crate to reveal a dozen 5.56 mm squad machine guns.

"I have M-203 over-and-unders here," Blancanales called, "and enough ammunition to hold off Attila the Hun."

Lyons looked at a case of M-67 fragmentation grenades marked Lake City Arsenal 1997. "It looks like all of this is stolen government property," he said. "Which means the end of our Mr. Dingo Jones one way or the other. We won't need phony kidnapping warrants to put him out of business now. We can call in the Feds any time we want and take him down."

"Except for the fact that this stuff is no longer on his premises," Schwarz pointed out. "We bust him, and he'll bring in his lawyers and be out on bail before he even has time for lunch courtesy of the county. You know that. He's a rich man, and they don't have to pay the price when they screw up."

"This is one rich bastard who will pay," Lyons promised.

"Damned straight," Blancanales added. "But I don't want the Feds getting to him before I can. I want it to be a good old-fashioned Able Team payback this time."

He shrugged. "If there's anything left after that, they can have him."

"But remember," Lyons said, "revenge is a dish best eaten cold. We're not done with that guy yet and now that we have a firm hook in him, I think we should go ahead with the original idea. If it doesn't work, then we can put on our Fed suits and hand him over to the Justice Department."

AFTER SEEING THAT Anne was secured in his suite, Dingo Jones went into his secret control room and reviewed the past two days of market news. He had intended to wait a few more months before launching his plan, but it was beginning to look as if he was running out of time.

As least, though, he had settled his account with that Rosario Perez. He still didn't know what or who the bastard had really been. Anne was sticking to her story that he was just a guy who had picked her up and made her an offer she couldn't refuse, but he didn't believe her. The things that had gone down since she had hit town, though, made him suspicious. There had to be more to it than that, there just had to be. The raid on his warehouse had him worried.

Caldwell had reported that the guards said that it

had been a gang of Cubans who had cleaned out the entire stock of weapons that had been intended to arm the first contingent of the strike force he would need when the bank collapse took place. For a man of his wealth, weapons were not difficult to buy. If, that was, he was willing to settle for Russian or Chinese arms. Buying front-line U.S. weapons, though, was a different matter, particularly in any quantity. But he had no time to worry about that now.

There was still one test that had to take place before he could say that his plans were completely ready to implement. And while he had intended to wait a couple more months before he made that last test, he was uneasy. The events of the previous week had shown that he had to be ready to act now.

The sole remaining mate to the microchip Anne had stolen from him was installed in his mainframe computer now. The development examples and the ones he had used to test the program had all been destroyed as had the patterns necessary to make more. The design was safely in his head, however, should there ever be a need for another one. He was confident, though, that he wouldn't and he was about to put that confidence to the test at the Bank of Rangoon.

Myanmar was the least technologically advanced of all the Southeast Asian nations that could conduct their banking on-line. Its social infrastructure was so deteriorated that it hardly ranked as even a Third World nation anymore. Nonetheless, the Bank of Rangoon was able to accept electronic transfers, and that was all he needed. When their system went down, no one would be alarmed. That it was up and running at all was seen as some kind of miracle of will over the forces of social chaos and fifty-year-old technology. The financial pundits would figure that some half-trained clerk had done something and fried the network.

Dialing up a number, he transferred a few thousand dollars from one of his anonymous offshore accounts into the Bank of Rangoon. When the transfer was completed, he sent another signal to read back the account. A brief alphanumeric code after the account number told him that the killer virus had been emplaced in the bank's computer network and was waiting patiently as only an electronic program could.

After so many years of planning and testing, though, Jones had no patience left. He broke the connection and dialed it up again. When it connected, he initiated a transfer of $6,666.66. Instantly, the connection broke.

Sitting back, he smiled and turned his attention to the market information feed. It would take fifteen minutes for the news of the Rangoon bank's wipe-out to be reported. Even in the cyberspace age when information moved at the speed of light, it still took time for some humans to wake up to a disaster. And even when they did, no one would have any comprehension of what had just happened, which was the only reason he had risked this test. As much as he wanted to, he couldn't take it any further just yet. But soon, though, very soon.

CHAPTER TWENTY-THREE

Stony Man Farm, Virginia

It took longer than usual for the President to come around to Stony Man's plan to take out the Mahdi with a nuke. Not only was there the religious consideration to get past, there was the nuclear issue to get over as well. No matter how well deserved, detonating a nuclear weapon wasn't undertaken lightly. The specter of nuclear devastation had been hammered so deeply into the human psyche that even the suggestion that the best solution for a particular problem was a nuke sent otherwise rational people who should have known better into raging hysteria. And that included almost every career politician on Capitol Hill.

The only reason that the President had finally consented to do it this time was that Hal Brognola had convinced him that the detonation would take place completely underground and wouldn't be visible. Even if it was determined that a nuclear explosion had collapsed the mountain, no one would ever be able to trace it back to the United States.

On his way to the chopper at Andrews Air Force Base, Brognola dialed his secure car phone. "We're go," he said when Barbara Price answered.

"I'll tell them."

Beirut, Lebanon

WITH THE GO-AHEAD from the Farm, Bolan and Katz called the whole team together for a briefing. This time, Bolan took the floor. "We're going after Vedik's boss," he said, "and the leader of these Assassins we've been dealing with here. The Farm agrees with us that they're the same guy."

"About time," Encizo growled.

Bolan smiled. "Kurtzman believes that he's based out of a hollowed-out mountain in northern Syria. Apparently this place had been extensively mined in ancient times, and the mine shafts were expanded to create an underground fortress. He also thinks that he's broadcasting the Mahdi messages from there as well so it'll be a two-fer."

That got a few grins. As long as the Mahdi was stirring up trouble, there would be no peace in the world.

"The plan is simple," Bolan continued. "We'll slip past the border and, after we're in the target area, Jack is going to deliver us a package and we're going to take it to the mountain and drop it off."

"What sized package?" Manning asked.

"One point five KT tactical nuke." Grimaldi grinned.

"One point five KT?" Hawkins arched his eyebrows. "That's a pretty good country-sized fire-cracker you're talking about there, son. We should be able to flatten garbage cans for miles around with that little cherry bomb."

"Just like the Fourth of July back in the old hood." James grinned. "We used to make match-stick-head pipe bombs to celebrate when I was a kid."

Manning smiled too. "Up north we used short-fused half sticks of stumping powder tossed into fifty-five-gallon oil drums. They make a hell of a bang that way."

Hearing the joking banter, Rust looked from one man to the next in complete disbelief. "You people are crazy, you know that?"

James grinned slowly. "Well, J.R. my man, you've got to look at it this way. You know how everyone's saying that the world's going to come to an end? Well, we're just going to set off the first firecracker to start the celebration."

Hawkins reached over to give James a high five. "Right on, bro."

"You're all nuts." Rust shook his head. "Completely out of your rabbit-assed minds. You're all going to go up in a radioactive cloud. It's suicide to even think of doing something like this."

"Oh, no." Hawkins shook his head. "If it was suicide, we wouldn't do it, no way."

"That's right," James cut in. "There's nothing in my job description that says I have to kill my-self."

Rust shook his head. He knew that unlike Islamic

suicide car bombers or Japanese kamikaze pilots, Americans didn't make good suicide troops. This wasn't to say that they didn't perform well under suicidal situations, because they did. The difference was that an American wanted to think that he would survive no matter what, and that's why he fought. Giving up and dying had never been a trait of American fighting men, and it was the same with the Phoenix Force commandos.

Since there was nothing else to say, Rust kept quiet while Bolan and Katz went over the details. This was even crazier than the mission to Pakistan that he had undertaken with them. If he thought they were nuts then, he realized now that he hadn't even scratched the surface.

AT THE END of the briefing, Bolan walked up to the Texan. "J.R.," he said, "when Phoenix moves out, Encizo and Katz are going to remain behind to hold down the fort and I'd like you to stay here and work with them."

Rust got his back up in a hurry. "What's the matter, Striker? You don't think a Company man's good enough to get blown up with the rest of you crazy bastards?"

"It's not that at all, and you know it," Bolan replied sincerely. "You've more than proved yourself with us both in Pakistan and here. You're as good a man as any and better than a lot I've worked with. This isn't about how good you are, though. It's a matter, I guess you'd have to say, of family connections.

"Phoenix and I have worked together for so long that each of us knows what the others are thinking without asking. An extra gun or two isn't going to make that much of a difference this time, but ultimate teamwork is."

"Plus," Katz broke in, "Rafe and I are going to have our hands full here and we're going to need the extra firepower you can give us. If Kurtzman's assessment of the Assassin mentality is correct, the Old Man's going to send all of his troops to take us out. He won't be able to maintain discipline among the Brotherhood when the word gets out that we put his nose in the dirt and he didn't try for some payback. If you want a chance to get your ass shot off, you can find that here."

"Okay," Rust said, "I'll stay. But I don't ever want to hear anyone say that I didn't step across the line when it was drawn."

"Believe me," Katz said, "no one's doubting your courage, J.R. This is just one of those times that guts is not enough. And I think you'll get more than a chance to show your stuff here. We haven't seen the last of these Assassins."

THE MISSION PREP for the operation took a little time. Operating in the city was a far cry from what they'd be facing in northern Syria. If they ran into trouble up there, more than likely it would be the Syrian army they'd have to take on, not back alley Assassins, and the Syrians wouldn't be pushovers. Except for the Israeli Defense Force, they were as modern a force as there was in the Middle East. The key to success, though, was to stay away from them, and that took planning.

Katz's Druze contacts were called upon again to lend a hand. After the success they'd had against the Assassins, there was nothing that they wouldn't do for al-Askari and his men. A couple of the weapons Phoenix Force had bought for the raid on the villa were borrowed, but mostly they needed to use a few vehicles and drivers again.

While the transportation and equipment was being assembled, Jack Grimaldi left Beirut for Israel on the first leg of his part of the mission. He would have the longest trip to make and, even though he would fly most of the way, it too wasn't going to be easy. The Mahdist uprisings were making any kind of trip an iffy proposition, even by air. The air forces that had remained loyal to their governments were taking no chances, and the military aircraft that had fallen into the hands of the Mahdists were raiding widely.

A UN chopper flew Grimaldi from Beirut to the border with Israel. From there, an IDF vehicle took him to the nearest airfield. There, he reported in to Brognola, and a call was sent to the Navy carrier task force steaming in the Mediterranean to send a COD to come and get him.

When the C-2 Carry Onboard Delivery aircraft landed, he boarded the plane and was flown to the nuclear aircraft carrier U.S.S. *Eisenhower*. On the way, he had changed into a Navy flight suit minus the rank badges and tiger patches. All the flight suit carried for identification was a Velcro name tag reading John Smith. He would have liked one reading Jack Doe, but he'd had to take what was readily available.

Upon landing on the aircraft carrier, Grimaldi was whisked directly into the captain's quarters where a satcom link to the White House explained who he was and what he was doing. At the end of the conversation, the captain offered the pilot the run of the ship until the F/A-18 Hornet could be prepped for the mission.

The last thing that needed to be done was to select a pilot to fly into Syria with him. The F/A-18F was a two-seat aircraft, and he would need a WSO to watch his back while he delivered the package. When he explained the need, the captain said that he would take care of that immediately and invited Grimaldi to rest in his wardroom until a selection could be made.

GRIMALDI WAS ENJOYING a cup of coffee and a late lunch in the wardroom when he heard a firm knock on the door. "Enter."

The pilot who walked into the room wore the silver oak leaves of a Navy commander on the shoulders of his flight suit along with the gold wings of a Navy pilot on his chest and the colorful patches of all of the carrier's squadrons.

Grimaldi instantly recognized him as the ship's CAG, the Commander Air Group. On a Navy carrier, the CAG had a lot of say in what happened to his planes because without them, a carrier was simply the biggest floating target in the world. His unofficial nickname was "Air Boss," and he was addressed as CAG.

CAG introduced himself and got right down to business. "Since I'm CAG around here, the captain suggested that I talk to you about this mission."

"That sounds about right."

"First off, are you carrier qualified, mister?"

Grimaldi could hear the sneer in the pilot's voice. This mission was going to be difficult enough to put together without having to go through a protracted flyboy-style armpit sniffing contest.

"Commander," he replied, "as you're well aware, as a civilian I don't wear the gold wings and I'm not officially 'carrier qualified.' However, this won't be the first time that I have flown fixed-wing naval aircraft. In fact, if I was allowed to show you my classified log book, which I'm not, you'd see that I have racked up quite a few hours in naval aircraft. You would also find that I have landed a number of various aircraft on U.S. Navy carriers. The last one, by the way, was a Russian Mi-24 Hind gunship, and that was just a couple of weeks ago in the Indian Ocean."

He took half a step toward the naval aviator. "But none of that really matters because I won't be landing back here. After the package is delivered, I will be landing at an Israeli airbase where I will depart and you will deliver the F-18 back here."

He paused. "If, that is, you turn out to be the flyer I choose to take. I'll need to go over your combat record before I can determine if I want you flying with me."

The Navy pilot looked like he was going to detonate. "Just who the fuck do you think you are, mister! I don't need some asshole civilian—"

"Put a sock in it, Commander!" Grimaldi lashed out. "You're dismissed."

"Goddammit, you don't tell me what to do on my own ship!"

Grimaldi was no stranger to aerial egos, but this guy was pushing it. "Would you care to discuss this with the National Command Authority, Commander?" he asked softly. "If you would like that, I can have the man on the horn in less than sixty seconds. If he thinks that I'm good enough to fly one of *his* naval aircraft, I think the least you can do is to try to go along with the program."

CAG's face suddenly went pale as he checked himself. He was on the shortlist to captain's rank, and the last thing he needed was a presidential veto to finish his Navy career.

"I...I'm sorry, sir," he said. "This is a little unusual and I—"

"Don't call me 'sir,'" Grimaldi snapped. "And don't piss on my back and try to tell me that it's raining. You think you're a real Sierra Hotel pilot and maybe you are, but you need to disengage your ego, Commander, before you find yourself permanently grounded for excess stupidity. Understood?"

CAG stiffened to attention. "Yes."

"Now, who can you recommend to accompany me on this mission? I need someone who's pilot qualified, but who can also run the ECM suite on the way into the target."

The pilot took a deep breath and swallowed his pride. "I would like to be considered for that job."

"I'm sorry, Commander," Grimaldi said, shaking his head, "but I don't fly with people who disagree with me. I find that's a recipe for disaster. I'm going into harm's way to deliver a package over enemy territory, and I won't have time to argue about every little pissant thing I want done. All I need from you is a recommendation for a good pilot who doesn't have an attitude."

Knowing that he was lucky to walk away without official reprimand, CAG capitulated. "I can recommend Lieutenant Roger Farris. I've flown with him in some hairy situations and he keeps his head."

"Send him in, please."

"Right away."

The man who walked in five minutes later didn't look like either Tom Cruise or Val Kilmer, and that was a definite plus in Grimaldi's book. Hollywood had ruined more aviators than bad landings.

"Lieutenant Roger Farris reporting, sir." He stiffened to attention but didn't salute. "I understand that you need a backseat."

"What's your call sign, Lieutenant?" Grimaldi asked.

"Merlin," the pilot answered proudly. "Because I'm good at what I do."

Grimaldi liked the man's confidence. At least he wasn't nicknamed "Ball Buster" or some other ultramacho tag. God knew that a combat pilot needed a healthy ego, but watching *Top Gun* too many times could get you in a heap of trouble.

"What have you been told about the mission?"

Farris smiled. "Only that you're going downtown down low and you need someone to keep your six clear and that's me."

"You understand that we're going in sterile, no dog tags, no photos from home and if we run into a Golden BB, no one's going to come looking for us?"

"That's most affirm."

Grimaldi stuck out his hand. "Welcome to history, Merlin. If this thing works, we're going to make the history books. But," he cautioned, "it's going to be classified for at least a hundred years."

"That's okay," Farris said, smiling slowly. "I plan to live a long time."

"Good." Grimaldi smiled in return. "I'm counting on it."

CHAPTER TWENTY-FOUR

Stony Man Farm, Virginia

As soon as the Phoenix Force convoy left Beirut, Barbara Price moved down into the Computer Room so she could more easily keep track of their progress. Since she'd been out of action for so long, she didn't have a good feel for what was going on. Being thoroughly briefed had helped, but being a successful mission controller required more than a working knowledge of the facts. To do her job, she had to be zeroed in on the actions of the men in the field as if she were a guardian spirit hovering over them.

Aaron Kurtzman had been able to finesse one of the NRO's Keyhole spy satellites into position to cover the area Phoenix Force would be passing through. The recent classified space shuttle missions to refuel and service the Keyhole satellite network had made that task a lot easier. Every time a satellite was repositioned, it expended maneuvering fuel and the recon birds could carry only so much onboard. Before the refueling missions, several of the deep space satellites had completely run dry and were almost useless.

With Keyhole Seven on station over Syria, he now had a full array of data coming in both day and night. He had the photo and digital imaging from KH-7 to match up with the IR and radar imaging from the NASA Vega bird orbiting from deep space. A Vortex military communications satellite also allowed him to intercept any and all electromagnetic signals from the Middle East. Little could go on down there that he couldn't find out about one way or the other. The only thing he couldn't do was send help to Phoenix Force if something went wrong. As deep as they were going in enemy territory with no backup, only God could do that.

But with each new report that came in, it was more and more apparent that God had taken a vacation from the Middle East. Each daily broadcast from the Mahdi sent even more ripples through an already troubled sea. The death toll was mounting and no one seemed to care. The Mahdi had come back to his people, and it would all work out in the end so it didn't matter how many people died that day. But the increasing civil unrest was the greatest thing the Stony Man commandos had going in their favor. With the region's governments fighting for their survival, no one was likely to be looking for a handful of men crossing the desert.

At least, that was the theory. The Stony Man crew had been in the business long enough to have learned the age-old mantra, ''no plan survives the initial contact with the enemy.'' It was the military version of Murphy's Law.

But taking things one step at a time was always the best way to deal with an unknown situation.

Price looked past Kurtzman's shoulder at the images cluttering his master monitor. ''How does it look?''

''Like the man said as he passed the fiftieth floor after jumping off the Empire State Building, 'so far, so good.'''

''Aaron!''

''Actually, they're in good shape,'' he said. ''The convoy is almost to their drop-off location at the Syrian-Lebanese border. The point they'll be crossing at is clear of troops and it looks like a clean shot all the way to the DZ.''

''How's Jack doing?''

''Our resident ace pilot has got the Navy whipped into shape. He had to invoke the Man's name, however, to get it done. The Carrier Air Group Commander got bent out of shape about a civilian flying one of 'his' planes and all the usual crap, but Jack got it sorted out. When Mack sends the word, he's ready to launch.''

''I thought we'd have more trouble about getting the weapon released.''

''So did I,'' he replied. ''But apparently the Navy doesn't care if someone nukes the Middle East.''

''What have you been able to come up with on the target itself?''

''After we decided to look at that mountain, Hunt ran back through a century of archaeology reports and found two expeditions that surveyed the region. They both reported that this mountain had extensive copper mine shafts dug into it dating back some five thousand years or so. If this is where the Mahdi is hiding out, God only knows what he has done inside there. With all that earth-moving equipment we saw, he could have a small city set up inside there by now.''

He shook his head. ''Not much shows on the optical runs as far as defenses. We have, however, used MAD and radar imaging to find a couple of openings close to the surface level that might make good entry points for the package. We're still looking, though, and I'll keep them updated on everything we find.''

''Keep scanning for defenses too,'' she cautioned. ''That place's got to be defended.''

Lebanon

THE STONY MAN TEAM rode out of Beirut in the back of a Syrian army truck in a small convoy of two other trucks and a Land Rover in the lead. With all of the military traffic on the city's streets, no one looked at them too closely. At the Syrian checkpoint going out of town, the commandos sat silently, their weapons ready while the Druze drivers showed their forged passes and orders. If they were discovered, the plan was to fight their way out and return to the villa to rethink the operation.

As the Druze had guaranteed, passing through the Beirut checkpoint was little more than a formality.

From there, it was only fifty miles up the coast to Tripoli, but it took almost two hours to make the trip. The nation's major highway was crowded with everything from local donkey carts and agricultural tractors to Mercedes long-haul tractor-trailer rigs. The normally heavy traffic was now chaotic as people fled the Mahdi-inspired chaos.

After passing through Tripoli, the convoy finally halted a few miles short of the Syrian border. After pulling off the road into a covered draw, the Stony Man team got out of their truck to stretch and to transfer their equipment into the Land Rover.

Ten minutes later, the team was loaded and ready to try the crossing. "Go with God, al-Askari," the Druze driver told Bolan as he relinquished his vehicle.

"And God be with you," Bolan replied.

Using the satellite photos and the GPS, McCarter carefully navigated as Manning drove the last few miles to the border. As Kurtzman had reported, there were no Syrian army units in place, but they stayed alert in case roving patrols were out.

Aboard the Eisenhower

JACK GRIMALDI AND Lieutenant Roger Farris went out on the flight deck to oversee the final preparation for the mission they would soon fly, the loading of the ordnance. Their fighter had been spotted on the Number One Cat, and a cordon of Marines was keeping the curious away.

The F/A-18F Hornet was the latest incarnation of

a well-proved combat plane. Originally, it had been designed as a naval fighter, but the attack mission had been tagged onto it, hence the double designation. This F model had extended wings and updates to give it more range and better target effectiveness in a hostile environment. Short of a Stealth fighter, it was the best aircraft for this particular mission.

This particular Hornet had had all of her insignia painted out including her tail number. It was no news that the U.S. Navy was the sole user of the F model Hornet, but the fiction had to be maintained that this was an unknown aircraft. If he screwed up and made a big hole in the ground, the pieces would be easily identified as being from a U.S.-made aircraft, but without the markings, it could be passed off as a pirate fighter.

The package was wheeled out on an ordnance dolly by a dozen of the carrier's Marines and four sailors with black stripes on their red jerseys. The red jersey identified an ordnance man and the black stripe signified a nuclear weapons handler. This particular package was an Mk 54 Mod 5 tactical nuclear weapon designed to neutralize tactical targets such as air bases or troop concentrations.

A lieutenant commander with a worried look on his face walked beside the warhead. He was the carrier's nuclear weapons deployment officer, and the worried look went with the job. He had been through this drill countless times before, but this was the first time that he was arming a nuclear weapon that he wasn't going to get back. It made his job a little more real.

Under his expert supervision, the bomb was hoisted and then bolted to the starboard underwing pylon. The parachute packs that were to let the bomb float to the ground were double-checked and the safety wires pulled out.

"It's been dialed to one point five," he reported to Grimaldi. "And I disabled the deuterium injectors to prevent an accidental higher yield."

"That's what I need," Grimaldi replied.

"What I can't guarantee, though," the lieutenant commander said, frowning, "are the additional retard packs. I've never rigged one with three parachutes before."

"If it doesn't work," Grimaldi said, "the worst it'll do is make a hole in the ground, right?"

"It won't go into a detonation sequence, if that's what you mean, no. But it might be recoverable at some later date and the nuclear material salvaged."

"If that happens, my people will insure that there's nothing left that anyone can use before they leave the drop zone."

The nuclear weapons deployment officer would have loved to ask exactly what was going on, but he knew better. The less he knew, the better it was for him and his people. He did, however, pat the bomb before clearing the deck for the launch.

With the nuclear package loaded, Grimaldi and Farris climbed into their cockpits to wait for the call from Phoenix Force.

Beirut, Lebanon

IT DIDN'T TAKE LONG for J. R. Rust to come to the realization that Striker had done him no favors by asking him to stay in Beirut with Katzenelenbogen and Encizo to help them hold down the fort. In fact, it was beginning to look as if this were going to be as much of a suicide mission as the attack on Mount Alamut.

Until now, Beirut had been a sea of calm in a Middle East that was going up in flames. While just as passionate about their religious beliefs as any other Middle Easterner, the average Beiruti simply wanted to go about his business in peace. Fifteen years of bitter religious civil war had driven home to them that how another man talked to God wasn't worth killing him over. But the madness inspired by the appearance of the Mahdi was too powerful to be ignored. The earlier millennium prophecies hadn't been able to greatly disrupt the battle-weary city, but the appearance of a savior was another matter entirely.

Against this new unrest, even the Syrian army was powerless to keep order. Almost within hours of the first Mahdi-inspired uprising, Beirut had gone back to the bad old days. The weapons came out of storage and, once more, the armed factions ruled the streets. The barricades were going back up, and most of the population was staying indoors.

Under the cover of religious mania taken to the streets, the Assassins struck.

This time, it was Rust who was in the tower standing guard with Manning's Springfield sniper's rifle. Like any kid from a North Texas ranch, Rust had been raised with a rifle in his hand. The Spring-field SAR-8 HB was a far cry from his old deer rifle, but a rifleman was always comfortable with any long gun.

The first shot came from a fourth-story apartment window directly across the street from their villa. The range wasn't that far, but the gunman hadn't compensated for the fall of the projectile on a down-hill shot. The AK round slammed into a sandbag an inch below the parapet James and Manning had put up around the tower.

Instinctively, Rust took cover behind the sand-bags but left the rifle where it was. Lying sideways to the rifle was awkward, but it kept him covered with only the weapon and his head exposed. Even though it was broad daylight, the front of the apart-ment was in shadow, so Rust switched the scope to IR to try to pick up hot muzzle gases.

When he had it, he flicked the scope back and saw movement behind the curtain. He hated to make a mistake and whack some nosy old woman by mis-take, so he held the sight picture until he saw the muzzle of an AK appear.

He triggered two shots on rapid fire, and the AK muzzle disappeared.

He started to relax, but as if he were back in the mesquite woods of north Texas, he felt eyes on him. He rolled over, bringing the rifle to bear on the apartment facing the other side of the tower. A sun-lit figure on the roof was raising an RPG launcher to his shoulder.

Rust instantly went into rapid fire, running the

rounds up the side of the building as he brought his scope to bear. The third round took the rocket gunner right as he was pulling the trigger.

The 85 mm RPG round went high, missing the tower and clearing the wall on the far side of the compound before impacting in the middle of the street. The detonation sent red-hot shrapnel flying into the cars and storefronts along the street.

The sounds of firing had brought Rafael Encizo racing up the steps of the tower. Throwing open the trapdoor, he rolled onto the flat roof and took cover against the parapet. "Where are they?" he asked.

"There was one in a window to the south and when I was taking care of him, another asshole on the roof to the north tried to put an RPG up my ass. I think Katz was right. They're back."

"Damn!" Encizo spit. With only three gunners, holding the villa against any kind of serious attack wasn't going to work. All it would take was for the Assassins to keep them busy from the rooftops while another group came over the wall. Even a first-year military cadet could figure that one out.

"Can you hang on here while I talk to Katz? I'm going to see if he can get us some help."

All of a sudden, dragging a nuke around in the desert didn't seem quite so dangerous. At least you'd be able to see the bastards coming. Rust started sweeping the rooftops with the sniper scope. "I'll try."

CHAPTER TWENTY-FIVE

In the Syrian Desert

When the Stony Man team reached the planned drop zone, a quick sweep of the area showed that they had the desert to themselves. Using the GPS to locate the exact center of the DZ, they parked the Land Rover and moved out into security positions to insure that they remained alone in their little patch of Syrian sand. From here on out, if the mission was to succeed, they couldn't afford a chance encounter of any kind. Burdened with the nuclear device, they wouldn't be able to cut and run, and fighting could be disastrous.

When they were ready to receive the package, David McCarter sent the launch message to the carrier and received confirmation.

"Grimaldi's launching now," he announced over the com link. "ETA a little less than an hour."

Aboard the Eisenhower

WHEN THE LAUNCH CALL was relayed to the *Eisenhower,* Grimaldi took the message. "We have a go," he called back to Farris.

"Let's do it."

The plane handlers in their yellow jerseys quickly spotted the F/A-18F Hornet on the cat track. Grimaldi ignited the turbines and carefully went over the prelaunch checklist. He didn't have a lot of hours in the Hornet, and had never flown the new F Model, so this was no time to get sloppy.

When he was ready, he gave a thumbs-up to the sailor in the brown jersey, the plane captain. The sailor held his right arm high in the air and twirled his finger to signal the pilot to run up his rpm. Advancing the throttles to their stops, the pilot engaged the afterburner, sending flames shooting out of the fighter's twin exhausts. When the tachs showed 110 percent from both turbines, he pushed his head back against the rest and showed a thumbs-up again. The plane captain swept his arm down and the steam cat fired.

Even though he knew what was coming, the cat shot was a bit of a shock. In less than the length of a football field, the F/A-18 Hornet went from a standstill to over 150 miles an hour at six Gs.

Since the fighter was carrying only the one special store, it accelerated quickly once the cat bridle fell away from the landing gear. Rather than climbing in a normal takeoff pattern and gaining altitude, though, Grimaldi kept the Hornet close to the water. The entire run in to the release point would be made on the deck to avoid showing up on anyone's radar, friendly or enemy.

As Farris settled in the backseat for the long flight, he activated his ECM suite and started looking to see who or what was sharing the skies over the Mediterranean with them. On a mission like this, it was never too soon to start looking for trouble.

Stony Man Farm, Virginia

"GRIMALDI'S ON THE WAY," Aaron Kurtzman announced to the Stony Man crew. "A clean launch."

"What's his ETA?" Brognola asked.

"I make it a little over fifty minutes."

"Are we set up to track him in flight?"

"Not till he gets into Syria," Kurtzman stated. "Plausible deniability and all that crap. It would have been easy to have the carrier launch an E-2 Hawkeye mini-AWAC to track him all the way, but that would have meant more people who would know where he's going. Only his backseat knows now, and he only has it as the coordinates for the DZ."

Brognola knew that was the best decision. But considering the serious repercussions that would come from a mistake this time, he would have liked to have had a real-time view of what was going on.

"Once he's crossed into Syria," Kurtzman continued, "we'll have him covered."

Half a loaf was better then none, so Brognola sat to wait like everyone else.

Above Syria

"FEET DRY," Farris announced as the Hornet reached the Syrian coastline.

"Roger," Grimaldi replied.

"We've got an MiG headed our way," Farris called out from the rear cockpit. "It looks like a Fulcrum."

The MiG-29 Fulcrum was one of the best dog-fighters in the world and was equipped with a look down-shoot down fire control system. If he spotted them before they could make the drop, they would have no choice but to turn and run. Dogfighting with the package in place wasn't on.

"He's painting us," Farris said, telling Grimaldi that he had picked up the MiG's targeting radar.

"Confuse him," Grimaldi snapped back as he nosed the Hornet closer to the ground. As long as the MiG didn't have a lock, Farris's ECM suite wiz-ardry and a little belly-in-the-dirt, terrain-following navigation should keep them inconspicuous.

It was too bad that the F/A-18 was painted Navy air superiority gray. A coat of Air Force desert sand paint right now would go a long way toward hiding them in the sand. At six hundred and fifty knots an hour, though, they didn't have too much farther to go. The desert and hills on either side were going past in a classic case of tunnel-vision blur. Grimaldi could only concentrate on his immediate front and the information ticking off on the HUD screen in front of him. Two more minutes and he would be at the zoom point for the over-the-shoulder bomb toss.

"We lost the MiG," Farris reported, "and we're coming up on the IP in six zero,"

"Roger. IP in six zero."

THE INSTANT THE PACKAGE left the pylon, Grimaldi racked the fighter in a tight Immelmann turn. Although that maneuver had been invented by a German ace back in World War I, it was still the fastest way to turn an airplane and get it headed in the opposite direction.

"The chutes are deployed," Farris called as he looked back over his shoulder. "I have three good canopies."

"Now let's see if we can get the hell out of here before the dickhead in that Fulcrum up there finds us again."

As soon as Grimaldi was leveled out and headed back the other way, he put his Hornet's belly in the dirt again. More than anything in the world, he wanted to go up there and tear apart that MiG pilot. He hated letting anyone get away with intimidating him, particularly when he was flying something like a Hornet. Plus, he hadn't yet had a chance to put the new version through its paces. But that wasn't called for today.

"I think the MiG is back." Farris's voice on the intercom was calm.

"Oh, shit!"

Stony Man Farm, Virginia

"THEY HAVE THE PACKAGE," Aaron Kurtzman announced when McCarter radioed touchdown.

Hal Brognola automatically thumbed an antacid tab off the roll in his pocket and put it in his mouth. How calmly it was announced that a nuclear weapon was now on its way to be detonated in an undeclared act of war. And calling it a "package" as if it were a two-pound box of chocolates instead of 1.5 kilotons of nuclear destruction was a fine fiction. The target was worthy of destruction, but it was sad that the millennium was going to be rung in a little early with a mushroom-shaped cloud.

He knew, though, that supposedly there wouldn't be the signature cloud of a nuclear detonation when this device was triggered. Since it would be so far underground, it wouldn't be able to form. That was one of the only reasons that the President had gone along with this idea. Anyone with half a brain would know what had happened to Mount Alamut. But without the nuclear cloud advertising it, they could pretend that it hadn't happened.

None of the surviving national governments in the region really wanted to fan the rage against the United States at this point in time. If this took the Mahdi out of the picture, they would desperately need all the international aid and support they could get just to survive. Rebuilding would take even more help from the West. And since the West meant the United States, this nuke might actually ring in a new era of peace in the Middle East.

If, that was, the team got through and was able to put it in place.

"How about Grimaldi?" Brognola asked. "Is he clear of Syrian airspace yet?"

"Not yet," Hunt Wethers replied. For this stage of the operation, he was monitoring the radar and communications input while Kurtzman kept track of the imaging input at the DZ.

"What's his ETA to feet wet?"

"Another fifteen minutes or so. Even flat on the deck, he has to be careful about not being picked up by the local air defense radars, even those of our allies. The Syrians aren't a problem, but there's only one route in and out that keeps him out of sight of both the Israeli and Turkish networks."

As much as Brognola wanted Grimaldi to get out of there as soon as aeronautically possible, he knew that it wasn't that simple. For the U.S. to be able to successfully say "What, me?" when asked about a nuclear weapon detonation in the region, the F/A-18 had to remain unseen by everyone, friend and foe.

"We have a problem," Wethers announced. "I have another aircraft in the area and Jack's altering his flight path to intercept it. I think he's being forced into a dogfight."

"Shit!"

Above Syria

"HE'S PAINTING US again," Farris said from the backseat of the Hornet. "Request permission to go weapons hot."

"Do it," Grimaldi ordered. "And arm the decoy flares."

"Bandit has lock-on and Fox One." Farris calmly announced that the marauding MiG had fired a missile at them.

Trying to keep this mission low profile was one thing, but Grimaldi wasn't about to let someone shoot him down without a fight. Not now, not ever.

"Go tracking hot and stand by to launch flares," he ordered as he slammed the fighter into an evasive maneuver to dodge the missile. "I'm on the bastard."

"Go get 'em!" Farris shouted.

According to the threat readout, the MiG-29 had fired an AA-7 Apex heat-seeking missile at them, and that was that pilot's second mistake. His first had been engaging them at all. Grimaldi wasn't about to give the guy a chance to make a third one.

Grimaldi knew that having a heat-seeking Apex trying to find its way up his tailpipe would make this a little easier. The Apex wasn't to be scoffed at, but it certainly wasn't the best air-to-air missile that had ever come out of Mother Russia. If it had been a beam rider, he might be in major trouble. As it was, he had a patented antiIR missile routine he had perfected.

"Launch decoys!" he ordered as he snapped the Hornet into a spiraling climb toward the sun.

"You've done this before, haven't you?" Farris asked, panting under the G force of the turn as he triggered the decoy flares in pairs.

Grimaldi grinned behind his visor. "You might say that."

When Grimaldi came out of his spiraling climb, the Apex had locked on to one of the flares and detonated harmlessly behind them. Best of all, when he rolled out, the Hornet was in a firing position to launch a missile of its own.

Flicking his selector switch, Grimaldi chose a radar-guided Sparrow missile for his first shot. The Sparrow had an active radar guidance system and once it was locked, nothing could save the target.

When Grimaldi's HUD showed that his fire control had a lock-on, he triggered the missile. "Fox One, Fox One."

The missile shot off the wingtip launch rail and streaked after the MiG, trailing dirty white smoke.

The MiG pilot had a lock-on threat warning blaring in his ears as he tried to break the Sparrow's radar beam, but to no avail. The tighter he turned to try to evade it, the closer it came. The missile hit the MiG right behind the wing and tore the fuselage in two. The detonation of the jet fuel engulfed the Fulcrum in a boiling fireball.

As the smaller pieces of the MiG fluttered to earth following the bigger parts, Grimaldi put the Hornet back down on the deck. He still had a hundred miles of Syrian desert to get past before he'd be safe. But even then, he had to keep low until he was well out to sea. Then he would pop up so he could be identified on Israeli radar and could land at one of their air bases without being blasted out of the sky as an intruder. They had good reason to be a little touchy about people who tried to fly jets into their territory.

WHEN GRIMALDI ARRIVED at the IAF base, he was directed to taxi the Hornet to a covered revetment.

Once inside, he killed the fuel feed to the turbine and opened the canopy.

"Just stay cool for a moment," he told Farris when he saw the armed Air Police surround the fighter. "I need to mellow these guys out before we get too active."

He stepped down from the plane first and stood until an officer came to talk to him. As soon as the formalities had been seen to, he motioned for Farris to climb out and stretch his legs while the F/A-18 was being refueled.

"Make sure that you tell your CAG to credit you with half a kill for that Syrian MiG," Grimaldi told the Navy flyer. "The gun's camera tape will confirm it."

"But I didn't do anything except go along for the ride," Farris protested. "That was your kill fair and square."

"Where I come from, Merlin, the GIB shares anything I have except my women and my last beer. You're one of the better guys-in-back I've ever flown with. You didn't choke, so we didn't die, and half the kill is yours."

"I really appreciate that." Farris grinned as he extended his hand. "Not too many hot rocks appreciate what goes on behind them in a dogfight. I still don't know who in the hell you are, mister, but if you ever need another GIB, let me know."

Grimaldi shook his hand. "Count on it, Merlin."

After waiting to make sure that the Hornet got off for its trip back to the carrier, Grimaldi arranged for an immediate ride back to the Lebanese border. Katz was a bit shorthanded, and he wanted to help hold down the fort.

upon a host of the system was called Manning found that it had been prepared to their specifications.

"The bomb on its pin," she announced.

"Just give us the LG-EX yields."

"That's exactly," Jonas said. "Now when a bomb on its LG-EX arm was formed it reducing its to minimums."

"Thomas," Hawk said ... "I've never been raised into legitimate families, safer, and I ended me out of our service income.

"It usually called some ..." the kid was ...

CHAPTER TWENTY-SIX

In the Syrian Desert

As soon as Grimaldi's aerial delivery package touched down on the sand, the Stony Man team moved in to recover it. After cutting away the parachutes, they saw that the bomb's casing appeared to have survived the landing intact. Beyond scraped paint and a small dent in the nose cone, it showed no damage. Since the weapon had been designed to withstand a carrier catapult launch as well as high-G maneuvering, Gary Manning expected the rest of it to be fully functional as well. He'd find out in a few minutes.

Most of the bomb's length was sheet-metal streamline and tail fins. Eight bolts were all that held on the tail section, and Manning made short work of them. Next off was the ballistic nose cone covering the instrumentation and fusing needed to detonate the warhead when it was deployed from the air. For their use, that had all been replaced with a simple battery-powered electronic firing system.

Examining the built-in readouts for the Pit, as the

nuclear heart of the weapon was called, Manning found that it had been prepared to their specifications. "It's been set up properly," he announced. "It'll give us the 1.5 KT yield."

"That's a relief," James said. "Now when it goes off, it'll only blow us up instead of reducing us to subatomic particles."

"Bummer," Hawkins said. "I've never been turned into subatomic particles before and I wanted to put it on my service record."

"It's usually called being dead," Manning replied.

"Forget it, then."

"Let's rig the slings and get it into the truck," McCarter said. "I want to get out of here in case anyone noticed Flying Jack's aerobatic show."

Stripped of its aerodynamic shell and excess instrumentation package, the device weighed 184 pounds. With four men on the carrying straps, they'd each be toting a little over forty-five pounds when they made the final approach to Mount Alamut on foot. It was a load, but it was doable.

As soon as the nuke was tied down in the back, the Stony Man warriors boarded the heavily laden Land Rover and headed to the southeast. The sun would be going down soon and they wanted to put as much distance as they could behind them before they stopped for the night.

Israel

JACK GRIMALDI THREW the IAF chopper pilot a snappy salute as he stepped off the bird at the UN checkpoint on the heavily fortified Israeli border with Lebanon. A little high-level skid greasing had been going on again, because he was processed right through and found that a UN vehicle with a driver and shotgun rider was waiting to take him to Beirut.

The UN troops were Italian Peacekeepers, and they had little to say on the drive back. They also knew better then to ask too many questions. Grimaldi had the driver drop him off a block short of his destination. Pulling his Beretta, he chambered a round, flicked it on safety and put it back in his shoulder holster. This was the kind of a town where if you weren't ready to rock and roll when the mood struck, you might not get a second chance.

Where before the neighborhood around their villa had been quiet, it was almost completely deserted now. From what little he had been able to learn from the two Peacekeepers, most of the Madhist unrest was taking place in the outer fringes of the city instead of at the core. Nonetheless, it looked as if the local residents weren't taking any chances.

"About time you dragged your sorry ass back here, Jack," Encizo greeted him at the villa gate.

"I thought you guys could use at least one good man around here about now."

"Grab this," Encizo said, handing him the extra MP-5 and a magazine pouch he was carrying, "and pretend that you remember how to use it."

"That serious, huh?"

"They've figured out that there's only the three of us left here and they're curious."

"Can't Katz get some of his Druze buddies to give us a hand?"

"He's trying, but with the Mahdi unrest, they're having problems of their own right now. They have women and kids to protect, so I think it's going to be just us until Striker gets back."

"How are they doing?"

"They got your delivery and they're on their way."

Katzenelenbogen greeted Grimaldi inside the villa. "We're going to need you on duty tonight," he said. "So get something to eat and grab a couple of hours' rest."

"What happened to 'nice to see you'? Or, 'did you have a nice flight'?"

Katz looked weary. "You're here, so you obviously had a good flight. The bomb was picked up and Striker and the guys are on the way. We, though, are still in deep shit. So get some rest so I can send you up to the tower to relieve Rust."

"Right, boss."

INSMIR VEDIK HADN'T BEEN idle while he had been incarcerated in his makeshift cell that had once been the villa's storage room off the kitchen. His captors had severely underestimated him if they thought that he was a helpless man. He was a medical doctor, true, but he was also a Bosnian who came from a long line of fighters, and his people weren't soft.

His captors had stripped the room bare before locking him in it, but they hadn't taken out the shelves that lined the walls. It had taken him some time to do it, but he had silently pried up one of the boards and extracted the big nails that had held them together. The villa had been built before World War II, and the nails were hand-forged iron, not machine made. They weren't as hard as steel, but the forging had made them tougher than modern nails.

Taking off his shirt, he had wrapped it around the end of one of the nails to pad the head so it wouldn't tear his skin. Using his improvised tool, he started picking at the plaster around the doorframe lock. It was slow work and when he reached the limestone blocks that made up the core of the wall, the nail started abrading as well. When it got too short to be of any use, he wrapped another one and continued digging.

When the back of the lock was exposed, he used his last nail to try to pick it. As he had expected, it was easy to trip the antiquated mechanism. He opened the door a crack to make sure that he had in fact unlocked it, then closed it and locked it again. There was no point in his trying to make his escape until night fell.

Gathering the plaster and masonry dust into a pile on the floor, he urinated on it to make a thick paste. Scooping it, he spread it over the area he had chipped away so that when his evening meal was brought to him, his captors wouldn't notice what he had done. Later, he could easily remove it, trip the old lock and escape.

His work camouflaged, the Bosnian laid on the narrow cot in his cell and tried to sleep. He would be busy in a few hours and wanted to be rested.

SINCE THERE WAS NO WINDOW in his cell, Vedik couldn't tell when night fell. His only clue was the subtle change in the faint background sounds he could hear though the thick walls. When his dinner came, an American Army meal packet called an MRE and a plastic canteen full of water, he saw that it was dusk. After eating what he could, he laid back on his cot to wait.

As he waited, he started making plans for what he would do once he had gained his freedom. The mutated anthrax had worked, but it hadn't been potent enough. He needed to find another pathogen, something he could mutate into an even more effective killer. And this time, he wouldn't work for a madman like Malik al-Ismaili. He would find a more politically savvy leader like Moamar Khaddafi.

AS SOON AS IT TURNED completely dark, Jack Grimaldi and J. R. Rust went up onto the tower. With the renewed fighting in the city, the power was being cut off at night to limit the damage from short circuits in case gunfire cut the lines.

"Damn," Rust said as he lowered his night-vision goggles over his eyes. "It's darker than the inside of a buffalo out there."

Grimaldi smiled as he followed suit. "That's good for us and bad for them."

"Unless they got their hands on some of those cheap Russian night optics."

The Russians were wholesaling their night-vision

devices and, while they weren't quite as good as the top-of-the-line U.S. goggles, they worked.

"They didn't have any the last time they came," Grimaldi pointed out.

"Let's hope they don't wise up."

Rust was on the Springfield sniper rifle again and was watching the apartment buildings in the south sector. Grimaldi had his MP-5 and was keeping an eye on the back of the compound. It would be a long night, and with Katz and Encizo securing the grounds, no one would be getting any sleep.

THE LEADER of the Assassins knew only too well of the foreigner's ability to see in the dark. He had been in one of the backup units during the first attack and had seen how effective the night optics had been. He had also seen how they had used radios to coordinate the defense and defeat his brothers.

He had been able to secure one set of Russian-made night-vision goggles, and each man had a small commercial radio so they could talk to one another. After testing the radios, he had decided that their voices were too loud to speak without giving away their positions, so he came up with a click code to communicate once they were inside the walls.

They were ready now and in position to scale the walls. It was time to send the infidels to hell.

THERE WAS a quarter moon, but haze and smoke from fires in the city made it as dark as a moonless night. Rafael Encizo crouched under one of the decorative shrubs and scanned the section of the perimeter wall in front of him with his night goggles. It was only a little after ten, and he was already tired. It had been days since any of them had had enough sleep, but he was an old soldier and knew all the tricks of night combat.

He had been in position for about twenty minutes and was standing to go to a new observation point when he thought he heard the faint carrier-wave hiss of an FM radio. It sounded like an old PRC-10 with the squelch turned up all the way. Since the Phoenix Force commandos were all using their com links, it had to be an intruder. Just then a neighborhood dog barked, and he lost the faint sound.

Dropping back into cover, he looked in the direction of the sound he had heard. A faint flash of green disappearing into the hedge told him that they had visitors. "They're here," he whispered into his com link. "On the south side."

"Roger," Rust's voice answered him.

Encizo backed away from his cover, keeping low so he could work his way around to the other end of the hedge. The minute he broke cover, a shot rang out from the west wall.

"Incoming," he called over the radio. "West wall."

AT THE SOUND of the first shot, Vedik came off his cot and grabbed his last nail. It took but a second to pry away the makeshift patch and get at the lock. Another second had the lock open. Opening the door a crack, he heard one of the commandos talking over a radio in the other end of the villa, then the sound of footsteps running out.

Opening the door farther, he peered around the corner into the darkened house. Seeing no one, he held the long nail as a dagger and slipped into the hall. His eyes were well adjusted to the dark, and he walked as silently as a cat. With the fighting going on outside, he expected the villa to be empty. For him to make his escape, he needed a better weapon than a sixty-year-old, hand-forged nail.

In the living room, he saw a stack of ammunition boxes and other military equipment. He looked for a weapon but couldn't find one. Then his eyes fell on an open box of hand grenades. They weren't what he wanted, but they were better than nothing. Snatching up two of them, he hurried back down the hall to the rear door.

OUTSIDE, A DEADLY GAME of cat and mouse was in progress.

At Encizo's call, Rust swung the Springfield to cover the west and caught what looked like the head and shoulders of a man aiming a rifle from the top of the wall. A quick shot made the silhouette disappear, and he started to scan the other walls.

"You stay here," Grimaldi told him. "I'm going down to help Katz and Rafe."

"Let them know you're coming."

Encizo and Katz were at opposite ends of the compound working alone. Katz had his favorite silenced Uzi and a chest-pack magazine carrier full of reloads. Since there were so few of them to cover the grounds, he had taken a well-protected position in the villa's front portico and was ready to do a one-man Alamo.

A burst of AK fire from his left rear sent bullets slashing into the stonework he stood behind. Rather than turn to fire back, he kept watching his chosen sector. As he had thought, they had counted on him to take the bait and another one was running toward him. Lining up his Uzi, Katz put a long burst into the Assassin.

"One down," he called out.

Encizo had chalked up one down and two more probable for the cost of a graze along his hip and a hole in his jacket. He was changing magazines in his MP-5 when he heard a noise from his right rear. Slamming his bolt forward to chamber a round, he rolled toward the sound and came up firing.

"One down," he called when the Assassin crumpled to the ground.

Katz was exchanging bursts with an Assassin hiding behind one of the big stone urns in the garden when he heard Grimaldi's voice over the com link. "I'm coming up on your right flank, Katz."

"Get that bastard in the garden for me."

"Roger."

A few moments later, two quick bursts sounded, followed by a scream.

"Splash one," Grimaldi called out.

THE ASSASSIN LEADER held back, watching the fire-fight through his night-vision goggles. Once again, the foreign devils were fighting like night demons.

Most of his men were down, and they had made no kills that he had seen. It was time that he joined the battle himself.

Pulling out from his cover, he scanned the area in front of him and saw a figure making his way toward the small outbuilding next to the west wall. Stepping out, he took aim and fired.

Vedik felt the AK round slam into his left leg, knocking it out from under him. As he fell, he pulled the pin on the grenade and pulled his arm back to throw it. A second round hit him in the right shoulder. The armed grenade fell from his nerveless hands and landed a few feet in front of him.

His scream echoed through the compound.

The grenade detonated with a flash, and Vedik was riddled with dozens of chunks of razor-sharp wire frag. He died from the sliver of frag that went through his left eye and sliced into his brain.

The flash of the grenade blinded the Assassin and lit him. Rust caught his outline vividly in his scope and pumped two rounds into him. "One down," he called out.

For the next few minutes, everyone held their places and waited. "No one's moving," Rust called out from the tower.

"Keep tight," Katz said. "We can wait all night if we have to."

CHAPTER TWENTY-SEVEN

Stony Man Farm, Virginia

Now that the Stony Man team had its package and was on its way to Mount Alamut, Barbara Price had a chance to disengage for a moment and see how her other mission was going. She'd been so focused in on the Syrian operation that she'd scarcely paid any attention to what Able Team had been doing in Miami. As far as she was concerned, Carl Lyons and his teammates were big boys, and they shouldn't have any trouble taking care of Dingo Jones and his cyberdreams of conquering the world. At least this Jones wasn't threatening death and destruction to half of the world.

There was also the matter of timing with the Jones affair. From what Sarah Carter had told them, her old boyfriend wasn't planning to do his cyber dirty work until the millennium arrived. That factor alone put him on the back burner. The dangers posed by the Madhist uprising and the threat of another anthrax attack was a reality now, and first things always had to be dealt with first.

This was the problem that always arose when both the action teams were in the field at the same time. For the work the Stony Man crew was required to do, it was a minimalist group to say the least. Any other government agency doing the job would have had a cast of hundreds. Entire shifts of people would be available who could work around the clock and still stay fresh. But Stony Man wasn't the CIA. One of the main reasons the Farm had been so successful at staying hidden for so long was that it was so small.

It was times like this, though, that she wished that they had just a couple more people to fill in and give the mission crew more breaks. It was late afternoon and the crew was trying to get what rest they could before the sun came up over Syria. When the team moved out again, everyone would have to be on his toes.

Kurtzman was catnapping at his work station while Hunt Wethers was actually laying down to sleep in the back room. Price was starting to really feel the residual weakness of her near brush with death herself. Usually, she could go for several days by taking Kurtzman-style catnaps of half an hour or so on the cot in the back room. Right now, though, she was completely wiped out, but she didn't dare lay down. She was afraid that if she did, it would be at least a day before she would wake up.

At the far side of the room, Akira Tokaido was manning the Miami Desk. Since the Coast Guard had recovered Blancanales from the Caribbean, however, he'd had little to report.

"Barbara, I have an anomaly here," he called out. "The Bank of Rangoon just went off the Net."

"What do you mean?"

"I mean they're completely gone, evaporated," he replied. "Aaron put together a program to notify us of any major change in the international banking system, and it just tripped off. The Rangoon bank just disappeared from all the financial and market feeds. It's like someone turned off their lights and went home."

"Hit the CNN raw feed and see if there's another coup in progress."

"No one is sending feed on any unrest in Myanmar. In fact, all they're covering in the region is an annual Burmese folk festival."

If this wasn't a coup, it could be that the antiquated infrastructure that burdened Myanmar had blown another fuse. But with power shortages being so common in the cities, most major buildings had their own backup power generators. If that was all it was, the bank should be back on-line in a few minutes.

"Keep an eye on it," she said, "and let me know if they're not back up in fifteen minutes."

"Will do."

Walking across the room, she watched the imagery coming in from the Keyhole satellite keeping watch over the Syrian desert. The sun would be coming up there before long, and the team would move out again.

Miami, Florida

NOW THAT Dingo Jones's computer-killer chip had been battle-tested and he could put his plan into operation at a moment's notice, he was free to turn his attention to other matters. The one thing he intended to look into first was the raid on his warehouse. The barrios of Miami were the same as the outback towns of Australia had been—a man could only call his own that which he could protect. The loss of the weapons was bad enough, but sitting by while someone ripped him off would only invite more of the same.

The first step he took to keep that from happening was to order the security chief to double the guards at all his other sites. "And," he told the chief, "they are to fire on any intruders. Further, no one is to be allowed into any of my sites without my personal signature on a facility pass. And even then, they will be escorted by armed guards at all times even when they take a piss. Any questions?"

"No sir," the security chief replied. To have given his boss any other answer would have put him in the unemployment line. "I'll make these changes immediately."

"Get back to me when you have."

Next Jones called Gunner Caldwell and Roy Bogs into his office. "I want you two to hit Little Havana and find who ripped me off. With that many guns out there, they're going to have to do something with them. Pose as buyers and tell them that you only want U.S.-made pieces, not any of that Chinese or Russian crap."

"We're going to need some flash money to make them believe us," Caldwell said.

Jones unlocked a drawer in his desk, opened it and pulled out a double handful of bank-wrapped packs of hundred-dollar bills. "That's ten thousand."

"That should be enough to spark somebody's interest," Gunner said.

"Interest the right someone and tell them that you want to buy in quantity. I want those weapons back. And when they're back, make an example of the bastards so no one else gets any ideas about ripping me off."

"We know the drill."

WITH HIS TWO ABLE ASSOCIATES put to work, Jones was left with one nagging loose end that needed to be tied up. As hard as he had tried, he hadn't been able to get Rosario Perez out of his mind. Even though the bastard was feeding the sharks in the Gulf Stream right now, he couldn't make the image of him and Anne together go away. Worse than that, he also couldn't shake the feeling that the bastard had had something to do with everything that had gone wrong since he had brought Anne back to Miami.

Part of the reason for his uneasiness was that he hadn't been able to find a background on Perez. From everything he had learned, the man barely existed. He had a driver's license, an IRS file, a few credit cards and that sort of thing, but none of it went back more than a few years. His current mailing address was a PO box in Dallas, Texas, but his driver's license had been issued three years before in California. Perez had the history of a man who was trying to keep out of sight. And if he was a hustler of some kind, it would fit. He hadn't been able to find him in the National Criminal Register, so if he was on the wrong side of the law, he had never been caught. The other thing his brief résumé could indicate, though, was the invented cover of some kind of federal undercover agent.

When those two Feds had visited him a couple of days ago, he had taken their assertion that Perez was a protected witness at face value. And the computer records of his life would fit that. But what if he wasn't a protected witness, but a Fed himself? That would also fit the evidence. What if it wasn't true that he had picked up Anne as they both had claimed? What if she had gone to the Feds and put the finger on him and Perez had come to investigate what she had told them?

Jones knew that he tended toward paranoia, but it had never greatly concerned him. He had been persecuted enough on his way to the top that it had come in handy at times. Beyond Roy Bogs and Gunner Caldwell, he trusted no one and he had been a fool to have ever talked to Anne about his plans for the killer chip.

When he'd asked her about the second copy of the chip she had taken with her, she had claimed to have lost it while she was in California. But now that he'd had time to think about it, he didn't believe her. She had known its unique value and he had never known her to throw away anything of value.

Getting out of his chair, he headed for his bedroom suite to ask her a few more questions. Part of being a good engineer was being persistent when you ran into a problem that looked unsolvable, and he was a good engineer.

CARL LYONS PICKED UP the phone in the hotel room on the first ring. "Yeah?"

"This is Gutierrez. You might want to know that Jones's two gunmen have been in Little Havana asking if anyone knows about any guns for sale. And they're asking about the kinds of guns we lifted from the warehouse."

"Make sure that no one says a word," Lyons warned.

"That might not be easy," the Cuban said honestly. "They're offering big money for information."

"We'll match it," Lyons replied. "And we'll meet you at your club as soon as we can get there."

"Hurry, amigo," Gutierrez said. "Money talks big in this neighborhood."

"YOU DON'T NEED TO TRY to protect your lover anymore," Dingo Jones said with a sneer as the woman he knew as Anne cowered at the foot of the bed. "So you might as well tell me who he worked for."

Carter didn't even try to hold back her tears, but she wouldn't let him hear her sob with pain. "I don't know how many times I've told you, Dingo.

I don't know anything about him or his past. He was just a guy I met. That's all there is to it."

"You still think he's coming back to get you, don't you?" He trailed the thin leather lash through the blood oozing from her breasts and rib cage. He drew back the lash for another strike. "Don't you!"

When she turned her head aside to protect her face, he lowered the whip and took her jaw in his hand and turned her head toward him. "Well, he's not coming back to get you, not now, not ever. Do you remember that bump you asked me about when we were out in the *Digger*?"

Her eyes flicked over to his face and she saw triumph.

"Your lover, Mr. Perez, followed us out of Miami, but I shook him off during the night. The next morning, I came up behind him while he had his head up his ass and I cut him in two at better than forty knots."

"No!" she screamed.

"He's dead!" he shouted as he slashed the whip across her as-yet-unmarked belly.

Her scream echoed off the walls and sent him into a frenzy. "You bitch! You bloody bitch!"

As she felt herself slip into welcoming darkness, Sarah Carter vowed that she would someday find a way to be free.

WHEN ABLE TEAM STEPPED OUT of its van in front of Gutierrez's social club, they were dressed for the occasion in their night combat suits and full kit. If this was going to be the showdown they had been looking forward to, they didn't want to be without the proper tools of their trade. Jones and his thugs had had things their own way so far, but that was about to change.

"*Madre!*" Gutierrez hissed softly when he recognized his visitors.

Jumping to his feet, he ran to the door and waved them inside. "Come in, come in quickly."

"My friends," he said, shaking his head. "You cannot go around here dressed like that. The cops will shoot first and ask who you are afterward."

"Where are Jones's boys?" Lyons got straight to the point.

"Let me try to find them for you." Gutierrez reached for the cellular phone in his shirt pocket.

"He's asking around." Blancanales translated the rapid-fire Spanish Gutierrez was speaking as he made one call after the other. "It sounds like they just left another Cuban hangout and are headed for a bar not far from here."

He paused to listen. "Apparently, one of our host's homeboys likes the sound of folding money a little too much and he's willing to talk."

"No problem." Lyons's face didn't break a smile. "He can have his share of what we take off the bodies. If, of course, he doesn't get caught in the cross fire first. I don't like snitches."

Gutierrez was concerned when he put down the phone. "You aren't going to go in there shooting, are you?"

"Not at all," Lyons said. "We only shoot at people who shoot at us first. We do, however, always make sure that we get in the last shot.''

Gutierrez could well believe that. These three were as hard-core as any of the mercenaries he had ever run into. ''Can I help you take care of this?'' he asked.

''Only by pointing out the target for us. After that, get your ass out of the area and take your people with you because we won't have time to check IDs if this goes down.''

''I understand.''

''Make sure your people do as well,'' Blancanales cautioned. ''This is no time for bullshit macho street games because we won't be reading anybody their rights tonight. Anyone who pops a cap on us is going down.''

Gutierrez eyeballed the ordnance the Able Team commandos were carrying. He had been in the business long enough to recognize full-auto subguns when he saw them, and these guys weren't carrying semiauto look-alikes. These crazy people were armed like an FBI SWAT team.

''I will do what I can,'' he said. ''But that bar is not on my turf. I don't have any control over it.''

''That's too bad.'' Lyons turned his rock-hard gaze on the Cuban. ''Someone's mother is going to be crying tonight.''

''Let me go in with you,'' Gutierrez asked again. ''Maybe I can talk to the people there.''

Lyons nodded and Blancanales said, ''Okay, but you're going unarmed. I don't want any mistakes.''

Gutierrez nodded. ''Okay.''

THE BAR WAS ONLY A FEW BLOCKS away, but Lyons had them all ride over in the van. On the way, Gutierrez called the bar owner and learned that Caldwell and Bogs had brought a couple of local toughs with them as backup.

"How many men are in there all told?" Lyons asked.

"The two gringos, their two men, six men from another gang and my man Paco."

"That's the guy who tried to shake me down, right?" Blancanales asked.

"He is the one, yes." Gutierrez nodded. "He was told to keep his mouth shut about the job we did for you and, if he has talked to them, he has betrayed me."

"So you won't mind if we have to kill him?"

The casual way Blancanales asked that question chilled the Cuban. He wasn't an innocent by any means, but these guys were a little too cold for him. "He has sold me out," he replied. "So it is on his head."

"Good. I don't want to waste one of your valuable assets."

CHAPTER TWENTY-EIGHT

Miami, Florida

Hermann Schwarz cruised past the front of the Papagayo Bar before rounding the block and parking on a side street. The bar was in the middle of the block with only one front door. The two large windows had been painted over to keep passersby from getting too curious about what was going on inside. That was both good and bad.

"Is there an alley behind the bar?" Blancanales asked.

"Yes," Gutierrez replied. "And it's usually locked, with a key behind the bar."

"Good," Lyons said, "That'll make it easier for us. Pol, you take the back door."

"Let Gadgets handle that," Blancanales replied. "I want the entrance this time."

"Are you sure?"

Blancanales was firm. "This one's mine."

"But, what are you going to do?" Gutierrez asked. "There are at least a dozen people in there, and most of them will be packing."

Lyons smiled slowly. "We're going to invite them to come out like gentlemen and be arrested."

"But you said you guys weren't cops."

"We aren't, but they don't know that. If they come out, we'll take their pieces and turn them loose. If they don't, it won't matter."

On the way out of the van, Blancanales grabbed the rotary grenade launcher loaded with flashbang rounds from the rack. When they went in, they'd do it with a bang.

Gutierrez followed Able Team, his cellular phone still in his hand. "Wait, amigos!" he said. "Let me try to talk to the owner and tell him that they need to get out of there. They aren't my people, but they are Cubans, my brothers, and I don't want to see them hurt."

He shrugged. "You can have Paco and the two gringos, I don't care."

"Make the call," Blancanales said. "But be careful what you say. And tell them that if they come out with their guns in their hands, they die."

GUNNER CALDWELL WAS about to lose patience with the Cuban who said he had information about the stolen weapons. Meeting in a bar full of macho street punks was no way to conduct business, but Paco had insisted on it. Now that they were there, though, the guy was asking them to pay for the guns first with drugs, then with diamonds. He also insisted in seeing the payoff before telling them where the goods were.

Roy Bogs was watching the two Cubans they had

hired as back up, and letting Caldwell talk to the kid. He barely noticed when the phone behind the bar rang and the bartender started speaking rapid-fire Spanish at the top of his voice. But he noticed that when the bartender called out something in a low voice, several of the gangbangers got up and headed for the front door.

"What's going on?" he asked Paco.

The Cuban looked scared and started to get up. "Not so fast, mate." Caldwell grabbed his gun arm and held him back.

Bogs was reaching for his piece as the last of the gangbangers cleared the door, leaving him and Caldwell with their two hired thugs and Paco when the window blew in with a bang. The noise and flash from the explosion momentarily blinded him, but he sought cover on the floor.

When his vision cleared, he saw Caldwell shooting at black figures rushing through the door. He snapped off a couple of rounds, but the return fire drove him back down.

Roy Bogs had been with Dingo Jones for a long time, but that didn't mean that he was a brave man. It also didn't mean that he was willing to stand and die for his employer. When he saw Caldwell take a hit, he panicked.

One of their Cuban guards fired his sawed-off shotgun, and the blast took out the front window close to him. Seeing an out, Bogs dived through the empty space, heedless of the glass fragments still in the frame. Rolling as he hit the sidewalk, he scurried out of the line of fire and took off running.

The sounds of gunfire followed him down the street.

WHEN THE LAST SHOT echoed away, the silence in the Papagayo Bar was eerie. The two hired guns were dead on the floor. Paco had a round in his shoulder and another in his leg, but he was alive. Gunner Caldwell lay slumped over the table in front of him, a dozen exit wounds showing on his back.

"He's dead," Blancanales said as he reached down to check Caldwell's pulse. "Where's Bogs?"

Lyons looked around and didn't see him either. "Damn!"

"Amigos," Gutierrez said, sticking his head through the open window, "the police, they are coming."

"Get your man," Lyons said, pointing at the dazed and bleeding Paco, "and get him the hell outta here."

"One of the gringos, he ran away."

"We know."

WHEN ROY BOGS SKIDDED to a stop in the Rainbow Cybertech parking lot, he flung open the car door and dashed for the express that would take him to Jones's suite. On the way, he used the elevator phone to call ahead to warn his boss that he was coming.

Jones met him in his private office. "What the bloody hell happened down there!"

"I don't know. Two guys came charging in and started shooting at us."

"You're sure Gunner is dead?"

Bogs nodded. "He got hit three or four times at least."

"Bloody hell!" Jones's eyes darted around as if he expected to see his number-two man. "Who were they?"

"I don't know, Dingo, they had masks on. But their builds looked a lot like those two guys who came here claiming to be Feds looking for Perez."

Jones frowned. "They had masks on, you say?"

"Right, black ski masks like the SAS wear."

Reaching for his phone, Jones punched in the number of his command center. "Put the facility on full alert," he ordered. "Tell the security chief to make sure that no one gets in without my say-so. And, I mean no one."

When Jones turned back to Bogs, his face was set. "Call the pilot and tell him to get the chopper here immediately. We're going back to the *Digger*."

"What do you want me to do?"

"Stay here and help me with the woman," Jones ordered as he turned back to the door of his suite.

Bogs just stood there. He had been through some dicey times in his years with Jones, but nothing like this. He didn't know what was going to happen next.

WHEN THE ABLE TEAM ARRIVED at the front door of the Rainbow Cybertech building, two of Jones's security men were standing guard in front of it.

"Federal agents," Lyons snapped as he flashed his badge. "Open the door."

"I can't do that, sir," one of them said. "Mr. Jones said that—"

Blancanales triggered the grenade launcher, sending a flash-bang grenade through the glass and into the lobby.

"Don't even think about it," Schwarz said, his MP-5 leveled at the guard, who looked like he was going to go for his side arm. The man stiffened and put his hands in the air.

"Disarm them," Lyons told him, "and stay down here so we're not bothered."

"You got it."

The three guards in the lobby were on the floor stunned by the grenade when Lyons and Blancanales stepped through the empty doorframe, the hardware in their hands discouraging any foolishness. When Schwarz herded the two door guards into the lobby as well, Lyons and Blancanales headed for the stairs to the upper levels and Jones's penthouse.

"Just have a seat on the floor, gentlemen." Schwarz motioned to the guards with the muzzle of his subgun. "Keep your hands where I can see them, and you'll all go home to mama when this is over."

WHEN LYONS and Blancanales reached the top floor, the corridor outside Jones's office was empty. Taking each side of the hall, they cleared all the rooms on the way to the receptionist's office. The door leading into Jones's inner sanctum was halfway open and through the frosted glass, they could see a figure.

Exchanging hand signals, Blancanales booted the door and Lyons rushed in. Roy Bogs was standing in the middle of the room with his pistol riding in his belt holster.

"Freeze, Bogs. It's over."

Bogs reacted to the sight of the weapons aimed at him and went for his piece.

Lyons tripped the trigger of his subgun and the burst took Bogs in the chest. He looked surprised as he crumpled to the floor.

The door to Jones's suite burst open and he came out holding Carter in front of him as a shield. The woman was wearing a bathrobe, but it was hanging open and Blancanales could see that she had been badly beaten. Fresh blood was running in rivulets down her breasts and belly, and her face was bruised.

Reaching up to pull off his balaclava, Blancanales stepped forward. "Let her go, Jones."

"You're dead!" Jones shouted.

Blancanales smiled grimly. "Not yet and it's going to take a better man than you to kill me."

He lowered his subgun to hang from its sling. "I knew that anyone named after a dog would be the kind of coward who'd hide behind a woman. Why don't you try to beat me up, Dingo?"

Screaming with rage, Jones threw Carter to the floor and started for Blancanales with his bare hands.

Carter crawled to the 9 mm pistol that had fallen

from Bogs's dying hand. Snatching it up, she took a two-handed grip and fired at Jones's back.

Her first shot hit Jones in the right leg, and it went out from under him. Ignoring Blancanales completely, he turned back to the woman just in time to catch the second round low in the gut.

"Anne!" he groaned with the impact.

The third and fourth rounds hit him in the chest, and the gun clicked on an empty magazine when she tried to fire it again.

"That's enough, Sarah." Blancanales stepped up to take the gun from her hand. He shrugged off his jacket and placed it over her shoulders. "Call an ambulance," he told Schwarz.

"Is he dead?" she asked in a small voice, averting her eyes from the body.

"He's dead and he won't hurt you again."

"He told me you were dead," she said, starting to cry silently. "He told me that I'd never get away from him no matter what I did and, that if I ever tried again, he'd kill me."

"He won't kill anyone again," Blancanales said as he led her to the couch in the receptionist's office.

"Do you know that he killed Captain Johnson? He had Gunner and Roy throw him off the *Digger* after he ran over your boat."

"Those two guys won't ever hurt anyone again, either," he assured her.

"The ambulance's on the way," Schwarz said.

"Let me stay with you." Carter looked up at him, her lashes wet and her tears streaking the blood on her face.

"You need to go to the hospital and get taken care of," he said gently.

"Will you go with me?" she asked.

Blancanales looked over at Lyons who nodded. "Sure. I'll come with you."

WHEN THE LOCAL COPS showed up, Lyons and Schwarz showed their photo ID cards naming them special agents of the Justice Department.

"If you don't mind my asking," the officer in charge said as he looked around Jones's private office, "just what happened here?"

"Apparently," Lyons said with a straight face, "Mr. Jones and his associate had a falling out when they learned that they were facing rather serious federal charges."

"What federal charges?"

"Murder on the high seas," Schwarz chimed in. "Bank fraud, firearms violations and kidnapping a protected witness, to name just a few."

The cop shook his head. "Look, gentlemen, I don't want this to turn out like a TV movie where the local cop has to go head-to-head with the Feds to solve the crime, but Mr. Jones falls into what I'd have to call the prominent citizen category around here, and I'm going to have to explain to the city fathers what happened to him."

Lyons put on his reasonable face. "And I assure you that we don't want this to turn out to be the movie where the Feds have to bust the local cops because they were in on a major crime committed by a wealthy local citizen. Mr. Ian 'Dingo' Jones was being investigated for serious federal crimes and in the course of our investigation we uncovered several more offenses that he had committed. Were he not deceased, he would never be getting out of jail. Nor would those two thugs he had working for him ever see the light of day, either.

"But," Lyons went on, "since everyone of interest in this case seems to be dead, I don't see a need for further investigations."

"However," Schwarz added, "if the local authorities insist, I can have a federal task force here in the morning. I'm sure that we can interest the DEA, the ATF and the FBI as well as the IRS and the INS. As I'm sure you realize, once a task force like that gets started, it can take months, if not years, for them to make sure that all the bases are covered. But, like I said, we're always more than willing to work with the local authorities to the fullest extent of the law. It's your call."

"Okay, guys." The cop opened his hands in mock surrender. "I get the message. This is your turf and you're welcome to it. But I still need to know what went down here. I understood there was a woman involved."

"She's the protected witness we were talking about. She was being held here against her will for several days, and she's been taken for medical examination."

The Miami detective understood the code. The woman had been sexually mistreated and needed medical attention. But with her being a federal witness and the apparent perpetrator dead, again it was none of his business. The way this was going, all his people would be allowed to do here was to string out the crime-scene tape and keep back the crowds.

"If we could ask a favor," Lyons said as if he was reading the Miami cop's mind, "there's something you could do to assist us."

"What's that?"

"We don't have a forensic team at hand, so I wonder if your forensic people could record this crime scene for us? Since this is a federal investigation, we'll be glad to reimburse your department for any expenses incurred."

"No problem," the cop said sarcastically. "My guys need the practice."

"They'll also get the credit," Lyons assured him. "My office will make sure of that. In fact, we know of a rental storage space of his that's full of stolen U.S. military weapons that needs to be recovered if you can spare the personnel."

"You're kidding!"

Lyons shook his head. "Not at all. That's part of why we wanted to talk to Jones and his associates. We developed a lead on them, and there might be even more contraband in his other warehouses. Your good citizen Mr. Jones had been up to a lot of things I sincerely hope that your city fathers don't know about."

The cop was experienced enough to understand the second implied threat. Leave the Feds alone to play out their game, and they wouldn't look too closely at who else might have known about Jones's dirty dealings and maybe taking payoffs to look the other way. In the world of law enforcement, it was a common enough trade-off, and he didn't want to have to explain to the police chief why he hadn't gone along with the deal.

"Give me the address of that storage place, and I'll get someone on those weapons immediately."

Lyons smiled.

The cop's cellular phone rang and, after listening to the man on the other end, he looked up at Lyons. "There's been a shootout at a bar in Little Havana. Is that one of your operations as well?"

Lyons's eyes went wide with surprise. "We don't know anything about it."

CHAPTER TWENTY-NINE

Mount Alamut, Syria

Malik al-Ismaili faced Mecca as he said his early-morning prayers. He felt as blessed as any man could ever expect to be. A merciful God had put out his hand and had raised him to be exalted among the faithful as the Mahdi. His inspired message was sweeping from one end of the Muslim world to the other like the sword of God. More and more councils of imams were replacing corrupt governments, and they were ruling their people by the Sharia, the Holy Law of Islam.

The only dark spot on an otherwise bright new dawn that was bringing the faithful out of the darkness of Western corruption came from Beirut. The Lebanese capital had always been a blot on the glory of Islam. The poisons of greed and corruption could be found at all levels there, and it had sunk deeply into the fabric of Beiruti society. The people were so fond of their corruption that they were turning their faces away from God's messenger.

He had expected that the Christian population

would ignore the Mahdi's words, and he knew that the Sunnis would have to be forced to turn their backs on the Western decadence they had come to enjoy. But even the Shiites of Beirut weren't responding as they were in other Islamic states. God had said that he would bring his vengeance to those who didn't heed his word, and as soon as the rest of Islam had been pacified, Beirut would pay the price for her disobedience. Part of the dark cloud over Beirut was tied to al-Askari and his commandos. Since they had overrun the Brotherhood's stronghold in the city and slaughtered his men, they had disappeared. They had left two or three men behind in their villa, but the rest of them had vanished.

It was apparent now that their real mission had been to kill or capture Insmir Vedik. And from the reports of the few Assassins who had survived the battle in East Beirut, they had captured him. Of itself, that didn't bother Malik. He didn't fear that Vedik would betray him. The Bosnian knew who he was, but the name would mean nothing to any Westerner. And all of the important information had been withheld from him. While he knew that the Brotherhood fortress was in a mountain, he didn't know where that mountain was. He had been blindfolded anytime he had been taken to and from it. He also knew nothing about the appearance of the Mahdi.

Being a Bosnian, Vedik had been corrupted by living so close to the West, and he would have scoffed at the idea of the Mahdi coming back to bring the promise of paradise. He'd had no idea that his work on the mutated anthrax had been merely one small part of a much larger plan. Vedik had just wanted to kill infidels not knowing that, of itself, killing was useless. Killing in the name of God, though, brought glory.

Vedik hadn't had God's name in his heart when he manufactured his deadly disease. Al-Ismaili, however, had used the Bosnian's effort in God's work as the first step to cleansing the Islamic World. And, if needs be, he would use it again. Enough of the bacillus remained to turn both Europe and America into a graveyard, if that was required.

He would like to think that the disappearance of al-Askari meant that the infidel had taken his Bosnian prize and had returned to his homeland, but he feared that wasn't what he had done. Were that the case, he wouldn't have left his men to guard the villa. Al-Askari was still loose in the lands of the faithful, working his evil, and he had to be found and stopped.

He had sent warnings to all of the cells to be on the alert for the infidel commandos, but they hadn't been spotted. The problem was that with the Mahdi's appearance, the Brotherhood's human resources were stretched to the limit. None of the Assassin cells in the major cities of the Middle East could spare a single man for this task. All that was left of the cells he had sent into Beirut was a mere handful, and most of them were new men. The experienced Assassin cadre had been wiped out when al-Askari made his daring daylight raid on the Beirut stronghold.

For the first time in his life, al-Ismaili wished that he could think like a Western infidel. His entire life had been devoted to the word of God as written in the Koran. From childhood, he had been trained to seek God's path, and he had never trodden the infidel's path of evil and deception. Al-Askari's mind was unknowable, and al-Ismaili had no way of discerning what the man might do next. All he could do was to continue making his appearances, knowing that every day the Mahdi spoke, the Muslim world was one day closer to being the paradise God intended it to be. And he would trust in God to protect him while he was doing His work.

THE STONY MAN WARRIORS woke before dawn and immediately broke camp. After checking to make sure that their weapons were free of sand, they boarded the Land Rover and headed out again. Manning drove at no more than thirty miles an hour. Any faster would raise a dust plume and the last thing they wanted was to announce their presence. The men ate breakfast as they drove, all the while scanning the horizon for any signs of hostile activity.

This desert was barren. Every now and then, they passed a cairn of rocks stacked by only God knew who, when or why. The only other sign that life had ever passed that way was a few scattered animal bones. Terrain this deserted was a perfect place to hide, particularly underground.

They drove throughout the morning and were within sight of the mountains in the distance when McCarter thought he smelled hot oil.

"Striker," he said and tapped the oil-pressure gage on the Land Rover's dashboard.

Bolan caught the note in the man's voice and saw that the oil pressure had dropped to almost zero.

"We've got to shut it down."

Knowing that they didn't have oil with them, only extra gas, Bolan made a decision. "No, keep driving until it quits. We need the miles."

The rapidly overheating vehicle made another four miles before the engine seized. Eyeing the mountains, the men got out and worked out the kinks from the long ride.

"Now what?" James asked the obvious question.

"I don't know about the rest of you," Bolan said, "but I feel that we can't pull back now. There's too much at stake here for us to walk away. If nothing else, we need to try to destroy the stocks of anthrax and the best way to insure that we can do that is to continue with the original plan."

"I've come this far," Hawkins said, "and I'd hate anyone to say that I let a little inconvenience get in the way of my doing the job."

"We're all in, Striker," McCarter spoke for the rest.

That settled, the map came out and they clustered around it to see what they had gotten themselves into.

"It's a little over ten miles' map distance," McCarter said after taking a GPS reading. "And we were going to stop short of it by a mile or so anyway, so call it nine miles."

"How about the water?"

"There's that oasis Kurtzman found for us about three miles away. We should be able to fill up our canteens there and carry away enough to last us till we get there."

"I'll call the Farm and let them know what happened," Bolan suggested.

"Okay, lads," McCarter said. "Let's get in marching order and get that bloody bomb ready to go."

Stony Man Farm, Virginia

THE ENTIRE Stony Man mission team was in the Computer Room, following the commandos as they made their trek across the desert. As expected, there were no clouds over the Syrian desert, and the KH-7 imagery could pick up their vehicle. They had seen that it had stopped.

"Do you think there's something wrong with the truck?" Barbara Price asked Hal Brognola.

Brognola hoped against hope that was not the case, but he could think of no other explanation.

"Stony Base, this is Stony One," Bolan's voice said over the satcom radio.

"Stony One, go," Price answered.

Bolan briefly outlined what had happened and their decision to try to carry the nuke the rest of the way.

"Are you sure?" Price asked him.

"We're sure. We've come this far and we knew the odds before we left Beirut. This has to be done, Barbara."

"But without a vehicle, you won't be able to get far enough away before it detonates."

"We'll try to think of something," he said. "But we have to try it."

Of all the people in the room, she knew firsthand what could happen if they couldn't destroy the stockpiles of the anthrax. "I understand," she said.

"Good luck, old buddy," Brognola added.

"Thanks, we need all the luck we can muster. Stony One out."

"Hal," Price said. The strain of the last few days was showing plainly and he knew she was running on sheer willpower.

"I know," he replied. "I'll talk to the President and tell him that we may need to go in there and get them out."

"Do you think he'll approve it? I mean the only reason they're there is that he didn't want to risk an American presence in the region."

He looked into her tired, red-rimmed eyes. "I'll see what I can do."

Syrian Desert

HAWKINS WIPED his forehead with his hand before changing his grip on the carrying strap. Now that they were into their second hour, the load was starting to tell on all of them. Though the nuclear device might not have been considered all that heavy somewhere else, carrying it in a place like the northern Syrian desert was a chore.

"I sure as hell wish some good ole boy would mosey past here right about now with an extra donkey he wouldn't mind parting with."

"How about a Hummer or a nice four-wheel-drive instead?" James asked. "My mama always said to aim high when you're wishing for things."

"Nope," Hawkins replied. "It's got to be a donkey. I don't think the madman in the mountain would take too kindly to someone driving a strange vehicle up to his back door."

"I wonder how in the hell he handles his logistics anyway. A place like that has got to be resupplied every now and then."

"I'm sure he has his own convoys bring the supplies in, but I'm also sure that he keeps them well protected all the way in. This guy is not supposed to be here, and he probably has to watch out for the Syrian army as much as we do."

"How far is that water hole the Bear found for us?" Manning asked.

"Another couple of klicks," McCarter said, checking his watch. "We'll be there within the hour. And not a bloody minute too soon."

As they approached the rise in the ground that the map indicated lay right in front of the oasis, McCarter called out, "Take a break."

They had traveled a little over three miles and were more than ready to refill their canteens. Since he was the man who hadn't been carrying one of the bomb straps, the Briton went ahead to scout out their hoped-for watering hole.

THE OASIS Kurtzman had picked off the geological survey map wasn't one of those palm-tree shaded spots. It was just a spring that flowed from a rock formation, and not a very large spring at that. The only vegetation it supported was an equally small patch of thorn bushes and one stunted tree of unknown species. As for animal life, none could be seen except for the three men with the tan-colored Toyota four-wheel-drive pickup parked under the tree.

Focusing his glasses, McCarter could see that the men were all dressed in Arab robes, but they were packing what looked like the new favorite tool of the Middle East, Kalashnikov AK-74s. Like the older AK-47s they had replaced, they were almost indestructible and worked well with sand in their guts. The difference was that they fired a 5.45 mm high-velocity round instead of a 7.62 mm bullet.

"We're going to have to fight if we want a drink, lads," McCarter announced.

"Can we leave this damned thing here while we do it?"

"I don't see why not," Bolan said. "It's not like anyone's going to run by and snatch it."

"Thank you, Jesus," Hawkins said. "I thought that I was going to have to shoot one-handed."

Leaving the bomb sitting in the sun, the five commandos moved out in two groups: Bolan and Manning in one; McCarter, Hawkins and James in the other. They weren't planning a fair fight, more of a massacre, as they were still short of their objective and they needed the water.

Bolan and Manning went the long way around to set up the anvil while McCarter and his team waited to play the hammer.

"We're in place," Bolan called over the com link.

"Tea time, lads," McCarter stated.

When the three Phoenix Force Commandos rushed the oasis, the Arabs spotted them and went for their weapons. But before they could get off a shot, Manning took out one of them and Bolan got a second. The survivor fired off one long burst from his AK-74 and took off running. James and Hawkins teamed up to put him down with short bursts.

"Man, I could sure use a cold one right about now," James said as he lowered his piece.

"That was the idea," Hawkins replied. "Those guys were hogging the keg."

"THEY'RE ASSASSINS." Hawkins pointed to the curved dagger in the belt of the corpse at his feet. "And that means we're inside the Old Man's security ring."

"Which also means that he might just send someone to look for these guys when they don't show up as scheduled," James cautioned.

"But we might be able to sneak this truck in a little closer and cut some time off this jaunt. We can borrow a couple of robes from these guys and see how much closer we can get dressed as them."

"But there are only three robes," James pointed out.

Hawkins grinned. "Who's counting?"

When Bolan nodded, Manning slid behind the wheel of the truck and fired it up. "It's got almost a full tank of gas, so we've lucked out."

Rubbing sand into the worst of the wet blood, James, Hawkins and McCarter donned the Assassins' robes and drove back to where they had left the nuke.

"Now I know why you wanted this truck," James told Hawkins as they lifted the device into the Toyota's bed. "I'd forgotten just how heavy this bastard is."

"I hadn't." With the nuke in the back of the pickup, the Stony Man team headed for Mount Alamut and Armageddon, now only six miles away.

CHAPTER THIRTY

In the Desert

The Phoenix commandos had no way of knowing that with so many of al-Ismaili's Assassins leading the insurrections in the cities, he didn't have much of a defense force at Mount Alamut. And the fighters he did have were inside the underground fortress. Following the lowest terrain, the commandos cautiously drove to within a mile of the mountain's base, parked the truck in a draw and off-loaded the device. That they had made it that far without being spotted was no guarantee that they were home free.

"Before we leave," Manning said, "I want to set the 'last man' function on this thing."

The electronic detonator that had been fitted to the bomb could be programmed for various functions. The "last man" setting Manning was referring to would allow it to be instantly detonated if it was in danger of being captured.

"Okay, lads, smartly now," McCarter said taking his place on the end of one of the carrying straps. "Just one more mile."

"That's what the farmer told his old horse," Hawkins said as he took his strap. "And we all know how that turned out."

"I don't," James said.

"You don't want to know."

Their maps showed that there was a slight depression that led almost all the way to the foot of the mountain. Following that route would keep them out of sight of anyone on the ground. But if the Assassins had lookouts on the sides of the peak, they'd be as obvious as cockroaches running across the kitchen floor, only far more vulnerable.

If they were spotted now, there was no way that they could abandon their package and run for their lives. They could only try to fight their way out with the bomb in tow. Or the last man standing would detonate it and hope that the blast would still do the job.

It took almost an hour to reach the base of the mountain, where the commandos turned south and headed for an outcropping a few yards above the desert floor. Kurtzman's space spies had noticed a heat anomaly in that area that might indicate an opening. When they reached the location, McCarter and Bolan stayed with the device while the others fanned out to look for a camouflaged entrance.

"It's over here," James called out from between two giant boulders. "I think it's an air vent, and it's got a grate covering it."

The grate turned out to be made of half-inch-thick rebar rods embedded in sand-colored concrete. "We don't have any way to cut through that,'' Manning said.

Bolan looked up the side of the mountain, but could see no other openings. He knew they had to be there, but not even the sensors on Kurtzman's spy satellites had been able to tell him where they were. It was this or nothing.

''Can you blow it?''

''That's kind of like knocking on the front door, isn't it?'' Hawkins asked.

''I can use small cutting charges and tamp them with sand,'' Manning offered. ''That should muffle the sound.''

''Do it,'' Bolan said.

While James and Manning worked on the demo job, the three other commandos spread out and took security positions around the device. Until it was in place and the detonator set, they couldn't let it out of their sight.

With James assisting him, Manning took a small roll of linear-shaped charge out of his demo bag and started to cut it into short lengths. Stripping the tape from the adhesive backing, he wrapped a length of the explosive around each of the bars. When that was done, he linked the charges with detonation cord and attached a fuse lighter to a blasting cap embedded in the first charge.

''Okay,'' he told James. ''Help me bury this in at least a foot of sand.''

When Manning fired the charges a few minutes later, the resulting thump sounded like anything except an explosion. When the dust cleared, the rebar rods had all been cut along the bottom where they went into the concrete.

"All right!" James smiled as he reached to try to bend the rod out of the way.

It took all five of them to work the rods far enough apart to allow the device to pass through the opening. It was a little less than three feet in diameter, but it couldn't snake its way through like the men were doing. Once inside, they continued up the dim tunnel.

A dozen yards away, they encountered a ventilation fan the diameter of the tunnel. "I knew this was too simple," James muttered.

"There's an alcove in the rock over here," Manning announced, "and it has a door so we can get around the fan."

Again, getting the device past the narrow door was the difficult part. But standing it upright, they were able to pass it through.

Now that they were inside the Assassin stronghold, McCarter passed off his hold on the device to Manning and motioned that he was going ahead to scout the tunnel. Sixty yards farther, the ventilation shaft ended in a T with another tunnel. Both sides were clear, but McCarter chose the left-hand branch as it looked like it headed toward the center of the mountain.

"We're going left at the junction," he radioed.

THE MEN OF THE Brotherhood usually carried their AKs with them in place of the swords their predecessors had proudly worn. It was the mark of a warrior. The Assassin hurrying down the outer ring corridor that connected all the tunnels had his assault rifle slung over his back. He was to open the arms room so the brothers of his cell could clean their weapons. The master had ordered them to leave for Beirut in the morning.

As he passed one of the access tunnels leading to the air shafts, he thought he heard a scraping noise. Bringing his Kalashnikov off his shoulder, he peered into the dimly lit corridor. A flickering shadow alerted him. "Brother?" he called out.

"What is it, Brother?" Another Assassin coming from the opposite direction stopped.

"I heard a noise."

The second man unslung his AK and took a step into the darkness. "Is anyone there?" he called out.

A short burst of 9 mm rounds from McCarter sent him staggering. "Brothers!" the first man's voice rang out. "To me!"

Aiming into the tunnel, he emptied his magazine and stepped back to reload.

"Attack!" he cried out when the brothers of his cell reached him.

"THIS IS AS FAR AS we go!" McCarter radioed over the roar of the AKs. "Set that damned thing up and let's go!"

The four lowered the bomb and Manning knelt to arm it while Bolan went up to take the other side of the tunnel mouth with McCarter.

They had decided that they would set the device for a fifteen-minute delay. That wouldn't give them much time, but it also wouldn't give the Assassins much time to try to disarm the weapon, either. The detonator had a built-in fail-safe so that if the main power was interrupted, a backup system would fire the implosion blocks anyway and initiate the detonation sequence.

Punching in a code, Manning twisted a key and the digital clock lit up. ''We're go!'' he said over the com link as he pulled out the key and put it in his pocket.

''Pull back,'' McCarter yelled.

Bolan stood beside McCarter to put out covering fire for the others.

''We've got you!'' James called out from the next turn in the tunnel. ''Pull back!''

Pulling a flash-bang grenade from his harness, McCarter armed it and threw it well past the device. ''Go!'' he told Bolan.

Covered by the explosion, the two sprinted back into the tunnel. When they rejoined the others, Manning led off as they hurried back the way they had come. Sporadic fire followed them as they ran.

When they reached the bypass door at the ventilation fan, Manning held back and reached into his demo pouch as the others went past. After passing through himself and locking the door behind him, he slapped a quarter-pound charge with a ten-second delay to the outside of the steel doorframe. When it went off, it would warp the frame so the door couldn't be opened behind them.

Hitting the switch, he turned and raced back down the tunnel to the grate.

"Run for it!" Bolan shouted from the rocks outside.

Manning ran.

MALIK AL-ISMAILI STOOD in the control room with an AK slung over his shoulder as his men reported on the intruders. They said that the infidels had fled, but that they had left a strange device behind. "What kind of device?"

"I do not know of these things, Master," the Assassin replied.

"Wait there until I come," al-Ismaili said.

"Follow me," he ordered two of his technicians as he strode out of the room.

The technicians had never seen anything like the device the foreigners had left behind. They could make the TV and radio equipment work because they had been trained to do it. That didn't mean that they had any idea how it worked. The digital readouts on the face of the control box on the device didn't mean anything to them, but the flashing numbers counting down were ominous.

"Could it be a Yankee atomic bomb, Master?" one of them asked fearfully.

"Never!" al-Ismaili said firmly. "God is protecting us, and the Americans would never use an atomic bomb. They are too afraid. And it is too small to be that powerful. I don't know what it is, but we drove them away before they could do what they wanted to with it."

The technician started to back off, avoiding his

master's eyes. That demon device looked like it was doing something on its own.

"Block off this corridor," al-Ismaili ordered. "And get back to the control room. The Mahdi must make his appearance on time today."

ARMS AND LEGS CHURNING, the Stony Man team raced down the side of the mountain, scrambling between the rocks. It was truly a race against the clock. After clearing the rocks, they sprinted flat-out over the sand, each step taking them that much farther from the nuclear sun that was going to burst into life deep underground.

"Ten seconds!" Manning panted as he called out over the com link. "Take cover!"

There was no cover in the desert to take and, if they weren't far enough away from ground zero, it wouldn't have helped them anyway. But everyone went flat with their heads pointed away from Mount Alamut. It might be interesting to watch what happened when the device detonated in the heart of the mountain, but not interesting enough to risk taking the shock wave headfirst.

With their elbows tucked close to their sides and their hands over their ears, the men counted down the last few seconds to detonation.

Stony Man Farm, Virginia

EVERY EYE IN THE Stony Man Computer Room was on the big screen monitor as Hunt Wethers calmly

read off the countdown from the digital clock.
"Four...three...two...one...zero. Detonation."

Since the Keyhole satellite was several hundred
miles in space, there was a slight delay as the images coming from the cameras were transmitted to
them. But when they came, they were stunning.

It looked as if Mount Alamut had suddenly
jumped into the air. Dust mixed with smoke and
flame jetted out of several vents around the peak.
Solid rock seemed to dance in an ever-growing ring
of dust as the shock wave propagated outward, rip-
pling the ground as it grew. The image was silent,
but each of the watchers heard the roar in their
minds as if the fist of God were hammering the
earth.

When the dust cleared enough for the satellite's
cameras to see again, Mount Alamut was gone. It
hadn't disappeared nor had it been blown away. It
had been pulverized from within, ground to powder,
and the remnants had sunk into the cavern that had
been created in its heart. Scattered boulders still
showed on the surface, but most of what had been
a towering mountain was as smooth as the surrounding desert.

"Jesus!" Hal Brognola said softly.

"'I am become death,'" Hunt Wethers said, re-
peating Dr. Robert Oppenheimer's words quoting
from the Rig Veda, the Hindu holy books. He had
said them at the detonation of the first nuclear bomb
in Nevada in August 1945. They were as valid now
as they had been back then at the dawn of the

Atomic Age. The awesome power of a nuclear detonation would always be linked with death.

"We have lost communication with the team," Kurtzman announced. "The dust must be blocking their transmissions."

No one wanted to suggest that the commandos might not have been able to get far enough away from ground zero to escape the effects of the underground blast.

"Keep trying," Brognola ordered.

In the silence, every eye was on the monitors as if they could spot five specks moving in the vast expanse of the Syrian desert.

"I'm switching to IR," Kurtzman announced. "I might be able to pick them up that way."

Price knew that trick wasn't going to work this time. The surface temperature of the desert was well above that of the human body, and there was no way he'd be able to pick them out against the sand. But she also knew that he felt like he had to do something. Waiting for the butcher's bill was always the hard part.

Syria

WHEN THE SHOCKWAVE passed, the five men picked themselves up from the sand and looked back toward what had been the Mahdi's hideout. Through the dust that still hung in the air, they could see that the Assassins' Mount Alamut fortress was gone, taken down to the level of the surrounding desert. The ground was still rumbling as the shattered rocks settled in the underground crater the bomb had carved from the rock.

"Man," Hawkins said as he picked himself up, "what a ride! If I could figure out how to package that puppy for amusement parks, we'd all be millionaires. That beats the hell out of any roller coaster I've ever been on."

"You got that right." James grinned as he dusted off his battle-dress jacket. "That was some ride."

"Not as bad as I had expected, though," Manning commented. "Considering how close we were to it, I really thought we'd get knocked around a lot more."

"Speak for yourself, mate," McCarter said as he bent over and massaged his thigh. "The bloody thing damned near broke my leg."

"You should have found a softer place to fall."

Bolan turned and saw that Manning was already on the radio to the Farm. "Are you getting through?" he asked.

"Not yet," the Canadian replied. "Either the dust or the ionization in the air is causing too much static. I can't uplink to the satellite."

"Keep trying," Bolan said. "I want to let them know that we're okay."

"I suggest that we do it on the road," McCarter said. "Even with all the local governments going down like tenpins, someone is bound to notice that one of their mountains just went missing. We need to make ourselves scarce before they start pointing fingers."

"If the truck will start," Manning cautioned.

"We don't know how much EMP that thing put out and if it was blocked by being underground."

A powerful electromagnetic pulse was one of the effects of a nuclear detonation. And while it wasn't destructive like the blast and heat given off by the explosion, it did fry unshielded electronics. Unlike military vehicles, civilian vehicles weren't designed to withstand it.

It took half an hour to get back to the Toyota pickup. The truck was covered with a thick layer of dirt and airborne debris that had once been part of Mount Alamut, but it hadn't taken any major damage. Manning climbed into the driver's seat and hit the ignition.

"Hang on guys," Manning said as soon as everyone was on board. "We're out of here."

As the Toyota sped across the sand, Bolan pulled out his tactical radio.

CHAPTER THIRTY-ONE

Beirut, Lebanon

In the Beirut villa, the Phoenix Force rearguard had had a busy morning starting at first light. Their discovery of Insmir Vedik's body among the attackers hadn't been a big surprise, but it had solved the problem of what they would do with him. He had been anonymously disposed of with the rest of the bodies.

When that chore had been attended to, Jack Grimaldi and Rafael Encizo drew the short straws for tower duty while Katzenelenbogen and J. R. Rust went into their radio room. They were on-line and watching the satellite feed as Mount Alamut was erased from the landscape.

"That takes care of the anthrax problem," Rust commented, "as well as our most recent Mahdi. Now maybe things can calm down around here."

"It'll be awhile," Katz said. "There are several governments that are going to have to put themselves back together again and a few cities that will need a good cleanup."

Neither man mentioned the thing that was foremost on their minds, the fate of their comrades. Both men knew that nuclear detonations did weird things to electronics and, if the men had survived, they might not be able to contact them.

Suddenly, the tactical radio burst to life. "Katz, this is Striker on the tac push, over."

Katz scrambled for the short-range radio and hit the talk button. "Katz, go."

"The satlink's down and I can't reach the Farm. Send bingo, over."

"Wilco, any further?"

"Keep the light burning, out."

"Outstanding!" Rust smiled.

Katz's smile threatened to split his face. "Go tell Rafe and Jack what happened while I talk to the Farm."

"Gladly."

Aaron Kurtzman looked over at Barbara Price and Hal Brognola, who were riveted to the big monitor showing a deep space view of the Syrian desert. "I have Katz on the phone from Beirut."

"Put him on the speaker."

"I just had a call from Mack," Katz said. "Their satellite radio's not working, but they're okay and they're on their way back."

"Thank God," she said, the relief plain in her voice.

"He didn't stay on the air long enough to chat, but I heard an engine in the background. So you might want to put the Keyhole to work and look for a vehicle heading away from that general area."

"Will do."

Brognola put his hand on her shoulder. "You need to get some rest now, we can take it from here."

"But they're still in Syria."

Brognola smiled. "Barbara, Striker's got more time in Syria than damned near anyone other than Hafez Assad himself. They've got a vehicle and we can keep track of them all the way back in. I'm going to get a UN Peacekeeper detachment to meet them at the Lebanese border and escort them back to Beirut. It's over, and it's time for you to go to bed."

Suddenly, she realized how tired she really was. "I guess I could use a nap. I'll just go into the back room."

"No, that damned cot in there is a monstrosity only fit for torturing prisoners. Go up to your room and get some real sleep. I'll call you when they're back in Beirut."

"Okay," she said in surrender.

As he watched her walk off, Brognola knew that the end of the millennium-inspired incidents hadn't yet come. They would have to go through something like this again in the not too distant future. But as long as they could keep going, they had no choice. Someone had to do it and the lot had fallen to them. When they could no longer keep the pace, someone else would have to take over to give the world a chance. He admitted that sometimes it didn't seem like too much of a chance, but it was all there was and as long as Stony Man existed, they would do their job.

Turning away, he went to call the President.

THE ABLE TEAM NOTICED that the media hardly carried anything about the mysterious electronic burnout at the Bank of Rangoon. Both the headlines and the top-of-the-hour reports were focused on the even more mysterious underground nuclear detonation that had occurred in the northern Syrian desert. According to the reports, the explosion had completely obliterated a sizeable mountain in a remote restricted military zone.

Since this was the biggest event that had taken place since the millennium countdown had kicked off in earnest, the blast was being explained in a dozen different ways. The top four explanations were that it had been: an act of God's displeasure, a warning from the vengeful Hebrew God of the Old Testament, an alien demonstration of what they will do to us if we didn't obey them when they land, or evidence of a secret Syrian nuclear weapon program. The other explanations were variations on the top four, but leaned toward the religious and apocalyptic angle.

There was no doubt in the minds of the trio that the nuclear blast had been a sign from Stony Man, not God, and that it meant Bolan and their Phoenix Force buddies had scored again. They didn't know the details yet, but that could wait until they got back to the Farm.

The cleanup of the Rainbow Cybertech operation

had been more involved than usual. Jones's main-frame had been taken apart and its electronic guts were now en route to Aaron Kurtzman. As soon as he located and recovered the killer chip and its pro-gramming, the entire thing would be pulverized. Now, they were ready to leave and only had to deal with Sarah Carter.

Two days' recuperation had done wonders for her. The signs of her ordeal weren't entirely gone, but makeup, sunglasses and a high-neck blouse cov-ered the worst of it, and she was well on the road to recovery.

"I'm going to miss you, Rosario," she told Blan-canales as he handed her the packet that contained her new identity and enough money to get set up again.

From now on, she would truly be Sarah Carter and she would never have to worry about being taken for anyone else again. She had also really been put into the Witness Protection Program, but more to keep an eye on her than to protect her. With Dingo Jones and his thugs gone, she was safe, but she still knew too much. And for what she had in her head, she would be watched over the rest of her life.

"I'll miss you too," he answered honestly. "But like I said, it's better this way. Now you can go back to California and get on with your life."

She got a far-away look on her face. "I never thought that I'd ever really be free again."

"We've got to take off, Rosario," Schwarz called out from the Caddy parked in the no-parking zone at Miami International. "Carl's chewing nails. He wants to get on the road."

"I have to go, Sarah."

"I know." She reached up, pulled his head down and gave him a long kiss. "I'm going to miss you more than I thought I would."

He brushed his hand lightly across the side of her face. "Take care."

"You too."

On the ride back to the hotel, Blancanales stared out the windshield of the car. "Does this ever bother you?" he asked.

"What?"

"That we'll never be able to settle down."

Schwarz shrugged. "I never really thought about it."

"Me neither, till now."

"And?"

As a departing plane roared overhead, Blancanales looked out at the palm trees and the sun glinting off the Gulf of Mexico. "I guess it's too late."

The ultimate weapon of terror...

JAMES AXLER

DEATHLANDS®

Dark Reckoning

A secret community of scientists gains control of an orbiting transformer that could become the ultimate weapon of terror—and it's up to Ryan Cawdor to halt the evil mastermind before he can incinerate Front Royal.

Book 3 in the Baronies Trilogy, three books that chronicle the strange attempts to unify the East Coast baronies. Who (or what) is behind this coercive process?

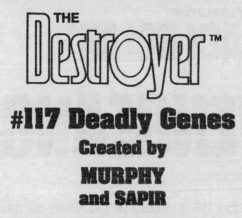

American justice...

DON PENDLETON's

MACK BOLAN®

VENGEANCE

When four U.S. Embassy staff in Algiers are murdered, Mack Bolan is sent to see if he can put a stop to the growing violence. At the root of the problem is a former U.S. citizen who hopes to unite the Algerian terror groups under one banner—his!

Available in December 1999 at your favorite retail outlet.

James Axler

O∴TLANDERS™

ARMAGEDDON AXIS

What was supposed to be the seat of power after the nuclear
holocaust, a vast installation inside Mount Rushmore—is a
new powerbase of destruction. Kane and his fellow exiles
venture to the hot spot, where they face an old enemy
conspiring to start the second wave of Armageddon.

Desperate times call for desperate measures. Don't miss out on the action in these titles!

#61910	FLASHBACK	$5.50 U.S. ☐
		$6.50 CAN. ☐
#61911	ASIAN STORM	$5.50 U.S. ☐
		$6.50 CAN. ☐
#61912	BLOOD STAR	$5.50 U.S. ☐
		$6.50 CAN. ☐
#61913	EYE OF THE RUBY	$5.50 U.S. ☐
		$6.50 CAN. ☐
#61914	VIRTUAL PERIL	$5.50 U.S. ☐
		$6.50 CAN. ☐

(limited quantities available on certain titles)

TOTAL AMOUNT	$
POSTAGE & HANDLING	$
($1.00 for one book, 50¢ for each additional)	
APPLICABLE TAXES*	$ _____
TOTAL PAYABLE	$ _____

(check or money order—please do not send cash)

To order, complete this form and send it, along with a check or money order for the total above, payable to Gold Eagle Books, to: **In the U.S.:** 3010 Walden Avenue, P.O. Box 9077, Buffalo, NY 14269-9077; **In Canada:** P.O. Box 636, Fort Erie, Ontario, L2A 5X3.

Name: _____

Address: _____ City: _____

State/Prov.: _____ Zip/Postal Code: _____

*New York residents remit applicable sales taxes.
 Canadian residents remit applicable GST and provincial taxes.

GOLD
EAGLE®

GSMBACK1